P9-DIZ-753

View from Pagoda Hill

View from Pagoda Hill

MICHAELA MacCOLL

CALKINS CREEK
AN IMPRINT OF BOYDS MILLS & KANE
New York

For information about permission to reproduce selections from this book,
please contact permissions@bmkbooks.com.

This is a work of fiction. Names, characters, places, and incidents are
products of the author's imagination or are used fictitiously. Any
resemblance to actual events, locales, or persons, living or dead,
is entirely coincidental.

Calkins Creek
An imprint of Boyds Mills & Kane, a division of Astra Publishing House
calkinscreekbooks.com

Printed in the United States of America

ISBN: 978-1-62979-782-3 (hc)
ISBN: 978-1-63592-372-8 (eBook)
Library of Congress Control Number: 2020932007

First edition
10 9 8 7 6 5 4 3 2 1

Design by Barbara Grzeslo
The chapter numbers of this books is set in Futura Std, light condensed.
The titles of this books is set in AE Prosperity.
The text of this books is set in Sabon LT Std.

To the following descendants of Neenah:
Petra, Madison, Max, Margaux, Rowan, Gunnar,
Susan, and Barbara.

And

For Patricia Reilly Giff, who never let me forget
this book should be written.

Part One

Shanghai 1878

chapter *One*

Ning tiptoed across the small courtyard lit only by the full moon. She lifted the iron latch and opened the gate slowly, praying it wouldn't creak and wake up Number One Boy. She had already heard enough from him.

"You were not invited. A young lady doesn't go where she isn't wanted."

What Ning wouldn't give to be wanted! She should have been invited to Hui's betrothal party. Hadn't she and Hui played together as children? Even though Hui was a few years older, they had been inseparable until the day Hui's mother kept Hui inside to begin her foot-binding. Suddenly alone in her courtyard, Ning could hear Hui's cries of pain as her feet were broken and molded into perfect tiny flower shapes. Ning's heart wept with envy. Why wouldn't Ning's mother do the same for her? Didn't Mama love her just as much?

But that was years ago. Ning knew once Hui married, she would go to her bridegroom's house and might never return to her family's home. Ning wanted to see her old friend one last time.

The alley was deserted. The smell of cooking oil and fish entrails was trapped in the humid air, filling her nostrils. Four houses down, Hui's door was decorated with lanterns that cast a joyful, red glow. Red for luck and wealth and happiness. As Ning approached, she could hear shouts and laughter. She pushed open the gate and froze. Hui's father, Master Feng, blocked her path. He was bragging to his friends about the fine match he had arranged for his daughter. Hui's fiancé was well-to-do and a widower with no children. If Hui gave him a son, her prospects were excellent.

Hui was sixteen and marrying a man who had already outlived one wife. A shudder ran down Ning's back; soon she would have to worry about a husband, too. Ning edged along the wall of the courtyard and darted inside the open door. Behind her, she heard Master Feng inquire, "Who was that? I don't know him."

In her plain clothes, Ning knew he meant her. Even her hair, braided in a plait down her back, resembled a boy's queue. She wished she could have dressed in finery to honor Hui, but Mama saw no reason for Ning to have festive clothes. Where would she go?

She found herself in a parlor identical to her own, even the altar to honor the statue of Buddha was in the same corner. But Hui's house was filled with aunties and grandparents chattering and clattering while silence lay like a thick carpet in Ning's parlor. Only she and Mama and

Number One Boy lived in her house, a fact that baffled the neighbors. Shanghai was such an expensive city that frugal families crammed as many people as possible into the small, narrow houses.

Hui stood next to the altar with her mother receiving her guests. Ning caught her breath—she looked so grown up. Dressed in a red silk robe with embroidered flowers, her trousers fell gracefully to just above her ankles. Her satin shoes peeked out, advertising her tiny feet. It was impossible to make out Hui's expression behind her white makeup. Her old friend had become a stranger.

Hui's mother spied her. "Foo-Tai Ning! What are you doing here?" Her shriek stopped every conversation. Hui's eyes snapped wide open to glare at Ning.

Bowing quickly, Ning said, "I came to wish Hui well." Her whisper barely traveled across the room.

Madame Feng tottered toward Ning, arms outstretched to shove her away. "Out. Out. My daughter should not have to see a yellowfish on her betrothal day! You are a bad omen. You will wreck all her good luck!" She scanned the foyer behind Ning. "Your mother didn't dare come, did she? She knows better than to associate with decent people."

"Hui, it's me, Ning!" Although her throat felt like Madame Feng's fingers were choking her, Ning managed to raise her voice. "I meant no harm. I just wanted to see you . . ."

Staring at Ning as though they were strangers, Hui slowly lifted a fan to hide her face.

"What's happening?" Master Feng appeared, his beady black eyes glaring from under his thick brows.

His wife jabbed a lacquered fingernail at Ning. "It's Foo-Tai Sun's odd daughter!"

"You're not welcome here. Get out!" He grabbed Ning's arm and hauled her outside. As he pushed her through the gate, he shouted, "Stay away!"

The heavy door slammed shut. Ning put her hand to the wall; even her broad feet couldn't keep her steady. Mama had always been clear: the only way not to shame her family was to be invisible. Ning had not listened. Of course, it had ended badly.

"I told you not to go."

Number One Boy's deep voice behind her wasn't surprising at all; he was always there to clean up her messes and bring her safely home.

She turned to look up at him. Despite her height, she barely reached his shoulder. His house slippers and his misbuttoned tunic were proof that he had dressed hurriedly.

"How did you know?" she asked.

"You were as loud as an ox," he said. The lanterns cast an eerie glow on Number One Boy's shaved forehead.

"I was silent as a mouse. Only your big ears could have heard me," she muttered.

"What happened?" he asked softly.

"They didn't want me there," she whispered. "Not even Hui. Madame Feng said I was a bad omen."

"That is unkind," he said. "I would say you are a mischievous girl who snuck out of the house when her loyal servant thought she was safe in bed." His half smile invited her to smile back.

As her eyes filled with tears, she asked, "Why do they all hate me?"

His smile disappeared. "Little dumpling, they just don't know you."

"Because Mama keeps me a prisoner at home!" she retorted.

Shaking his head, his queue flicked like a cat's tail. "Shhh," he said. "Your mother only wants to keep you safe."

"She is ashamed of me," Ning whispered.

His broad face hardened, as frozen as Hui's expression. "That is not true."

"My hair, my eyes, my feet—Mama hates everything about me."

A burst of laughter from Hui's house made her cringe. They were laughing at her. "And the neighbors think the same."

"I still love you, no matter how disobedient you are." He held out his hand. "Let's go home."

Ning let her only friend lead her down the dark alley away from the colored lights.

chapter *Two*

Number One Boy did not release Ning's hand until they were safely through their own gate. "Upstairs to bed before your mother comes home."

"Please don't tell Mama what I did," she begged.

"I am her servant," he said. An answer that was not really an answer at all.

"Mama will blame you because you let me sneak out," she cautioned.

"Very clever . . . but somehow I think I will be punished less than you."

He was right, of course. She tried again. "How would she find out? Mama talks to no one."

"Someone will want to be unkind . . . don't you think?"

"Maybe not?" she said, but her voice lacked conviction. Madame Feng would leap at the chance to embarrass Mama.

"We'll see in the morning," he said. "Now go to bed before I drag you there by your hair."

"You'd be out of breath before we reach the stairs," she shot back.

"I will count. If I reach three, you will stay home the next time I go to the market. One . . ." He held up one finger.

"The merchants will cheat you blind without me." Even as she threw out the insult, she started for the door. If it weren't for Number One Boy's shopping trips, she would never leave the house.

"Two . . ." he growled. His upper lip twitched despite his best efforts to look stern.

"I'm going." She slipped past him and ran up the rickety stairs.

"Straight to bed!" he called after her.

At the landing in front of the small room she shared with Mama, Ning paused and listened. The wide-bottomed chair in the kitchen creaked as Number One Boy settled in to wait for Mama. After the scene at the Fengs, she couldn't lie down and sleep as though nothing had happened. She pulled off the boys' shoes she had worn to Hui's and threw them under her cot.

Feet bare, she crept up the next flight of stairs to the attic. Only her own footprints marred the dust on each step. (Mama couldn't navigate the steep steps and Number One Boy was too lazy to climb so high if he didn't have to.) Ning had built her own ladder to the window out of old boxes she'd found in the alley. Pushing aside the rice paper curtain, she climbed out to the windowsill. She braced her feet against the stone tiles that lay over each other like fish scales. The iron gutter spout was shaped like a dragon's head, its forehead worn smooth by years of salty breezes from the Huang Po River.

"Master Dragon, what should I do?" she asked the spout. "Hui looked at me and didn't see her friend. She saw only an ugly half-Chinese girl with peculiar green eyes, ugly feet, and no father. I embarrassed her the same way I embarrass Mama," she whispered. There was no answer. Dragons were supposed to be wise, but this one had been on the roof too long to offer Ning any useful advice.

She glanced down to the communal courtyard where the Fengs were still celebrating. Hui's little brother lit a long straw and used it to ignite a firecracker. He ran off laughing with his hands over his ears. The noise would drive out the evil spirits—just like Ning had been pushed out of the party.

Ning's home was one in a row of identical skinny wooden houses. They were connected by shared walls so thin the neighbors' snores at night made the rafters shake. During the day, the women gathered in the shared yard behind the houses. Ning and her mother were not welcome. She had only known about Hui's engagement from listening to gossip from their kitchen window.

"Women never praise while gossiping." Number One Boy had a proverb to fit every occasion. From her eavesdropping, Ning could attest to the truth of that. The neighbors thought Mama arrogant. "Who does she think

16

she is putting on airs? She lives with us in the slums of the Old City, doesn't she? Her house is no better than ours!"

"Where does she get her money?" one neighbor would ask. The answer: "A foreign devil brings her a chest of coins every month." Another would disagree, "I hear she gambles." Both answers were true, but it was rude of them to speculate about Mama's money.

They wondered why she lived alone with only a daughter and a servant. "Where is Foo-Tai Sun's husband?" they whispered. "He is a foreign devil. Maybe he tired of her and went back to the West." The first speaker might add, "He left because his daughter is so ugly!" No matter how tightly Ning covered her ears, that one echoed in her skull.

Most unforgivable of all to the nosy neighbors was Mama's refusal to satisfy their curiosity in any way. She wouldn't even answer Ning's questions! And there was so much Ning wanted to know.

For instance, Ning wondered about Mama's family. Family was everything in China, but Ning had never met a single relative. And what about the father she had never met? Who was he? Was he English? Or French? Or German? Why did he leave? Did he run away because Mama scolded him too much? Maybe he beat Mama and she ran away from him? No matter how often Ning asked, Mama only said, "He is a ghost." At first Ning thought he was dead, but Number One Boy explained he was alive but must not be spoken of. Why couldn't Mama just tell her the truth? Why did she have to hide the past the same way she hid Ning?

She rested her cheek against the dragon's head. A gust of wind caught a stray hair that had escaped her braid. She took a big breath and tasted . . . possibility. If she were a bird, like the red-billed seagulls that hunted the river eels, she'd soar above the rooftops, over the walls around the Old City to the river. Swooping between the flat-bottomed Chinese junks and the sailing clippers from Europe, she would glide on the wind to the deepest water to greet the enormous steamers with their belching smoke-stacks. One of those ships must come from a place where people were kinder. Where Ning wouldn't be mocked because she was different. Where she might belong.

The party guests started to make their farewells. Below, a watchman patrolled the alley, his bamboo sticks clacking to ward away anyone with evil thoughts.

He's warning ME I was disobedient.

As if her thoughts had summoned Mama home, Ning's ears caught the rumble of wooden wheels slipping along the greasy cobblestones. Mama was here. Clutching the roof's edge, Ning peered below to see a rickshaw stop in front of their gate. After a long moment, the door swung open. Number One Boy's lantern cast a circle of light in the dark courtyard. Mama's querulous voice scolded him for keeping her waiting.

Ning scurried inside, nearly falling off the ladder in

her haste. She slipped into their shared bedroom and hopped on her stool next to the lattice window, tucking her feet out of sight. As he did every night, Number One Boy deposited Mama in the doorway.

Ning watched his face to see if he had a message for her. He put his finger to his lips. He had not told Mama that Ning had tried to go to the party.

"Thank you," she mouthed.

Mama didn't notice their silent conversation as she tottered into the room. She swayed like a lily but smelled of jasmine. Despite the late hour, her pale white makeup was still smooth. Her face was perfectly oval and her eyes dark and mysterious. Ning wished so much she could look like her. Maybe Mama would love her daughter more if she saw something of herself reflected in Ning.

Mama clicked her tongue, "You should be in bed."

"I waited up to help you."

Mama's carefully painted lips pursed. "So help me then."

Touching the wall lightly for balance, Mama moved gingerly to her platform bed.

Taller than her mother, Ning lowered her down to the thin mattress. A basin of water and clean rags at hand, Ning cleared away Mama's makeup with quick, sure strokes. The final step was to take off Mama's shoes. She sighed at the blood oozing from the knuckles of Mama's big toes.

As a child, Mama's mother had broken her feet and bound them so tightly that her toes folded permanently under the arch of her foot. Mama's "lotus blossoms" were no larger than a child's fist. They were a mark of her good breeding.

Mama made no sign as Ning gently wiped away the traces of blood and rewrapped Mama's feet with clean cloths. With quick practiced movements, she tied Mama's sleeping slippers with red ribbon—red for good fortune, like Hui's wedding dress or the lanterns that adorned her courtyard.

Staring down at Mama's golden silk rug, Ning asked in a low voice, "Were you favored at the tables?" She held her breath—if the mahjong tiles had been cruel, Ning would be slapped for reminding Mama of her losses.

"I was," Mama said with satisfaction. Her eyes rested on Ning's bare feet. "How are your feet so filthy when you never leave the house? Wash them so you don't soil the bed linen."

Reusing the dirty water, Ning wiped the dirt from the roof away. Under Mama's disapproving gaze, she scrubbed quickly. Especially when her own lotus blossoms were aching, nothing irritated Mama more than the sight of Ning's natural, unbound, ugly feet.

chapter *Three*

The room lightened with the pale rising sun. Ning had slept very little, staring at the ceiling in the dark trying to forget the night before. If only the shadows could crowd out the memory of Hui's glare—or her face disappearing behind her fan. Ning touched the sore spots Master Feng's grip had left on her arm as he forced her out of his house. She squeezed her eyes shut. Think of anything else. Anyone else.

Another memory of a so-called friend, Abigail, crowded out Hui. But that memory gave Ning no comfort.

Abigail had been an English girl at the Presbyterian Mission School for Girls. They were both new at the same time, and Abigail had seemed kind. Ning hoped that she could finally make a friend who didn't care how big Ning's feet were. Ning had begged Mama for days to allow her to invite Abigail home.

That morning, as they hung their cloaks on a peg, Ning burst out, "My mama said you could visit my house."

"Where do you live?" Abigail asked.

"In the Old City."

21

"Only Chinee live there," Abigail said in the pidgin English that made a Chinese listener feel as though she was no better than the slime on the bottom of Abigail's leather shoes.

"I am Chinese," Ning said, being sure to stress the second half of the word.

Abigail gave her a sharp look with her light blue eyes as if to check for herself. She touched Ning's hair, holding up the dark brown tresses. "You don't look it." She glanced at the half dozen Chinese girls with their bound feet who always huddled in the corner together, like frightened sheep. "Your feet are normal."

"My mother is Chinese. I am Chinese," Ning said.

"An English girl can't be friends with a Chinee girl," Abigail said. "My father would never allow it." After a moment she added, "I'm sorry." But she didn't sound sorry.

The anger and hurt exploded inside Ning like a hundred firecrackers held in a fist. How dare this pale, white girl say Ning wasn't good enough? She shoved Abigail to the ground. "Foreign devil!" Ning shouted. "You don't belong here! Go home."

That was her last day at the school.

The rice paper at the window rattled and Mama stirred slightly in her sleep. Ning exhaled in time to her mother's snores. The sun was taking its time rising. Not that she was eager for today to begin. Why would this day be different than any other day? Mama's schedule never varied. First breakfast, followed by calligraphy and embroidery. After lunch she and Mama would engage in painfully dull conversation in English to keep up Ning's language skills. They would read articles in the English paper, *The North China Daily News*, about polo matches and cricket. After dinner, Ning learned stories demonstrating the Confucian Three Obediences and Four Virtues. Every day the same.

It wasn't always this way. Ning dimly remembered when she was little. Mama took her to the theater or the puppet shows in the market. They had giggled at the street performers, and she had bought Ning sticky rice buns from the vendor on the corner. But then Ning grew taller. The other girls disappeared into their homes to have their feet bound. Mama faced impertinent questions about her daughter. Then they stopped going out at all. Soon after that, Mama forbade Ning to play outside. Mama seemed as much a prisoner as Ning; she left the house only to play mahjong or go to the temple. But Ning was trapped at home.

It's not fair. Why can't I have friends? Why can't I play mahjong?

Ning's fingers itched at the thought of the lovely, smooth tiles with their intricate designs carved into the ivory. She loved how when she looked at her wall of tiles she could see all the possible combinations. It was as if mahjong's Four Winds were at her beck and call. She was a good player, maybe even good enough to win *yuan* at the mahjong tables, but Mama said it was inappropriate for a young lady to gamble. Once Ning had been foolish enough to point out that Mama wagered on the tiles. Ning's bottom had ached for days. Mama looked delicate, but she had a strong arm.

From its table in the corner, Mama's prized mahjong set beckoned. Ning was supposed to ask before she took it out, but Mama had come in so late the night before she'd be asleep for ages yet. She would never know. And a game would carry Ning's mind away from unpleasant memories.

Ning swung her legs to the floor. Mama's prized silk carpet felt soft to her bare feet. Soundlessly, she pulled on her trousers and tunic and fetched her three dolls from beneath her bed. Tiptoeing, she brought the mahjong set out to the landing. Closing the door silently behind her, she listened. When she was sure Mama's breathing was still deep and steady, she opened the lacquer box and drew twelve tiles for each player. Mahjong required four players so Ning pretended her dolls were friends eager for a game. She would play each hand in turn through their eyes.

Examining the three dolls, she sighed. She should be grateful that she had not one but two dolls and a horse, even if the horse was missing a leg. But Ning wished that at least one of the dolls looked like her with dark brown, waist-length hair and light green eyes that were too round. It couldn't be helped. She began to play.

Ning was the dealer, or the East Wind. Mama always said all good things begin in the East. To play the West Wind, Ning chose the wooden horse with a broken leg. Finding it discarded in the courtyard one day, Ning had polished it until it shone. She pretended the horse was her father. He was an unpredictable player.

Her favorite doll, a Chinese girl in formal robes, was the North Wind. Ning liked her pale, white face and long, black hair. She called this doll Hui, after her former friend. "You and your family were very cruel to me last night," she said to the doll. "Your mother called me yellowfish." Even whispering the word to herself felt like a blow to the stomach. Yellowfish were long and flat, like Ning's feet. It was a terrible insult.

The doll's dark eyes were as blank as Hui's. "Yellow-fish, you should know better than to come where you are not welcome."

"We are in my house now, and my feet won't keep me from winning!" Ning said.

She turned to the other doll. "Abigail, you are the South Wind." A doll with golden hair, she looked like Ning's old schoolmate. She was a gift from the ladies at the Mission School. She wore a white pinafore. Out of spite, Ning said, "You do realize that white is the color of funerals, don't you?"

Mimicking Abigail's British accent, the doll said, "Only the Chinese could be so superstitious." She lifted an imaginary cup of tea by its handle, sticking her pinkie in the air.

Ning sniffed. She didn't like the English with their fussy ways. Sometimes English ladies, like Abigail but grown up, wandered into the Old City to see how the "real" Chinese lived, as if the locals were animals in the circus. They moaned about the noise and walked around pinching their noses. Soon they retreated to the International Settlement where the only Chinese people were servants.

Good riddance to them!

The game began. Ning was lucky from the start, laying down four identical tiles to create a *kong*. "Take that, Hui."

"You play well, daughter, almost as well as a real Chinese girl," Horse said with a hint of a French lisp. Since she didn't know where her father came from, one day Horse might be French, another day as British as a cricket match.

Ning scowled. "I am as Chinese as Hui."

"Half as Chinese," Horse corrected in his gravelly voice.

"One look at your feet, and we know you aren't one of us," Hui said in the high-pitched Shanghai-style Chinese.

"I am more than just my feet!" Ning replied. "You were my friend once. You should know that."

"Shush!" Hui hissed. "You'll wake your mother. Does she approve of you playing mahjong?"

"She taught me to play," Ning retorted. "When she was a child, she played every day in a room with a cherry tree outside the window."

"Your mother was raised properly, anyone can see that," Hui said. "Her lotus blossoms are exquisite. But somehow she married a foreign devil and had a daughter like you." After a deadly pause, she added, "Your parents were married, weren't they?"

Making a face, Ning collected three red dragons to make a *pung* and win the game. "Take that, Hui." She flicked her finger at the doll, knocking it over. "And I've had enough of you, too." She shoved the horse inside the tile box and let the lid drop with a thump.

"What are you doing with my mahjong set?"

Ning started, shoving the box away as though she could deny playing. "I'm just practicing . . ." she said in a small voice. How long had Mama been standing there? Ning tried to remember everything she had said aloud.

"You are not allowed." Mama's smooth accent couldn't disguise her anger. Her indoor slippers had a platform to provide support for her lotus blossoms, but she was leaning on her cane.

"I'm sorry, Mama," she said, scooping the tiles up to put them away.

"Careful! You will break one!" Mama scolded.

Ning ducked her head. "Yes, Mama." Expecting Mama to go downstairs, she was surprised when she lurched closer to examine the tiles Ning had played.

"A good hand," she said, grudgingly. "But you take too many risks."

"I won!" Ning protested.

"Playing against yourself," Mama pointed out.

Her gaze on the broken tile wall, Ning muttered, "If I had friends, I could play with them."

Mama lifted her right eyebrow—something Ning couldn't manage no matter how much she practiced. "I spent much yuan to send you to school so you could make friends. And then you were expelled for fighting. Be patient in one moment of anger and avoid a hundred days of sorrow."

Instead of quoting proverbs, Ning wished that Mama, just once, could be on her daughter's side. "I've apologized a thousand times. If you let me go to another school, I will do better," Ning promised.

"You are twelve now. The time for your education is over." Mama added as if she were reminding herself, "Besides, I have other plans for you."

Suddenly, Ning was worried about more than a scolding for using Mama's mahjong set. "What kind of plans?" she asked warily.

28

As though it had just occurred to her, Mama asked sharply, "You said I played mahjong as a child. Did Number One Boy tell you that?"

Ning gulped because Number One Boy had been her source. Was it better to be honest with Mama or protect him? She thought of all the times he had kept her secrets, including his silence the night before. A lie then. "*You* told me, Mama, a very long time ago. Don't you remember?"

Mama watched her with suspicion, but Ning looked back not flinching. "Remember, you said that you lived with your rich uncle. And you and your cousins spent your days playing together in the garden."

The frown on Mama's forehead smoothed itself out. "Those were good times."

"Before you had me."

"Yes." Mama sounded distant, the past holding more interest for her than the present. "I was happy then."

"It would be nice to have a garden," Ning said, fingering a dragon tile. "It would be even nicer to have an uncle and cousins." She stole a glance at Mama. "Can we visit them?"

"We would not be welcome," Mama answered. "You have no family except me."

Hurrying to ask the question before Mama remembered that she kept her secrets close, Ning asked, "Is it because of me? Did I ruin everything?"

Mama took a long time to answer. "You did not ruin my life." Her words sounded strained as though she had to force them past her lips. "I did that myself."

chapter *Four*

After Mama started down the steep stairs, Ning swept up the tiles and her toys. Once her mother was out of earshot, she whispered to Hui the doll, "What does she mean? How did she ruin her life? Why does she have so many secrets?" The doll stared blankly at Ning. "You're on her side!" Ning accused as she shoved the doll under the bed.

Ning barreled down the steps, bringing herself up short as she caught up to Mama midway. Mama's progress was painfully slow as she had to balance all her weight on the knuckles of her toes.

When they finally reached the kitchen, Number One Boy was stirring a pot of *congee*, Mama's favorite.

"I thought you had decided to sleep until afternoon," he said. In other households, Number One Boy would be beaten for his brashness. But the three of them had fallen into familiar habits.

"I will wake up when I choose," Mama said.

"Not *congee* again," Ning whined. It wasn't fair,

after last night, that she had to eat watery porridge for breakfast, too.

Turning so Mama couldn't see, Number One Boy winked and placed a bowl of his special wheat noodles with sesame oil in front of Ning.

"That's better!" she said. "Thank you."

He scattered spicy peppers from Szechuan on top of her dish. Mama swatted at his hand but missed. "You waste my money with expensive delicacies for a child," she accused. "Frugality is the mother of prosperity."

"You have more money than the tax collector!" he retorted. Every quarter, a bank clerk arrived with a thick envelope of yuan for their living expenses. Ning assumed the money came from her father. Yet another question she wasn't allowed to ask. Mama didn't spend half the amount, yet she complained bitterly about every expense. The neighbors thought Mama put on airs, but really she was very cheap.

Mama and Ning ate slowly, Mama to aid her digestion and Ning to avoid a lecture from Mama. As a compliment to Number One Boy, Ning slurped her noodles.

"Tomorrow morning, you must get to the bakeshop very early to buy the freshest sweet cakes," Mama said. "I'm expecting a visitor."

The noodle on its way to Ning's mouth slipped off her chopstick. A visitor?

"Who is coming, Mama?" she asked. Did this have to

do with Mama's plan for Ning? Behind her she sensed that Number One Boy was alert with curiosity, too.

"Madame Wu will be here at noon," Mama said.

"Who . . ." Unnoticed by Mama, the servant put his finger to his lips; Ning would learn more if she listened.

"Ning is too young," he said.

"She is already well past the age when we should start looking," Mama said.

"Looking for what?" Ning almost shouted.

Ignoring Ning's outburst, Number One Boy asked, "Did she come to you or you to her?"

"What difference does it make?" Mama said.

"All the difference in the world," he answered.

"I don't understand," Ning said, struggling to keep her temper. "What are you talking about?"

"Madame Wu is a matchmaker," Number One Boy explained.

Matchmaker! Ning felt her face grow hot. She should have known this was coming; hadn't Hui just celebrated her engagement? But Ning, behind the other girls for so long, thought perhaps marriage was not for her. Even as she dreamed of life outside her house, she had never stopped to think there would be a husband, too. She would have to leave Mama and Number One Boy. She shivered at the thought.

"I'm too young!" she said quickly. "I'm only twelve"

"You're thirteen at the next New Year. It's not too

soon to start negotiations," Mama said. "The marriage will come later."

Thinking of Hui in her red engagement robes, about to marry an old man who'd already buried one wife, Ning's chopsticks trembled in her hand.

Much later I hope!

"What if I don't want to marry?" she asked.

Mama snorted.

"Marriage is the only choice for a girl of good family," Number One Boy said, his hands clasped before him in the manner of a wise man.

Ning's mind raced. There must be another choice. "I could get a job in an English bank," Ning said. "I'm good with sums."

Number One Boy hooted. "As if a bank wants a girl-child!"

"Then I'll go to sea," Ning cried. "I'll become a pirate like Ching Shih." Number One Boy had told her stories of the Pirate Queen who led an army of ruthless cutthroats. "She ruled the Seven Seas and the emperor himself bowed down to her."

Mama picked up her bowl and shook it at Number One Boy. "I blame you for filling her head with nonsense." She leaned forward and grasped Ning's chin in her thin fingers. "Why do you suppose I spend my time gambling at the mahjong tables? For my good health? No. It's to increase your dowry so that you can marry well. And you talk of banks and pirates!" Mama hissed. "You must marry."

"But what if he takes me far away?"

"Then you will go."

"What if his mother hates me?" A young bride was like a servant in her new family.

"Then you will remember the Virtues and strive to please her."

"What if she beats me?"

"Then you will stay out of her way," Mama snapped.

She doesn't care what happens to me.

From his stove, Number One Boy returned to the subject of the matchmaker. "Madame Wu's reputation is not the best."

"She was the only one who would come."

• • •

At Mama's insistence, they waited in the tiny parlor long before the matchmaker was due to arrive. Mama sat perfectly still in a teak armchair, like a doll, dressed in a black silk overcoat embroidered with red poppies. Ning wore a pale blue tunic, slippery in its newness. Unused to pants so long they brushed the floor, she found it difficult not to trip. For the first time, Ning wore her hair up like an adult. She felt like a stranger to herself.

Everything was going to change after this meeting.

Who would the matchmaker pick for Ning's husband? Would he own a flat-bottomed junk so she could travel up the Yangtze River to see the Emperor's palace? Or would he be a butcher who smelled of raw meat? She hoped he would not be a farmer because it would be terribly dull to live in the country. Most of all, she hoped he would not take her far away from Mama and Number One Boy.

She ran her finger under her hair to keep the comb from poking her scalp. "Stop fidgeting," Mama said without even glancing at her.

Adjusting herself on a long bench, Ning wished the cushion was a little thicker. She kicked and scuffed at the polished mud floors until her mother sent her a black look under her carefully penciled eyebrows.

This waiting was interminable.

Tick tock. Tick tock.

"You wound the clock," Ning said, surprised. Made of polished red wood, the clock looked as if it were British but it had been made in Shanghai. An expensive item, it usually sat mute in the corner.

"Madame Wu will notice every detail," Mama said.

Ning considered the parlor, trying to see it through a matchmaker's eyes. A vase of fresh lilies was on the table near the front door. The furniture was good but not too extravagant. A set of Mama's painted landscapes hung on rods on the wall. As in Hui's house, the small altar was in the corner. A stick of sandalwood incense sent tendrils of smoke into the air. Number One Boy was perched on a stool in the corner.

Tick tock.

"Where did the clock come from?" Ning asked.

"I have had it for many years," Mama said. "It was a gift."

Ning's mouth was forming the words "From who?" when Mama unexpectedly offered more information.

"Your father gave it to me."

Number One Boy's deep voice intoned, "Not an auspicious gift."

"Why not?" Ning asked.

"Listen . . . To give a clock," Number One Boy said. "What does that sound like?" Chinese words were often judged by the phrases they resembled.

"Go to a funeral?" Ning guessed.

He nodded. "Such a gift invites death into the house. Unlucky."

"Who asked for your opinion?" Mama asked, scowling at him.

"Did someone die?" Ning asked, breathless.

The long hand circled the clock face before Mama answered. "No one died, but I should have been more careful." Mama sounded so mournful that Ning thought her father might as well be dead.

Madame Wu's visit had already cracked Mama's silence like a quail egg. Ning was almost looking forward to the matchmaker's arrival: who knew what other revelations there might be?

Finally, Number One Boy went to answer a knock at the gate.

"Avoid looking Madame Wu in the eye," Mama said as she stood up to honor the matchmaker's arrival. "Do not speak unless directly addressed. And whatever you do, don't forget to slouch."

"Yes, Mama," Ning said dutifully. It would be so easy to sabotage this meeting. Was it worth Mama's wrath to try?

A woman teetered into the parlor behind Number One Boy. Her lotus blossoms were larger than Mama's, a fact both of them were sure to note. And her red dress was just a little too brown, more like dried blood than crimson.

"Madame Wu, you honor my house." Mama bowed from the waist, just shallowly enough to show that although she might need Madame Wu's services, Mama was of a higher rank.

"Madame Foo-Tai." Although the matchmaker was a tiny woman, her voice was loud and grated on the ear. Ning winced, and Mama's expression stayed carefully blank.

Staring at the floor, Ning stole quick glances when she could. Madame Wu's black hair was streaked with gray. She had piled it high on her head and fixed it with white jade combs. Her makeup was thick on her cheeks and cracking around her eyes. It seemed impossible that Mama would do business with such a vulgar person, much less invite her into the house.

They settled themselves in Mama's polished teak armchairs. Madame Wu's eyes darted about the room as if she were toting up the value of every piece of furniture and wall hanging. Number One Boy brought in a plate of sweet buns and chrysanthemum buds steeped in Mama's favorite celadon teapot, the one she only brought out for special occasions. The grassy aroma of the flowers as they unfurled in the water was usually Ning's favorite smell. But today she wouldn't smell it at all. Madame's peony perfume was so thick that Ning thought she could see it hanging in the air like the fog that rolled in off the Huang Po in winter.

Madame Wu sipped her tea noisily, then put the paper-thin cup on the table so carelessly it rocked. Ning held her breath until it found its balance. The gracious smile on Mama's face became fixed.

Not auspicious at all.

Madame Wu pointed as though Ning were a dog. "Is that the girl?"

Ning's hands were damp with sweat. She clenched her hands at her sides to keep them from her new clothes.

"Yes." Mama beckoned to Ning to come forward, ducking her head to remind Ning to hunch.

Madame Wu craned her neck as if to look for a bird in the sky. "She's a giant."

"She's stopped growing now," Mama assured Madame Wu. That was a lie; just last week Mama had complained that Ning had outgrown all her trousers but one.

Comparing mother to daughter, Madame Wu said, "You're a normal size, so I suppose the father was tall?"

Mama hesitated, then nodded. Through her nervousness, Ning found herself enjoying Mama's predicament: Madame Wu's questions could not be ignored. No matter what else happened, Ning would learn something about her father today.

"British?" Madame Wu asked.

"American."

Ning's mouth dropped open. Most of the foreigners in Shanghai were British or French; how had Mama even met an American? Mama's eyes narrowed, and Ning closed her mouth with a loud snap.

Madame Wu let out a long sigh. "That's bad; half her ancestors are useless. Is he still alive?"

"Yes."

Madame Wu looked about the room suspiciously as though Ning's father was hiding under a chair. "I should be consulting with him."

"He is not part of this," Mama said in that resolute tone Ning knew so well. Madame Wu recognized it too and moved on.

"Does she speak English?"

"Very well," Mama said.

Madame Wu waggled her hand as if that might be a benefit or might not.

"She's quick with numbers, too," Mama added.

"Men don't want a clever wife," Madame Wu said. "Confucius said, 'Ignorance is a woman's virtue.'"

"A clever horse needs only one touch of a whip," Mama replied, not to be outdone.

"Who would want a stupid wife?" Ning muttered. "I don't want a stupid husband."

Madame Wu's plucked eyebrows arched on her broad forehead.

"And I don't want to be whipped either!" Ning straightened up to her full height.

"Shhh, Ning!" Mama hissed.

"She needs work on her Obediences," Madame Wu said sharply.

In addition to his Virtues, Confucius had set out Three Obediences for a girl. First, she must obey her father. Second, her husband. Third, her eldest son. Since Ning didn't have a father, she had not mastered even the first one.

Madame Wu beckoned Ning with a finger heavy with gold rings. Ning came close and the matchmaker leaned forward and tugged hard on her hair. "It's healthy and long—but if her prospective groom sees her in daylight, he will know that her hair is not black." She peered into Ning's face. She threw up her hands. "No Chinese girl has green eyes."

"Perhaps not," Mama said, "but green symbolizes wealth and harmony."

Straining against Madame Wu's tight grip, Ning tried to catch a glimpse of Mama's face.

Mama never compliments me.

"Her eyes are still odd." Madame Wu made the word sound like a final judgment. She poked at Ning's legs. "Let me see your feet."

Ning took a deep breath; the worst was still to come. She lifted the pant legs to reveal her slippered feet.

"Ai yi yi!" Madame Wu leaned down to measure Ning's foot against her closed fist. "Twice as long!" she cried. "I can do nothing here."

Ning's feet felt cast in iron, weighing down her prospects. The unfairness of it all made Ning want to scream. None of her flaws were her fault—except perhaps disobedience.

"I was told you could find a husband for anyone." Mama's perfectly painted mouth was pinched with dismay.

"A yellowfish cannot be helped," the matchmaker said.

"Don't call me that!" The words sprang out of Ning's mouth before she could stop them. It was bad enough the woman looked at her like a slab of meat; Ning wouldn't stand to be insulted, too.

Madame Wu sucked air through her teeth. "Such terrible manners!"

"Ning, you dishonor our family," Mama said, her neck reddening with shame. She turned to Madame Wu, speaking quickly. "You found a match for that man who killed his first wife. And that girl who lived on Nanking Road, she had a lisp and a limp, yet you got her a husband. I thought maybe you could find someone in the country who would appreciate a girl who could walk easily. Someone not too particular."

"You come from an excellent family, Foo-Tai Sun, why didn't you bind your daughter's feet?"

"Her father did not approve." Mama answered flatly.

So it was her father's fault?

"The best I could do for her is second wife and that would never do for a girl from your family. I am surprised that the Mandarin Foo-Tai did not insist you follow tradition."

"My uncle was not consulted," Mama said quietly.

Mama's uncle was a Mandarin? If Hui knew that Ning was from such a wealthy and important family, she would have made Ning a honored guest at her party. Everything would have been different. Why had Mama kept this from her?

"I cannot work miracles. And I dare not offend such an important man by arranging a poor marriage for his grandniece," Madame Wu said. "It is impossible."

Madame Wu rose out of her chair, but Mama grabbed her arm. "Surely there is something you can do. For you, I would double the fee . . ."

Ning felt a rush of shame; her mother should never have to beg someone like Madame Wu.

Greed shone in Madame Wu's eyes for an instant, then faded. "It is impossible," Madame Wu repeated as she removed Mama's hand from her arm and gestured to Number One Boy to lead her out.

Mama and Ning listened to the outside door slam. Without Madame Wu's perfume polluting the air, Ning felt as though she could breathe again. Trying to strike a light tone, she said, "We can do better than the awful Madame Wu, Mama."

"She said it was impossible," Mama said. "I thought it would be difficult . . . not impossible." The word floated in the air between them, shrinking Ning's future to nothing.

"We can go to someone else," Ning ventured.

"She was my last hope." Mama's voice sounded hollow.

"So, I won't marry. I didn't really want to anyway," Ning reassured her. "We can stay together in this little house forever."

"Don't be ridiculous," Mama snapped. "Do you think I want to spend the rest of my life here with you?"

chapter *Five*

At the midday meal, after Madame Wu had gone, Number One Boy tried to comfort Ning with an old favorite, lion's head soup. Mama quickly finished her meal and retired to the parlor, leaving Ning alone at the kitchen table. Usually the meatball's resemblance to a fierce Chinese lion delighted her, especially the bit of floating cabbage that represented the lion's mane. But what was the point of amusing food on a day like today?

Madame Wu's words were lodged in her memory, robbing Ning of her appetite. Useless. Impossible. Yellow-fish.

Ning poked at the giant meatball with her chopsticks until it lost its shape in the broth.

"I will put it out of its misery," Number One Boy murmured, taking away the bowl.

"Will someone put me out of my misery?" Ning said under her breath.

"Don't be silly," he said over his shoulder.

"I'm not!" she insisted. "I'm too tall and my feet are too long. Mama doesn't want me. Madame Wu can't help me.

No wonder I don't have a single friend except you."

His silence said more than all his proverbs could. He knew she was telling the truth.

"Did you know my father was an American?" she asked suddenly, watching his back. He became still, his long queue hanging down as though the end of the braid was weighted with lead.

He did know!

"What was he like? How did they meet? Where is he now?"

His massive arm moved in circles as he scrubbed the soup pot. He said, "You must ask your mother."

Ning snorted. "Then I will never know anything at all."

. . .

In the afternoons, Mama scheduled an hour to embroider. Of all the Virtues, sewing was Ning's worst skill; she dreaded this time every day. Mama's work, as always, was exquisite. She was sewing a scene from a fairytale of a fisherman pulling a golden carp from a pond. Ning was practicing her stitches on a useless, overworked bit of cloth.

"Those stitches are too tight," Mama said. "They will pucker the fabric. Unpick the thread and begin again." Ning sniffed, *I wish I could start fresh, too.* But there was no returning to who she had been yesterday.

Ning heaved huge sighs as she worked, but Mama ignored her distress. Sorting through skeins of silken threads for the right gold for the carp, Mama was lost in her own thoughts. Every so often, Ning glanced up to see her mother staring at her, brow creased as though she was trying to wedge Ning into a design as neat as the one in her embroidery frame. But Ning was too large to fit; her feet and body spilled over its edges.

Suddenly, Mama let out a sigh, almost a moan. Ning's head jerked to see what was wrong. Grim-faced, Mama nodded as if she had reached an agreement with herself.

She's made a decision.

Ning's limbs felt numb; the needle in her hand slid away from her fingers.

"What is it, Mama?" she asked.

Eyebrows lifted, Mama asked, "What do you mean?"

"You have a plan, I can tell," Ning pressed. "What are you going to do with me?"

Mama sewed in silence as the hand on her clock ticked for five whole minutes.

Before Madame Wu's visit, Ning might have stayed quiet. But today's events had changed everything, and Ning was no longer willing to wait. Taking a firm grip on her needle, she stabbed at the cotton. "It is my life. Don't I have the right to know?"

"I will not be questioned by a child," Mama said.

The steel in her voice told Ning that Mama's mind was made up. Setting aside her sewing and pushing herself up from the chair, Mama added, "Whatever I do will be for the best."

Mama was gone, only her jasmine scent lingered. Ning let herself crumple into her chair. Tears began to flow down her cheeks. Number One Boy appeared silently and handed her a napkin to dab her eyes.

. . .

The next morning, Ning woke to an empty room. Mama was already downstairs with Number One Boy.

When Ning came into the kitchen, Mama greeted her cheerfully. A long lock of hair had come loose from her chignon and dangled by her cheek. Dressed in a simple cotton dress, Mama wore no makeup. Without the armor of the white powder, Mama looked younger. Kinder. "Come and put an apron on," she said.

"What's happening?" Ning asked warily.

In a voice so gentle that Ning was struck dumb, Mama said, "We're making ginger pork dumplings. I know you love them."

"It's not a holiday," Ning said.

"I have never taught you the recipe for my *jiaozi*. My mother taught me when I was younger than you."

"But why now?"

"We need to bring luck into the house," Mama said. Dumplings were lucky because they were shaped like gold ingots.

"There aren't enough dumplings in the world to make up for Madame Wu," Number One Boy observed as he pounded the pork with a mallet.

"Forget Madame Wu—both of you!"

"I can't forget the things she said," Ning said.

Tucking the lock of hair behind her ear, Mama asked, "Ning, do you want to make dumplings or not?"

Ning slipped Number One Boy's apron over her head. As she wrapped the ties several times around her body, she made her own decision. She would make the dumplings and take the luck—but also keep her ears and eyes open for clues. Ning had been blindsided by Madame Wu. That wouldn't happen again.

First, Mama taught Ning the exact ratios for the flour, salt, and water. When they finally started rolling the dough, Ning pushed too hard on the dowel.

"You must take care, Ning," Mama said. "Too thin and the dough will tear."

Ning's next effort was better. Slowly, the questions in her mind receded, and she began to enjoy herself. Next, Mama showed her how to cut squares that were all the same size.

"Very good," Mama said. "Now for the filling." They mixed the ground pork, scallions, cabbage, and ginger in a large bowl with a long wooden spoon. Mama made Ning memorize the ingredients and repeat them back to her.

"I can always ask you if I forget," Ning said.

"I won't always be here to ask," Mama answered.

"You found another matchmaker!" Ning accused. "You are teaching me so I can make them in my new home."

"Calm yourself," Mama said. "You don't need to worry about marrying for a long time."

Ning's eyes darted to Number One Boy—he looked as surprised as Ning. Mama hadn't confided in him either.

Mama tapped Ning's hand. "Now pay attention. It's very important that you put in just the right amount of filling."

Ning scooped out a spoonful and dropped it on the first square.

"The first time I made these for your father, I put in too much and they were raw in the middle," Mama said matter-of-factly as though she often reminisced about Ning's father.

Ning forced herself to keep working, staring down at the dumplings so she wouldn't distract her mother.

"He got terribly sick and would never try them again," Mama said laughing. "He didn't care for Chinese food anyway—it was too spicy for him."

"What did he like to eat then?"

"He often said he missed cheese and tomatoes."

"What is a tomato?" Ning asked.

"I never really knew." Mama actually smiled.

Ning tried to paint a picture of her father in her mind: an American who didn't like spicy food and liked cheese and whatever tomatoes were. And one who didn't approve of foot-binding even though it was a thousand-year-old tradition. It wasn't much, but it was more than she knew before.

Number One Boy showed Ning how to fry the dumplings so that they got slightly charred on one side but remained juicy on the other. Finally, she placed the steaming tray of food in the center of the table and they could eat.

After she dipped a dumpling in a mixture of vinegar and soy, Ning popped it in her mouth. "Ai yi yi," she yelped. "Too hot!"

Mama and Number One Boy burst into laughter. "Always so impatient," Mama said. After they had eaten every dumpling, their bellies were full. They reclined back like the seals that sometimes appeared on the rocky shore of the Huang Po River.

Into the sleepy silence, Mama suddenly announced, "Tomorrow, I am going to the Longhua Pagoda for the festival."

Ning stared in surprise.

"You haven't gone in at least ten years," Number One Boy said.

"More," she corrected him. "But the peach blossoms are supposed to be very fine this year."

Sluggish from eating so much, Ning struggled to make sense of this new development. Only a day after Madame Wu's visit, suddenly Mama wanted to go to the festival. It couldn't be a coincidence. What was the Longhua Pagoda to Mama?

"Can I come, too?" Ning asked, her voice barely louder than a whisper.

"Yes," Mama said. "It's important that you go."

"Why?" Ning and Number One Boy said simultaneously.

Mama said, "It is time to introduce Ning to her ancestors."

Number One Boy said piously, "To forget one's ancestors is to be a tree without roots."

Madame Wu had said "Half her ancestors are useless" because Ning's father was American. But now Mama was going to introduce her to the useful half. Ning's mind felt as full as her stomach. After all these years of knowing nothing about her father, Mama was leaking information like a sieve. What would she learn tomorrow?

chapter *Six*

Sitting on her bed, watching her mother apply her cosmetics, Ning did her best to keep quiet, but her exasperated sighs escaped anyway.

"I will not be ready any faster because you are eager to leave," Mama said from her small makeup table. One eye painted, the other plain, Mama looked as though she was winking at Ning. "Patience and the mulberry leaf become a silk robe."

Ning glanced down at her plain linen tunic. "I don't have a silk robe."

"Because you have never been patient."

"We never go anywhere, but suddenly we have to go to Longhua," Ning said. "Why?"

"Don't you want to go to the festival?"

"Yes!" Ning assured her. "But why now, Mama? Is it because of Madame Wu? Just tell me and I'll be still."

"The peach blossoms are very fine this year . . ."

"You never cared for peach blossoms before."

"Nor do I care for rudeness," Mama snapped.

Folding her arms, Ning waited.

"Stubborn!" Mama cried. "Why can't you just wait until we get there?"

"You'll answer my questions then?" Ning persisted.

"Maybe a few," Mama promised.

• • •

Number One Boy hired a rickshaw to take them to the canal south of Shanghai. As they bounced along the cobblestones, Number One Boy trotted behind them, panting and sweating in his blue robe.

"It will be dark by the time we get there," Ning grumbled. "The festival will be over!"

"The sun has barely traveled a quarter of the sky. We have time," Mama said.

Ning twisted in her seat to make sure Number One Boy was keeping up.

"Sit still, Ning," Mama said. "He won't get lost."

"It's so hot, Mama. We should get a second rickshaw for Number One Boy," Ning suggested.

"I won't pay good money for a servant's comfort."

At the canal, they had to wait for Number One Boy to catch his breath before he could hire a boatman to take them the rest of the way to Longhua. Number One Boy carried Mama down the slippery stone steps from the road to the water. As if Mama were made of fine porcelain, he gently placed her in the flat-bottomed boat while the wiry boatman held it steady. Ning bounded in to sit next to her. Her long flat feet made it easy to keep her balance. For once, she didn't envy Mama her lotus blossoms.

Number One Boy climbed in next. His weight caused the boat to tip momentarily; dank water spilled in over the side.

"You'll sink us," the boatman shouted.

Mama lifted her skirt away from the puddling water. "You eat too much food," she berated Number One Boy.

"Mama, Number One Boy can't help how fat he is," Ning protested.

Number One Boy scowled at all of them and took his place in the center of the bench behind Ning and Mama.

The boatman shoved off from the bank with a long pole. Ning quivered with excitement. This was the real start of the journey. And once they arrived, Mama had promised to answer her questions. Well, a few anyway.

As they glided through the circular openings beneath stone bridges, Ning waved to the people on top who were climbing the steep stairs to cross the canal. Their boat outpaced the rickshaws, carriages, wagons, and people thronging the streets along the canal. Mama had been smart to travel by water. But even so, they weren't moving fast enough for Ning.

A boat came up suddenly and silently on her right.

So narrow and low in the water, Ning hesitated to call it a boat at all. It was powered by a set of long oars rowed expertly by a man wearing a white shirt and a woven hat. He nodded to them as he passed and said in English, "Good morning!"

A few more pulls of the oars and he was gone.

"The British are mad," Number One Boy said. "Who would go out on the water in such a boat?"

Unexpectedly Mama said, "He was not British. Only Americans are willing to talk to anyone, even Chinese."

Maybe that is how she met my father. He didn't know that he was supposed to keep his distance.

Although spring had just begun, the sun was strong. Mama opened her golden parasol to shield her smooth white face. Ning plucked her tunic away from her sweaty body.

The street along the canal was filled with people at first, but they all seemed to be heading into the city, not away. The houses and shops were also crammed together but thinned the farther out they traveled. The boat reached a part of the canal that was shallower. The stagnant water stank of sewage and rot. Ning carefully breathed through her mouth to keep from gagging.

The boatman navigated through the maze of criss-crossing canals without hesitating. Ning wondered if there was a map of the canals like there was of the streets of

Shanghai. Soon, they were floating through small farms and villages, and the air improved. But the lack of people made Ning uneasy.

"Where is everyone?" she asked her mother.

"Once you leave the city, neighbors are far apart."

"It's lonely," Ning said.

"But the air is fresher," Number One Boy pointed out. "I miss our old home in the country."

Mama stiffened. Ning pounced, "When was that?"

"Never mind," Mama said.

"For now," Ning said, ready to remind Mama of her promise.

Mama nodded so slightly that Ning nearly missed it.

Her secrets are like ice on a pond in the spring. Cracks are forming.

Once out of the city, the landscape was completely flat for miles. Far in the distance, she could see rolling hills. The boat began to feel very small and cramped. Ning wished she could get out and run along the canal.

"How long before we get to the pagoda?" she leaned back to ask Number One Boy.

"Another hour," he said.

"A whole hour!" she cried.

"Patience," Mama said.

Ning groaned. "I know. I know. Mulberry worms."

Mama and Number One Boy chuckled. Ning was

startled—they were hardly ever all happy at the same time.

The boat turned into a watery rice field with a thousand pale green shoots planted in neat rows. The water was only knee-deep here. Insects with shimmering wings sped across the water with a sound like a "zip." Then there was the sound of "gulps" when the white herons, standing on one leg, gobbled up the insects. Herons symbolized long life and peace. *But not for the insects*, Ning thought.

Ning dragged her hand in the water, letting the silky mud slide between her fingers. The stalks of rice had sharp edges, she discovered. "Why doesn't the rice drown?" Ning asked Number One Boy, sucking a cut on her palm.

He shrugged. "Do I look like a farmer?"

In the next field a girl not much older than Ning was bent over double, planting seeds by hand. When she straightened up to watch them pass, Ning could almost hear her spine cracking. What if Madame Wu had matched her with a farmer? She would be living like this, laboring in the hot sun, staring at the watery ground.

Squatting on a tuft of land at the end of the field was a tiny cottage. An old woman, her face leathered by sun and wind, sat on a bench singing a familiar ballad.

> *Dragon brother in the sky,*
> *Sister flower down below*
> *Dragon turns then spring rain falls*
> *Spring rain falls and flowers bloom*

Suddenly, Mama was singing, too.

On the mountain grows a tree
By the tree she waits for her love
Mother's asking why she waits
"I wait for the flowers to bloom."

When it was done, the melody floated in the boat's wake like iron filings to a magnet. Ning's heart twisted at the yearning in Mama's voice. Did Mama wait for her love? Did she miss her husband? Maybe that was *why* she never spoke of him! A wave of pity swept over her, and Ning wanted to smack herself for her selfishness. She had thought only of her own unhappiness when Mama was suffering, too.

Throwing her arm around Mama's shoulder, she whispered, "I'm so sorry."

For a moment, so brief that Ning might have imagined it, Mama hugged her back. "For what?" she asked.

"He left because of me, didn't he?"

Mama pulled away. "Don't be silly," Mama said sharply, all melancholy gone. "Not everything is about you."

chapter *Seven*

Ning felt Mama's words like a slap across the face. Crossing her arms tightly against her body, she tried to make herself invisible. What had she been thinking? Mama did not care for hugs. Nor pity. Hidden from Mama's view, Number One Boy squeezed Ning's shoulder.

For once, Mama noticed Ning's hurt feelings. Sighing, she said, "I promised to tell you why we're going to the pagoda."

Eyes fixed on the prow of the boat, Ning was silent.

"I married your father at the Longhua Pagoda," she said.

Ning gasped. Of all the things Mama could have said, this was the least expected. Dozens of questions went through her mind.

Start at the beginning.

"How did you meet him?" she asked.

Mama's tongue wet her lips. "I was always good with languages. My uncle had me learn English so I could be useful when foreign devils came to visit. One day, he asked me to translate for a young American who had come to dredge his canal."

"My father," Ning mouthed to Number One Boy, not wanting to interrupt Mama's thoughts. Watching Mama with worried eyes, he nodded.

"We spent much time together and finally fell in love."

"A romance," Ning breathed.

"A tragedy," Number One Boy whispered in Ning's ear.

"What happened then?" Ning asked.

"He asked me to marry him."

"Impossible," Number One Boy whispered. "A foreign devil should never look so high as the niece of a Mandarin."

Ning swatted him to keep him quiet "Mama, what did you do?"

"I sent him away," Mama said. "My uncle's rank demanded it."

"But then . . ." Ning's voice trailed off.

"I missed him," Mama confessed. "So I had Number One Boy steal a boat and we rowed through the night to catch up to him on the canal." Mama's fingertips skimmed the top of the water.

Ning stared. Her practical Mama would never do such a thing!

Barely audible, Number One Boy said, "Yes, *we* rowed through the night."

Mama ignored him. "It was the only time in my life I acted without thinking."

"It's like a fairy tale," Ning said.

"You can't build a life from fantasies," Mama said, regret laced through every word. "We were not welcome anywhere. But at Longhua, no one cared who we were. We came here to be happy."

And now Mama is bringing me.

Ning drew a breath to ask what happened next. Number One Boy cleared his throat, warning her not to push any harder. Ning took the hint and pressed her lips closed. He was right. Mama had said all she was willing to say.

They left the rice paddies to enter a slow-moving stream. Stunted trees along the banks offered a little shade but not enough. She was about to ask again when they would arrive when Number One Boy nudged her. "Look."

Shading her eyes from the midday sun, she caught her breath as she spied the silhouette of a tower lording over the flat marshes. No one could mistake this was a building of great importance.

Finally.

"Mama, there it is!" Ning cried, bending forward at the waist as though that could make the boat go faster.

Mama shushed her, but her eyes were fixed on the pagoda, too.

The boatman got closer. The pagoda was made of red brick and polished dark wood. The glazed terra-cotta tiles glistened in the sun. Ning counted seven stories. The roof at each level curved up and outward gracefully, like a bird's wings about to take flight. The pagoda was built on a pedestal to give it even more height. What was the view like from the top?

"It's so tall," she whispered.

"There are taller buildings in Shanghai," Mama said, but she seemed pleased that Ning was suitably awed.

"Those are for the foreign devils. This is Chinese."

"It is beautiful, isn't it?" Mama said.

Next to the pagoda was a tall stone wall. "The temple is inside the walls," Mama said.

"Is that where we are going?"

Mama nodded.

"Look!" Ning cried. A crowd at the base of the pagoda, too far away for her to make out their faces or hear their voices, had parted to make way for an enormous red dragon slithering like a snake in water. Ning knew it was really a dozen dancers holding up a cloth skin with long poles, but from this distance, it resembled a real dragon.

Echoing her thoughts, Number One Boy murmured, "Lustrous dragons. That is what Longhua means."

Tearing her eyes from the dragon, Ning turned to see his face. "Dragons?"

"The Emperor built the pagoda ten centuries ago to hold the ashes of the very first Buddha. The dragons are its guardians. And on this day every year they return to Longhua." His voice lifted in an enticing lilt, "It is said they grant wishes."

"First pirates, now dragons," Mama muttered.

"They'll grant my wishes?" Ning whispered.

He nodded.

"What do I do?"

"You must leave an offering at the feet of the jade dragons," he said. "If they are pleased, they will grant your heart's desire."

Ning frowned. "Just one?"

He shrugged. "You could ask for ten, but the dragons might think you are greedy and send you away with nothing."

"What would you wish for, Mama?"

Mama looked so sad. Suddenly Ning was sure that Mama's wish was about her.

A shiver ran down Ning's back.

Now her only wish was to know Mama's.

chapter Eight

Suddenly Ning was not quite as eager to arrive. Needing time to think, she slipped her hand in the water to slow the boat's progress.

Number One Boy's sharp eyes saw everything. He pulled her hand back inside the boat. "You cannot hold back the tide." His soft voice was for her ears only. "And you cannot keep your mother from doing what she thinks is best."

The day had been still and windless, but all at once Ning felt a breeze on her body. She lifted her face and heard notes of music floating on the wind. A whisper so joyful she had to smile despite her worries. She searched from the water to the land to the pagoda. Ah, there! Tiny bells at the end of the curved rooftops of the pagoda were greeting her in song.

"Be easy, Ning," hundreds of bells seemed to say. She let them calm her. Mama could be trusted to do the right thing.

They joined a line of boats jostling along the muddy bank. No sooner had one boat disgorged its passengers, then another took its place. After preaching patience all day, now Mama harangued the boatman to get to the front of the line.

Ning couldn't take her eyes off the family in the boat ahead of them. The father stood so straight and tall Ning thought he must be a soldier. His wife held tight to his arm, and a little boy followed behind. If her own father had not left, then Ning's family would look like that: a Baba, a Mama, and a Ning.

Maybe the dragons were giving her a hint: wish for your father.

Ning sat motionless, thinking furiously. That one wish would solve everything. Mama would be happy, and Ning would have a family. Everyone would understand why she looked a little different. She would have friends. She would belong.

At last, their boat bumped into the soft ground. Her doubts gone, Ning leapt off the boat.

"Don't be so reckless!" Mama scolded.

"But Mama, I didn't get dirty at all." She lifted a clean foot and presented it to her mother.

"We'll see how long that lasts," Number One Boy said. He stepped out and sank ankle-deep into the mud.

"Carry me," Mama ordered. In a moment, she was clinging to his back like a brightly feathered bird.

"Can we go now, please?" Ning begged. At least they could hurry without Mama's feet holding them back.

She tugged on Number One Boy's arm. What if the dragons only granted so many wishes a day?

Pilgrims arrived from all directions, drawn to the pagoda like ants to honey. Ning hadn't been to a festival in so long she had forgotten they drew all kinds: peasants and farmers, elegant ladies and their servants, scholars in dark blue robes, and children dressed in their finery.

At first, there was room for Ning to stride and swing her arms, but the crowd grew denser as they approached the pagoda. Tall as Ning was, she couldn't see ahead of her.

"Stay close to me," Number One Boy said to Ning as he pushed his way through.

"Keep steady," Mama ordered as she swayed on his back, "or I will fall."

"I won't let you fall," he said calmly. "We are almost there."

Without warning, they arrived. The pagoda loomed over them, casting only a slight shadow from the noonday sun.

A loud twanging of lutes and the beating of drums announced that the dragon parade was about to cross their path. Number One Boy stepped back so quickly that Mama nearly toppled to the ground. Ning squatted to see the dancers' feet underneath the dragon.

"Get up, Ning!" Mama scolded.

Something tapped Ning's head. She cried out and

hunched away from the threat from the sky. It was the feathered stick of a stilt walker. He wore a long blue gown like an Empress, if the Empress didn't mind mud clinging to the hem of her gown. Ning's head barely came to his knees. Ning grinned up at the masked face bobbing above her. "Number One Boy, give him a coin for his trouble," Ning ordered.

"You both waste my money!" Mama cried.

Out of Mama's sight, Number One Boy held out his hand behind his back. Ning grabbed the small coin and pressed it into the stilt-walker's hand. He nodded solemnly in thanks.

"Head for the temple gate," Mama said.

Blocking the gate was a pair of performers, a young boy and a gnarled old man. The boy wore filthy rags, but the old man's tattered maroon gown had once been very fine. Mama made a "tsk'ing" noise and tapped Number One Boy's shoulder to have him go around the performers. But Ning held back, mesmerized as the boy shoved a long sword down the old man's throat.

Ning's hands went to her own neck. "How does he not bleed inside?" she asked.

"It is magic," Number One Boy said. "The sword was enchanted by a sorcerer."

"Don't fill her head with nonsense," Mama said.

"It would be empty if I didn't," Number One Boy said, winking at Ning.

Finally, the three of them plunged through the stone gate.

An enormous smiling Buddha, arms outstretched, greeted them from the center of the courtyard. The temple monks, easily identified by their shaved heads and orange robes, walked in pairs, silently meditating. Ning felt warmly toward them; they had been kind to her parents.

Behind the Buddha was a large building with wide-open doors. That must be the temple because she could see dozens of lesser Buddhas inside. Off to the left was a path that led to groves of peach trees. Even though Ning could still hear the music and the noise of the crowd, the temple courtyard felt like another world. Ning realized that the point of this place was for contemplation, not games and parades. They were here for weighty reasons. And dragons.

Mama was battering Number One Boy's broad back with her umbrella. "Let me down."

He lifted her off his back as though she weighed no more than a sack of feathers. Mama, one hand at his elbow for support, dusted off her skirts and fixed her hair. All the while, her eyes flitted about the courtyard evaluating the other fine ladies who were visiting the temple today. Was she afraid to see someone she knew? It was possible. Opportunities for ladies to be seen outside their houses were rare, and these women were making the most of the festival. Like Mama, they moved on bound feet, clutching at each other or hanging on the sturdy arm of a servant.

Once Mama was satisfied she was among strangers, she sent Number One Boy to buy two bundles of incense sticks. She and Ning lit them from a brazier glowing with hot coals at the Buddha's feet and placed the sticks upright in a tray of sand. The tiny tendrils of smoke widened in the air until they disappeared in a puff of wind. Ning sniffed the air; the sandalwood was swamped by the heavy scent of peaches.

"Now that we have honored the Buddha, we'll go inside to pray to our ancestors," Mama ordered.

Her eyes watering from the smoke, Ning stared up at the cheerful Buddha whose sly grin encouraged her to be bold. "Are my ancestors buried here?"

Number One Boy's eyes rolled. Ning held her breath as Mama stared at the Buddha's expansive belly for a long while. Finally Mama said, "They are buried in Suchow."

Suchow was an important city to the west, famous for its canals and gardens, but most of all for the perfect lotus blossom feet of the women. No wonder Mama's feet were so pretty.

"Then why are we here?" Ning pressed.

"Suchow is too far to go. Many years ago my uncle's father endowed an altar here. The Foo-Tai ancestors have not forgotten. They will hear our prayers."

Mama began her slow walk to the temple.

Hanging back, Ning asked Number One Boy, "Where are the dragons?"

He pointed to the same doors where Mama was waiting for him to lift her over the threshold. The carved wood barrier in the doorway was too high for her to manage. The taller the barrier, the harder it was for evil spirits to enter. Ning hopped over on her own.

Does that mean I have a purer spirit than Mama? No. It's just that I have the feet of a peasant.

Inside the temple, her eyes took a moment to adjust despite the many candles. She had been in a few temples before, but none as rich as this one. Everywhere, she saw signs of an Emperor's favor and wealthy patrons. Dozens of small Buddhas lined the walls. A solemn bronze Buddha the size of a water buffalo sat on a gilded throne in the center of the room. A group of monks knelt on the floor in front of the statue. A small gong beat a rhythm for their prayers. Behind them were benches for the other worshippers.

Entwined about the Buddha's feet were two long sinuous dragons carved from green jade with white streaks like clouds.

The dragons! This is where the wishes happened. Her mind raced to compose the exactly correct request. Her thoughts were interrupted by her mother motioning Ning to sit beside her in front of a small, onyx shrine. How curious to think that this was her family's altar.

71

Quickly, Ning obeyed, but she kept her gaze on the nearest dragon. From his perch at the Buddha's feet, he stared back at her with eyeholes cut deep into the jade. What did he think of her round eyes? Would he think she was lesser the way Hui and the neighbors did?

I must believe that the dragons are wise and just. They will know I am entirely Chinese in my heart.

"Oh ancestors, this is your daughter's daughter's daughter, Ning." Mama whispered, "I am sorry you have not met her before. I was wrong not to introduce you sooner."

That was the first time Mama had ever admitted she had made a mistake. Maybe she had been shaken by too much remembering today. Ning tried to imagine what her life had been like in the household of the Mandarin Foo-Tai, surrounded by cousins and servants. Mama had turned her back on all of that for her foreign devil husband.

Mama murmured, "She may not look like your other descendants, but Ning is still my daughter. She will have need of you soon. Please do not fail her."

All of Ning's suspicions sharpened. "Why will I need help, Mama?" Ning whispered.

"Shhh," Mama hissed.

An elderly woman sitting behind them shushed Mama.

"Pay attention to your own prayers, grandmother," Mama snapped. "And I will attend to mine."

"Mama, please tell me. I'm begging you," Ning urged.

What plan was so terrible that Mama had to enlist the ancestors of the family she had left behind?

"Pray!" Mama commanded. "I brought you all this way so you could make a good impression on them."

Mama would have to make her case to them by herself, Ning decided. Rather than rely on distant ancestors, Ning was going to take action to get the life she wanted. She had a wish to make.

Mama closed her eyes to pray, silently this time, while Ning inched to the end of the bench and made her way to the nearest dragon. Its head was just at her eye level. In the flickering light, she could almost believe it was about to slither away.

She reached into her pocket and brought out a candied plum.

"I know it is not much, but this is all I have," she whispered. "Lustrous Dragon, please accept my offering and grant my heart's desire." She snaked out her arm and placed the plum on the altar.

Please bring my father home. Let me belong to a family.

chapter *Nine*

Ning heard a funeral dirge outside her gate. She peeked out into the alley. A dozen musicians were walking down the alley playing drums, pipes, and a zither. She heard wailing coming from Hui's house.

"What are you doing?" Number One Boy appeared at her side, holding a bowl of spring peas.

"I think Hui is dead!" Ning said. "Or someone else in her family."

He chuckled. "Hui is getting married today. The groom has just arrived to collect his bride."

"I thought the Fengs wanted this marriage."

"Of course, they do," Number One Boy said. "But once she marries, Hui is no longer part of the family. So her mother is mourning her now."

Ning caught her breath.

Would Mama wail like that for me?

The neighbors suddenly scattered, pushing up against the alley walls to allow the passage of a hired box carried on the shoulders of four servants. Through the velvet curtains, Ning caught a glimpse of her old friend inside a red lacquered box trimmed with gold. Hui sat perfectly still, like Ning's favorite doll. Next to her, face hidden in the shadows, was the groom in his dark coat.

"He should have hired a carriage for his only daughter," Number One Boy sniffed. "Master Feng is too cheap."

Ning ignored him, intent on seeing the crimson wedding dress. Ning poked Number One Boy and pointed at Hui's white headdress with beads that covered her face. "She can't even see!"

"She is not supposed to know the way to her new home," Number One Boy whispered.

"Why not?"

"So she cannot return to her old one."

Ning knew the bride went to the groom's house, but had never considered that she couldn't come back. The journey was in one direction only. No wonder Hui looked so stone-like.

How frightened she must be!

The procession moved past the house. At the end of the alley, they turned into the main road and were gone. The neighbors returned to their own courtyards. The alley suddenly felt very quiet and empty.

"She's gone," Ning said. She slumped against the gate, closing it with her weight. "So what happens now?"

"Now you help me make dinner," he said.

Ning waved away that suggestion. "Madame Wu said I'm not to have a wedding. And Mama says I'm too old to go back to school. It's been four months since Madame Wu came. Four months since we went to the pagoda. Four months since Mama made a decision to do . . . something! And what has happened? Nothing."

Number One Boy didn't answer. He sat on his bench next to the door and began shelling peas.

"And you, Number One Boy, you're the worst!"

"Me?" His eyes widened with surprise.

She jabbed a finger at him; a rude gesture to show her displeasure. "You told me the dragons would grant a wish. You gave me hope. But they have done nothing!"

A pounding on the gate startled them. Ning jumped up and opened the door to see a panting boy in the alley. "I have a telegram for Foo-Tai Sun. Is this her house?" he asked.

"Yes," Ning answered. He handed her an envelope with both hands then ran off.

The address on the telegram was typed in English. Ning held it up to the sun to see if she could decipher its contents. Quick as a cat, Number One Boy snatched it from her hand and hurried inside to Mama with Ning at his heels.

"A telegram," Number One Boy said.

Mama held her hand out to take the envelope; her face impassive. Then, excruciatingly slowly, she tore it open.

"I can translate for you," Ning offered as Mama scanned the few words on the paper then tucked it in her pocket.

"What does it say?" Ning asked casually, as if it didn't matter at all. "Is it about me?"

"That is none of your concern," Mama said. "You have become too inquisitive; it is disrespectful."

Ning started to protest, but Number One Boy placed his large hand over her mouth. "She will tell you when she is ready," he said quietly.

That will be never.

· · ·

Questions about the telegram tortured her all day long. Was it the answer to Mama's wish or Ning's? Maybe it had nothing to do with wishes. Perhaps her father was dead? Not knowing was torture. All day long, Ning stayed close enough to watch everything her mother did. Finally, Mama slid her strongbox out from under the bench in the parlor. And casually, as though it did not matter at all, Mama placed the telegram inside the box and locked it tightly again.

Perfect.

That night, after Mama was sound asleep, Ning slipped out of bed and tiptoed downstairs. She cringed at every creak of the steps. At the bottom, she waited and listened. Number One Boy should be sound asleep on his bed on top of the stove. He sighed loudly. Holding her breath, Ning stood motionless. Only when she had counted twenty Number-One-Boy breaths did she move into the parlor. She wished she could close the partition door between the kitchen and parlor, but that would certainly wake him. His ears were much too keen. At least the polished mud floors muffled her steps.

Careful not to rattle the contents and wake Number One Boy, she carried the box outside to examine it under the full moon.

It was locked with a bronze padlock, but Ning was prepared. While Number One Boy had been baking a whole fish at the communal oven, Ning had scoured the house for keys. She had found three in a drawer in the kitchen. One of them must fit this lock. She tried the first. No. The second. No luck. She inserted the third one, and realized that it didn't work either,

Suddenly Number One Boy was there. "I heard burglars," he whispered. "Or mice. I had to see which. Instead, I find a little pirate snooping!"

Ning rocked back on her heels. "Did Mama hear me?"

"Lucky for you, she is a sound sleeper." Number One Boy wore his pale blue sleeping robe, his queue hung over his shoulder.

"I need to read that telegram," she said simply.

He made the barest of nods and settled himself on the bench. "How will you do it?"

"I could break the lock," she said doubtfully.

"What would your mother do if she found out?"

"She would be furious." The thought of Mama's anger made Ning's skin itch like crickets were crawling over her body. She rubbed her arms as if to brush them away. "There has to be another way." Sitting cross-legged, Ning rested her chin in her palm, trying to think. Unfortunately, her experience with locks was limited. If only she knew a thief who could tell her what to do . . . Slowly, a smile formed on her lips.

"You have an idea," Number One Boy said.

She nodded happily and ran into the house. She returned holding two metal chopsticks. "Do you remember the story you told me about one of Ching Shih's pirates? The one who was locked in jail but used his chopstick to open the lock?"

"Your mother is right—I have filled your head with ridiculous ideas," he moaned.

Ning stuck a steel chopstick into the lock. She poked and pushed at the springs inside the padlock, but it stubbornly refused to open. "What am I doing wrong?" she whispered.

He shrugged. "Maybe try both of them," he suggested.

Using both sticks, one at an angle to the other, she pressed against one spring, while holding back the other. The metal sticks were damp from the humid air and slipped in her hands. At last, there was a click, and the lock surrendered Mama's secrets.

"I did it! I knew I could."

"Don't gloat," he said.

Ning lifted the lid. She pulled out a dozen bags full of copper yuan—more than she had ever seen in one place. What would Mama do with all this money now that she had no need to pay a dowry?

The only other item inside was a wooden box made of walnut and beautifully inlaid with white pearl and red coral in the shape of a tiger.

"Your mother bought that the year you were born," Number One Boy.

"Because I was born in the Year of the Tiger?"

He nodded.

Ning couldn't imagine her Mama being so sentimental. She tried to imagine Mama as a young woman, her belly swelling with a baby, shopping for a keepsake. On the other hand, Mama had never shared this treasure with her only daughter. But perhaps the girl was unworthy? After all, wasn't Ning sneaking behind her mother's back? Ning shook her head. It wasn't her fault that Mama was so mysterious. If Mama wouldn't tell her, Ning would have to find out for herself.

Suddenly nervous about what she might discover, she slid the lid off. The first thing she saw was a jade necklace, made with alternating red and green beads separated by gold ones. It was pretty but not unusual or very valuable. Why keep it here instead of wearing it?

Next was a folded piece of heavy paper. She unfolded

it to see a formal document handwritten in English with a red seal at the bottom. The letters were in cursive script which she found difficult to decipher. Finally, she made out the words, "certificate of marriage between George Hamill and Sun Foo-Tai."

"George Hamill," she said out loud. "Ham-ill." She sounded out the unfamiliar syllables. "My father."

"A name I hoped never to hear again," Number One Boy groaned. He glanced up at Mama's bedroom window. "Hurry up," he prodded. "Where's the telegram?"

"I found it!" she said, holding up a thin piece of onionskin paper. These English words were easier to read because they were typewritten.

2 JULY 1877

ARRIVE SHANGHAI EARLY MORNING
ONE WEEK FROM TODAY ON STEAMER
MANDRAKE.

GEORGE HAMILL

Ning had asked, and the clever lustrous dragons had answered! She laughed out loud, then shushed herself before Number One Boy could.

"My father is coming back," she said.

"I was afraid of that."

81

chapter *Ten*

"Everything will be better now," Ning said, pressing the telegram close to her heart.

"Will it?" Number One Boy asked doubtfully.

"When my father is here, Mama won't be lonely anymore. We'll be a family. It won't matter what the neighbors think." She grew breathless thinking of what might change. "Maybe we'll move to the international settlement and have a fresh start. I can make new friends."

He puffed his cheeks and then blew out a long sigh. "Your problems won't disappear because that man comes back."

"You always say 'One happiness scatters a thousand sorrows.' My father will be my one happiness."

"You'll still be only half-Chinese."

"But I'll also be half-American."

"That counts only among the Americans," he said. "Your feet will still not be bound."

This felt like a game where he threw an obstacle in her way, and she had to knock it down. "The foreign devils don't care about lotus blossoms," she shot back.

"But who wants to live with them?" He took a deep breath as if he needed a moment to speak calmly. "Don't get your hopes up. He's not the answer to your prayers."

"I wished for the dragons to give me a family, and they sent me my father," she said. "Why can't you be happy for me?"

He raised his eyes toward Mama's bedroom window. "I knew your father," he said. "I rowed the boat so your mother could ruin her life. And for what? The man was selfish. He abandoned her and broke her heart."

Ning covered her ears. "Don't say bad things about him."

He dragged her hands down. "He will break your heart, too. I speak only the truth."

Ning didn't want the truth; she wanted to be happy. This telegram was good news. "He wouldn't come all this way to break my heart."

Number One Boy rubbed the thick folds of skin on the back of his neck. "Then why is he coming?"

"To see me. And Mama." She paused. "Because we're family."

"Did he say that?"

"Of course," she said. She reread the telegram to prove him wrong. Actually her father didn't mention her at all. He didn't say he missed them. But perhaps that was just the way foreign devils wrote? Why waste money on words that could be better expressed in person?

She glanced from Number One Boy, so tall and wide that he blocked the moonlight, to the flimsy piece of paper in her hand. Why was he assuming the worst? "I want to be the first person he sees in China," she said. "I want to be there when his boat docks."

"Your mother will never permit that."

"Mama has her secrets; I will have mine," Ning declared.

"You cannot go out alone," he warned. "You'll get lost."

"You can tell me where to go," she said, feeling more and more confident in her plan.

"But you don't even know what he looks like."

Ning bit her lip. Number One Boy had a point. But surely Mama had a photograph of her long-lost husband. Ning rummaged through the wooden box again and found a photograph of a clean-shaven foreign devil at the bottom. On the back Mama had written "George" in her careful lettering.

She held the photograph to see it better. At that moment, a cloud crossed the moon's path darkening the courtyard. She groaned. How could the light fail now? If she were like Number One Boy who always thought the worst would happen, she would think this was a bad omen.

I choose to hope.

"I have his picture. I can find him."

Number One Boy opened his mouth to voice yet another objection.

She put her finger to her mouth. "Enough Number One Boy. George Hamill arrives in a week." Sliding the picture into the pocket of her sleeping pants, Ning said, "I'm going to meet him and you can't stop me."

• • •

Using a knife stolen from Number One Boy's kitchen, she added another slash to the five she had already carved on the windowsill of her rooftop hiding spot. The past six days had passed so slowly!

Only one night before I meet my father.

For the hundredth time she pulled out the photograph, searching her father's features for any resemblance to her. It was hard to find any . . . except his hair seemed dark. She'd grown up thinking the foreign devils were ugly—she was relieved that she didn't look like him at all.

If Mama was excited about George Hamill's arrival, she hid it well. Not only had she kept the secret of his return from Ning (or so she thought), Mama had not altered her normal routine even once. Ning kept calm as well; Mama mustn't suspect how much Ning knew.

To pass the time, Ning prepared herself for the auspicious meeting. She studied her father's picture so she would be sure to recognize him. She practiced talking

English with her polished horse. And she went over the route to the Customs House in her mind a dozen times.

At last the seventh day arrived. Greeting the dawn with relief, Ning eased out of bed and took the bundle of clothes she'd prepared out to the landing. She had deliberated for many hours over which items in her meager wardrobe to wear. Her finest outfit was the new coat and silk slacks purchased for the matchmaker's visit, but Ning didn't feel like herself in those clothes. She preferred her comfortable linen trousers and a plain tunic. Hopefully, her father would not mind.

At least they are clean.

After she dressed, she quickly braided her hair down the back. She took another look at the precious photograph of her father, then slipped it deep in her pocket to keep it safe.

Number One Boy was waiting for her downstairs, his shoulders slumped. "You are going through with it?"

"Don't try and stop me," she whispered, glad her voice didn't tremble; this was her first time out of the Old City alone.

"I'd sooner try to stop the tide," he sighed. "But let me go with you."

A lump came to her throat. He didn't approve of her scheme, but he was willing to help her. "No, I want to do this alone," she said.

"Remember, the boat docks by the Customs House on the Bund. It is the only Chinese building."

"I won't forget. Don't worry." She patted her pocket to be sure the photograph was safe. "Maybe I'll bring my father back with me!"

"I'm sure that will delight your mother," he said dryly. "You had best hurry if you want to meet the ship. The sun is rising."

As she closed the gate behind her, she heard him say "Be careful, my little pirate."

In the alley alone, she took a deep breath. Then another to calm the buzzing in her ears. She had wondered for so long about her father and how she fit in the world. Today, she would finally find out!

Glancing up at her mother's window, she felt that same triumph she did when she laid down a winning hand of tiles. She had escaped Mama and her secrets.

It's easy to be brave down here while she's asleep up there.

Tidying a stray hair behind her ear, she straightened her tunic and picked a bit of string off her pant leg. She was ready: it was time to meet her father.

She took off at a jog, heading down the alley toward Fang Bang Lu, the main road. First, she had to pass the opium den on the corner. It never closed, and there were always a few men slumped against the wall, their legs blocking the entrance to the alley. A fog of sweet, heavy smoke hung about the corner. She plugged her nose and hurried past.

This early in the morning, the street was full of farmers and tradesmen delivering goods by wagon or from baskets on their backs. A few rickshaws carried passengers, swerving in and out among the donkeys and people on foot. Boys were going to school in their uniforms. Ning plunged into the flow of people, only to be halted by a booming voice.

"Make way," a manservant ordered. "Make way for the Magistrate Trang." He swung his arm wide to shove Ning against the wall of the butcher's shop to clear a path for a sedan chair. Ning tried unsuccessfully to catch a glimpse of the magistrate behind the thick curtains.

Ning fretted at the delay, but she knew her place. Number One Boy had taught her to judge the importance of someone by how they traveled. Carriages were first, then sedan chairs, then rickshaws, followed by those in the wheelbarrows with the open seats. Only the lowest walked. Ning smiled to herself; she might be the most insignificant person on the street, but she had an important appointment at the Customs House.

She hurried past the storefronts crammed together into narrow spaces, their carved wood doors and shuttered windows shadowed by overhanging roofs. You could buy anything in the Old City from live snakes to carved jade. Inside the shops she saw the merchants, some already stripped to the waist in anticipation of the heat, arranging their wares for sale. She had no time to dawdle today, but she took note of a tankful of tiny turtles. Number One Boy made an excellent turtle soup.

Ning kept an eye on the road to avoid the muck and save her shoes. There were no sidewalks in the Old City, just deep grooves in the street that carried waste away from the shops and apartments above the stores. Coolies were already scraping the sewage into wheelbarrows to sell to the farmers for manure. It was one of the lowliest, meanest jobs in the city but necessary if the city wasn't to drown in its own waste. Even the word "coolie," bitter strength, matched their hard labor.

Suddenly, a stream of yellow liquid fell from the sky, splashing her shoes and pants. Ning was so intent on watching her feet, she forgot to keep an eye on the second-story windows. She looked up to see a housewife pouring the family's waste from a chamber pot.

"Watch what you are doing!" Ning shouted, shaking her fist at the window. The woman made a rude gesture in return and closed the shutters.

Father's photograph!

Ning patted at the photograph to make sure it was dry. It was safe, but she couldn't say the same for her pants below the knee. She picked at the fabric, pulling it away from her legs. She smelled awful. What was she going to do? She couldn't meet her father stained with urine. Going home was not an option; she would never manage to sneak out a second time.

Everyone passing by was much too preoccupied with their own business to notice her predicament. Glancing about the street for a solution, she spied a large barrel of water—there was one on every corner because of the threat of fire in a wooden city—and hurried over. The water was brackish and had a thin film of algae on top, but it was better than nothing. She scooped handfuls of water onto her pants until they were soaked through. Hopefully, only water was left now.

Ning's eyes traveled skyward. Despite all the red store signs with gold calligraphy obstructing her view, she was able to see that the sun was creeping higher. She had to go. Squishing and dripping, she pushed her way past those street vendors who couldn't afford a shop. There was Number One Boy's favorite barber who was shaving a clerk's head with a long, straight razor. A servant stood by to braid the customer's queue that sprung from the back of his skull and hung down to his waist. The flower seller was arranging baskets of peonies, chrysanthemums, and camellias on the corner. Mama was partial to white lilies and, every few weeks, Number One Boy spent his own money to buy a bunch for Mama. She scolded him for spending too much, but secretly she loved them. Ning hated lilies; the longer they stayed in the house, the more they smelled like rot and decay. Mama's lighter jasmine perfume was much more pleasant to Ning's nose.

Ning dodged an old woman who had a wooden yoke strapped across her back with baskets hanging off both ends. One contained a bleating young pig, and the other was filled with garlicky greens. All the ingredients of Ning's favorite meal—pork sautéed with garlic. She would have to ask Number One Boy to make a special meal for her father. Maybe as soon as tonight the three of them would eat at Mama's table. A family dinner.

Turning the corner to head toward the river, her heart sank when she heard her name being called in a querulous voice. "Foo-Tai Ning!"

Reluctantly, she slowed. Master Li, the apothecary beckoned her over. One of the most respected Chinamen in the Old City, his medications and potions were famous. He had no use for all the country women who sold ginseng, wolfberry, and the like from baskets on the corner. Let the poor and superstitious use their wares; his clientele was more discerning, like Mama. His special concoction was the only thing that eased the sores on Mama's feet.

"Master Li," she said, bowing deeply to the old man. Shrunk with age, his hair and wispy beard were a blinding white against the midnight blue of his robe. Despite the heat, he was buttoned up to his throat. Master Li was always very proper in his dress and speech.

"Good day, little Ning," he said, "How is your honorable mother?"

Ning felt a stab of guilt. "She is very well, Master Li," she answered. She started to edge away. The *Mandrake* might be chugging down the river at this very moment. Maybe it had docked already, and her father was gone.

"And where is your servant?" he asked.

"He is at home," she said. "I have to go there right now. Good day, Master Li."

Master Li's beard quivered with curiosity. "You live in the opposite direction. Where are you going?" He sniffed the air. Frowning, he stepped closer and examined her pants. "And what happened to your clothes?"

"Never mind, Master Li, I have to go," she said.

His hand reached out and grabbed her sleeve. "I think you should stay here. I'll have my clerk go to your house and tell your mother you are here." His grasp was surprisingly strong for such an old man.

"No, thank you," she said, growing desperate. "I am late." Wrenching her arm away, she ran toward the river as fast as she could.

Not even Master Li's lotions would soothe Mama when she discovered what Ning had done. But surely when Mama saw father and daughter together at last, her fury would dry up like water spilled on a hot brick.

I hope.

The fortified wall that separated the Old City from the international part of Shanghai rose up in front of her. The wall was built hundreds of years ago to protect Shanghai from invaders, but the foreign devils had come anyway. They claimed the land along the river for their own international settlements and insisted that the Chinese had to live within the original walled city. Number One Boy complained that the Old City had become a prison, but Ning preferred to stay on the Chinese side of the wall. Even if the neighbors kept her at arm's length, the Old City was her home, and the Chinese were her people. Besides, her experiences at the Presbyterian Mission School for Girls had not left her with a good impression of Westerners.

But today I am happy to be on the side of the wall where my father is.

The passage leading from the Old City to the river was only a hundred feet, not so very far to make such a difference. First, the noise and smells of the Old City faded away. Then, she felt a fresh breeze off the river on her face. She emerged from the passage, blinking at the sun reflecting off the water. There wasn't a cloud in the sky.

A perfect morning to meet my father.

The river teemed with ships of all kinds, crossing paths, often just barely avoiding collisions. She scanned the river for the smokestacks of a steamer. She didn't see any among the tall-masted wooden sailing ships.

Closer to shore were dozens of Chinese junks with their square flat sails. The junks had large painted eyes on their prows: they saw everything that happened on the Huang Po.

Have you seen my father?

If the junks could talk, they would say "Ning, he's not here yet. You still have time."

chapter *Eleven*

She was standing in the middle of the Bund, the street with the best views in Shanghai. The British had built a road out of brick that stretched from the riverfront to an imposing row of banks, hotels, and shipping offices. It was so wide that ten carriages abreast could drive down it. All this open space made her feel uneasy, like a tiny mouse venturing across an open field. It was only a matter of time before a hawk decided she was dinner. After all, the only Chinese who were welcome here were servants or those doing business with Westerners.

The exceptions were those Chinese who made their living from the river. A group of sampans, their decks loaded with carp, were being rowed to shore by men in homespun bleached cotton shirts and short trousers. The fishermen would gut and clean their catch on the bank of the river. She wrinkled her nose and began moving away; she didn't need to smell of fish, too.

Following Number One Boy's directions, she set off west. After a few steps, she had to wait for a dozen coolies to cross her path. The wooden yokes on their backs carried great buckets of river water to sell in the Old City. Their sandals squished water on the pavement. That reminded her to remove her own slippers and wring the water out of them.

Farther down the Bund were the piers, jutting out into the river like spokes on a wheel. That was where she would find her father. But which dock? There were at least a dozen, but none with a steamer in front of them. What if the ship had already come and gone? Ning should have left the house while it was still dark. She broke into a run, speeding past granite banks and marble hotels.

More than one foreign businessman, unmistakable in brimmed hats and dark suits, frowned at her as she passed them. Ignoring them, she searched for the building Number One Boy had described. When she reached the midpoint of the Bund she found it, the one Chinese building still standing here among the foreign devils' banks and hotels.

The pier was empty. Trying to catch her breath, she looked eastward where the river met the sea. There! Against the wind, a steamer was moving through the waves as though they were made of spun sugar. Puffs of smoke, white man-made clouds in a blue sky, announced the ship's arrival.

There were beads of sweat on her forehead. As she wiped them away with her hand, she realized her braid had come loose. Her hands worked quickly to redo it.

Then she looked with dismay at her still damp pants. She sniffed at the air.

My father will be pleased to see me. He won't care how I smell.

Keeping one eye on the slow-moving ship, she admired the Customs House. So much more elegant than the Western buildings, its sloping tile roof was held aloft by decorative towers made of carved wooden pillars. All Chinese public buildings were the same, so Ning knew the tall doors led to a calm, open courtyard—pleasing to the eye and mind. Her eyes went to the upturned curves on the roof. Number One Boy had told her that while they were useful to keep off rain, they also repelled demons and evil spirits.

The two newish banks on either side of the Customs House were four or five stories tall, dwarfing the fine old building. Their roofs were flat. What kept the demons out? Maybe they were afraid of heights.

A long, loud horn made her whirl back to the water. The ship was close enough that she could make out the lettering on the ship's prow: *Mandrake*. Her father's ship! A handful of passengers on deck faced the shore. Was her father searching the pier for his wife and daughter? Ning waved frantically, but no one responded.

She waited impatiently as the boat was tied to the pier and a gangplank was lowered from the ship's deck. Only three people headed down the ramp, an elderly couple and a younger man in a dark suit.

Ning moved closer, eyes drinking in every detail of the man from his dark hair to his polished shoes. Was it him? Pulling the photograph from her pocket, she compared the image with the man. He wore a hat that hid his face, but his narrow shoulders and long legs were exactly the same. Even the suit he was wearing was identical to the one in the photograph. It had to be George Hamill.

From her spot between the ship and the shore, she could hear every word of their conversation.

"What is that stench?" the old woman asked, grimacing.

"The summer is always unbearable here," answered her father. "The city is built on swampland, so it stinks to high heaven. In a month, the mosquitoes will eat you alive. I'm not pleased to be back, I can tell you."

His American accent was strange to her, but his voice was deep and purposeful. Just like a father should sound.

"Will you be in Shanghai long, Mr. Hamill?" the woman asked.

Ning nodded to herself; it was definitely him.

"It depends. I'm here to settle an old debt," he answered. "But I'll be returning as soon as I can."

Ning moved forward to stand in front of him. She smiled, waiting for him to puzzle about her for a moment then realize who she was.

"Boy, you're blocking my way," he complained. "What do you want?"

Boy?

Ning opened her mouth to introduce herself. "*Baba*," she said but her voice was too weak to be heard over the seagulls.

Father.

"*Zou kai! Zou kai!*," he said loudly. To the elderly couple watching, he said, "That means 'get away.' These urchins will rob you blind if you let them." He started forward, holding his arm out to safeguard his companions from Ning.

He has to look at me. Then he will know.

She grabbed at his wrist.

He swatted her hand away. "Don't touch me."

"I'm Ning," she managed to say. "Don't you know me?"

"Of course, I don't know you."

She clung to him with her fingernails, as if she could make him hear her if he would only stand still. "Please listen," she begged.

"I said . . . get away from me!" He pushed her hard, and she fell to the pier. Her face scraped the surface, and she felt a sharp pain from a splinter of wood in her cheek. Like a wounded animal, she froze. If she didn't move, he couldn't hurt her again.

The elderly woman stepped forward, hand out-stretched to help, but George Hamill stopped her. "Don't touch him, Miriam. You don't want to catch a disease."

"I don't think he's a thief," Miriam protested, but she let Ning's father take her arm and lead her away.

"A beggar then," Hamill said. "Either way, don't encourage them. They're like vermin. They won't ever stop."

Ning closed her eyes, wishing her body would just dissolve through the planks and disappear into the river. Only when his footsteps faded to silence and she was alone did Ning get to her feet. Blinking fast, she swore that she would not let George Hamill make her cry. He didn't deserve her tears.

She tore his photograph into pieces and let them fall to the ground.

chapter *Twelve*

Somehow Ning forced her feet back to her front door. Her hand reached for the iron latch, but she couldn't bring herself to lift it. To go inside as though nothing had happened was more painful than she could bear. Number One Boy's observant eyes would see everything: the foul muck on her trousers, the scrape on her face, the shame. She couldn't face his pity.

Without any warning, the door swung open. Ning stumbled and would have fallen if he hadn't caught her.

"Shhh, you'll wake your mother." Holding her at arm's length, he took a long look at her face. He reached out and very gently pulled the splinter from her cheek. "What did he say?" he asked softly.

"Nothing," Ning said, shaking off his hands. "He didn't know me. And he doesn't want to know me."

A blood vessel throbbed on Number One Boy's forehead, but his voice was soft. "I'm sorry."

"I don't want to talk about it," she said, brushing past him. "Ever."

As she slipped into the house, she heard him whisper, "Damn you, George Hamill."

. . .

The kitchen was unbearably warm.

"Why did you cook this morning?" Mama demanded. "It is too hot to use the wok."

Number One Boy shrugged. Ning knew why. He had prepared her favorite noodles to cheer her up. For his sake, she poked at the noodles pretending to have an appetite.

Mama glanced from him to Ning, who sat sullen and silent at the table. "Have both of you lost your tongues?"

"No, Mama, I'm just hot." Ning wiped her brow.

"It is always hot in the summer."

Ning's eyes slid sideways to study her mother. Her hair was clean. She had washed her hair only last week. In this heat, there was no reason for Mama to do it again so soon unless she was expecting a visitor. George Hamill was not worth the effort. Maybe long ago he had been different, a man Mama could love, but not now. Mama was going to be disappointed.

Mama finished the last of her noodles and lay her chopsticks across the bowl. "Ning," she asked, her casual voice not giving any warning of what was to come. "Where were you yesterday morning?"

Ning froze in the middle of slurping an oily noodle. Number One Boy quickly turned his back and scrubbed at a pan that was already clean.

"One of our dear neighbors sought me out yesterday to tell me you were seen sneaking out at dawn. You returned later with dirty clothes. And Master Li sent me a note as well."

Ning forced herself to swallow the noodle. She took a sip of tea. "I . . . went for a walk," she said.

"Haven't I forbidden you to leave the house alone?" Mama asked, eyes drilling into Ning.

Ning began to make up an excuse but then thought better of it. "I disobeyed you," she said.

Mama waited for the usual apologies and stammered explanations. Ning chose silence instead.

Mama looked puzzled by Ning's reaction. After a few moments, she said, "Go practice your calligraphy."

Why isn't she punishing me?

Ning pushed herself away from the table and stomped into the parlor.

"Start with the character for 'Obedience,'" Mama called after her.

"We always start with that one," Ning muttered, but she did as she was told. No sense in provoking Mama any further. She pulled out the small table in the parlor and laid out a clean sheet of paper, her brush, and a jar of black ink that Number One Boy mixed for her specially.

There were thousands of Chinese characters in calligraphy, and she had to use tricks to remember them all. The symbol for "Obedience" was like a tower with a long rectangle missing the bottom stroke and two crossing lines. Poised above the paper, her hand stilled. Obedience. One of the most important virtues. Even if she hated her father, she would have to obey him. What an idiot she had been to wish for his return.

If she squinted, the character she had painted looked a little bit like the Longhua Pagoda. She added a thin, sad dragon snaking itself around the base. Now it didn't represent obedience as much as a wasted wish.

"Why aren't you working?" Mama's sudden sharp voice at her shoulder startled Ning. Her hand knocked over the bottle of ink

"Ai yi yi!" Mama screeched. "Boy, come clean this. My floor is ruined."

Ning stared as the dark liquid flooded her paper, the table, the mud floor. "Obedience" disappeared in a smear of ink.

Number One Boy hurried in with a wet cloth. He pushed her to one side and began mopping the dark liquid before it was absorbed by the floor. If only she could get rid of George Hamill as easily.

"Go outside," Mama ordered. "You have done enough damage."

Ning slipped outside. Her hands covered with ink, she had to push open the door with her elbows. Mama would explode like a firecracker if Ning ruined the door, too. She rinsed her hands in a bowl of water that Number One Boy kept for cleaning.

Inside, she heard Mama shouting at Number One Boy. Ning knew Mama was on edge because she was expecting George Hamill today; she wanted the house to look perfect. Little did Mama know that he had changed. Once he had loved a Chinese woman, but now they were all vermin to him. Ning almost felt sorry for her—almost, but not quite.

Reluctant to go back inside, Ning paced around the small courtyard thinking about a new problem. Once George Hamill told her where Ning had gone the day before, Mama would never let her leave the house again.

There was a quick knock at the gate. Before Number One Boy could come, Ning opened it to a messenger younger than herself.

"What do you want?" Ning asked.

"I have a message for Foo-Tai Sun," he said.

"You can give it to me," she said.

"George Hamill will be here at six o'clock," he said, holding out his hand for a tip.

The bile in her stomach hardened. "*Xie, xie,*" she said. Thank you. She slammed the gate in his face.

She slowly walked inside to Mama who sat in the

parlor waving her favorite fan to cool her face. Mama only brought out this particular fan when her mind was unsettled. It was very old. The silken thread was cleverly woven to show a crowded court scene on one side and a country picnic on the other. The faces of the figures were painted on slivers of ivory. Preoccupied with her own thoughts, she didn't notice Ning at first.

"My father will be here at six o'clock," Ning announced, watching for Mama's reaction.

For a moment, Mama's hand froze, then she began fanning herself again, the rhythm never varying. "How do you know?" she asked.

"A messenger came just now," Ning said. "From George Hamill."

"That wasn't what I meant," Mama said. "How do you know about your father?"

Number One Boy appeared in the doorway to the kitchen wearing his apron and an anxious expression. Mama stood up, her hand resting on the back of her chair for balance. Her eyes glared at Number One Boy. "Did you tell her? You've gone too far this time."

"Leave him alone, Mama. He didn't tell me anything," Ning interrupted. This time she would not ask Number One Boy to take the blame. "I found out for myself. I broke into your strongbox and read the telegram."

Mama slapped Ning's face hard. "You ungrateful,

disobedient child. Thankfully, I won't have to tolerate your disrespect for much longer." She turned her back on Ning and hobbled out of the room.

Ning held herself still until Mama was gone, then staggered back until her knees hit the upholstered bench. She sank down, cradling her cheek in her hand. "What did she mean?" she asked. "Not for much longer?"

"I don't know." Number One Boy laid his hand on her shoulder. "You should not have told her."

"I'm tired of lying to her."

Of course Mama hit the side that was already sore.

"Both my parents hate me," she said.

"No," Number One Boy said, laying his hand on her shoulder. "It just seems that way."

• • •

Ning pushed a broom aimlessly about the parlor. Number One Boy, sweaty and exhausted from cleaning the house to Mama's exacting standards, watched her with an exasperated frown.

"You are making more dust than you clean," he accused.

With a sigh, Ning asked, "What does it matter? I could clean for a year and Mama would still be angry. Why should I bother?"

"Stop pouting. No one forced you to tell your mother the truth," he chided. "She wants you upstairs. It is time to get dressed."

"I shouldn't have to dress up for George Hamill. He doesn't deserve it," Ning said.

He lifted his eyebrows and waited.

"Very well," Ning said finally. "I'll go."

Mama sat in front of the mirror, piling her thick, glossy, black hair into serpentine coils on top of her head. After she whitened her face with rice powder, she darkened her eyebrows. With a pencil, she drew a tiny flower on her forehead. Next was a faint red line from the outside of her eyes to her hairline to make the outer corners of her eyes lift toward the sky while the inner ones angled down to the ground.

Ning stared at the two faces floating in the mirror's reflection. They looked nothing alike. Mama was beautiful and elegant and Ning was . . . Ning. But perhaps Ning could change that about herself and make amends to her mother.

While Mama was occupied painting her lips, Ning quickly dusted her face with white powder and used the pencil to elongate her eyes.

I almost look like a proper Chinese girl. Mama will be pleased.

Suddenly, Mama grabbed the hand mirror away. "You

look ridiculous." Her voice cut like Number One Boy's sharpest cleaver.

"I wanted to look like you," Ning whispered.

"Not today," Mama said grabbing a wet cloth. Ning winced as Mama scrubbed her sore cheek. Then she brought out a new tunic that was the color of a plant's first growth. "It brings out the green in your eyes," Mama said.

"You never liked my eyes before," Ning pointed out, but she couldn't keep her hands from stroking the satin cloth.

Green is the color for new beginnings.

"I do today." Mama brushed a stray lock away from Ning's face. "Don't hide your face or your height tonight. I want your father to see you clearly."

Ning pulled away. "Aren't you afraid my ugliness will frighten him away?"

Mama's perfect crimson lips pursed in annoyance. "I am more worried that you will be insolent and bring dishonor to my house."

"Why should I care about my father? He has never cared about me."

"You are speaking of things you know nothing about," Mama said.

"Why can't you tell me the truth?"

"You have changed these past few months and not for

the better." Mama shook her head. "Questioning me all the time! It is disrespectful." She said the final word as if it were the filthy stuff that collected in the street gutters.

"You have changed, too," Ning accused. "Ever since Madame Wu came you have acted like I am problem to be solved."

"Ever since you were born you have been my problem to solve," Mama snapped.

Mama's words stole all the air from the room.

Breathe.

Inhale. Exhale. Find the breath to ask the necessary question. The one she had always wanted to ask but feared the answer to: "Don't you love me?"

"We're not talking of love, but duty."

"You used to love me when I was little," Ning said, wiping tears away with the back of her hand. "We went outside and had fun. That wasn't duty. What happened?"

"You grew up." Mama's made-up face was impossible to read, but her voice was terribly sad. And angry. "You were not the daughter I thought I would have." Her eyes dropped to Ning's feet.

"But that isn't my fault!" Ning cried. "You made that decision."

"You asked what happened." Mama headed for the door. "Put on the tunic and come downstairs. Don't dawdle."

After Mama was gone, Ning curled up on her hard bed, pressing her ink-stained fist to her mouth. Mama had finally admitted the truth. Ning was not the daughter Mama wanted. The knots in her stomach hurt so much that she pressed her abdomen with her palm to make the cramp go away.

She only had an hour left before her father came. Another parent who didn't love her.

chapter *Thirteen*

Ning glanced sideways at Mama. How did she manage to sit there so serenely, as though their conversation had never happened? And she expected Ning to do the same!

It's not fair. I want to shout or break something—but my father will be here soon.

Too soon, but not soon enough. It felt as though they had been waiting in the parlor for hours. She looked at the clock. Its hands were frozen at 5:55. The number five was one of those numbers that could be lucky or unlucky. She waited for the clock to move on. Another tick. Then another. Time was passing . . . slowly. Mama beat the air with her precious fan, and Ning wished she had something to do with her hands. She adjusted the hem of her new tunic for the tenth time.

"Stop fidgeting!" Mama's words spattered like drops of water in a hot pan. "You are just like your father. He couldn't sit still either."

"I'm nothing like him," Ning retorted.

Like a cat hearing a mouse in the wall, Mama's head jerked toward Ning. "How do you know?"

Number One Boy's face appeared in the doorway to the kitchen. He shook his head and put his hands together in prayer. Don't tell your mother!

So much has already been said today. Why not this?

"I snuck out and met his ship," Ning cried out. "He was awful to me."

"What did he say?" Mama demanded.

"He pretended that he didn't know me."

Number One Boy covered his face with his palm. Mama waved the fan as though she wanted to create a windstorm in the parlor. "You foolish girl. The plans you might have ruined!"

Before Ning could respond, two things happened at once. The clock chimed six o'clock, and there was a loud rap at the door.

"He is here," Number One Boy announced.

Mama glanced at Ning. "Wait in the kitchen. You may come in when I call you. Not before."

Not budging, Ning asked, "Then why did you have me sit here all this time?"

"Impertinent!" Mama cried. "Go. Now."

Ning moved to the kitchen and stood behind the partition. The door creaked open and footsteps made with hard foreign shoes came into the house. Soon Number

One Boy joined her.

"Hello, Sun." The unfamiliar sound of a man talking in English reverberated in the parlor.

"Hello, George," Mama said. "Please sit down." Mama's voice had changed. It was gentler, like shallow water running over rocks. For George's sake? Or, perhaps, it was simply her speaking another language.

She heard the sounds of her father settling into a chair. "You look well," George said.

"Thank you. So do you."

Enough with the polite greetings, Mama. What about me?

"Tell me, Sun, the money I send, is it enough for your needs?" he asked.

"Yes," Mama answered. "I am very frugal."

"Then why are you living here?" Suddenly his voice was louder, less polite. "I left you in a decent house, but now I find you in the Old City living next to an opium den. If you needed more you had only to ask."

"We had another house?" Ning whispered to Number One Boy.

"What did they say?" he asked. "You know I don't speak English."

She hastily whispered a translation of the conversation.

"We lived in a house in the International Settlement with the foreign devils," Number One Boy said, nodding.

"Your mother sold it at a very good profit."

Of course she did.

Ning put her ear to the door again. Now Mama was telling George that she preferred the Old City.

"Why aren't they talking about me?" Ning whispered. He'd been gone for so many years, and he hadn't bothered to ask once about his daughter.

Number One Boy lifted his shoulders.

"I wanted to live among my own people," Mama said.

Ning snorted softly. Mama never spoke to any of their neighbors; they might as well live among the foreign devils.

"I wanted better for you than the slums," George Hamill said. "I told you . . ."

"You told me where to live," Mama said. "But I did not agree with you." Her voice was still soft, but Ning wondered how long it would stay that way.

There was a long pause. "I don't want to fight with you," he said.

"It is no matter, George," Mama said graciously. "Let us have some tea."

Too graciously, Ning thought. Mama wanted something.

Mama called for Number One Boy to bring in the tea. Ning slid the door open for him. As she pushed the panel door back, she left it open just wide enough so she could see George sitting in Ning's chair. His pants

115

were tailored to cuffs that brushed the top of his polished black leather shoes. Most noticeable of all was how stiff he looked, like a marionette doll waiting for the next performance.

George didn't take his eyes off Mama as she strained the tea into his cup. She handed it to him with both hands. He stretched his legs out in front of him, sighing as though a heavy burden was lifted with each breath. Ning felt a pang of surprising familiarity; she too found Mama's rituals calming. It was as if time stopped.

"I'd forgotten how nice it is to drink tea with you." His voice had mellowed now.

"Do you finally like green tea?" Mama asked.

"No, I still think it tastes like grass." His chuckle was a low rumble that set Ning's teeth on edge. "But I like sitting here with you."

Mama sipped her tea, and they were both quiet. Ning shifted from one foot to the other, almost tripping on the hem of her wide trousers. Number One Boy scowled at her and put his finger to his lips.

Finally, she heard George's teacup clatter on the tray. "All right, Sun. I've respected your traditions. No business until after tea. Why did you send for me?"

Ning gasped. "What . . .?"

"Shush." Number One Boy clapped his hand over her mouth.

She lifted it away and whispered, "Mama sent for him! Why?"

"I want to know as badly as you," he said. "Listen so you can tell me!"

"I have to tell you something," Mama said. Ning slid open the door a few inches more so she wouldn't miss a word. Mama's voice sounded as if she were at ease, but her hands were twisted together like strands of a rope.

"You couldn't just write a letter?" He sounded amused. Ning smiled grimly—he had no idea that something bad was coming.

"Not about this," Mama said.

He stirred in his chair, uneasy. "Just tell me, Sun."

"You have a daughter."

He chuckled as though she had made a joke. Then he saw her face. "I have a daughter?"

"He didn't know?" Ning felt as though the mud floor was dissolving under her feet. She caught hold of Number One Boy's arm to keep steady.

No wonder he didn't know me on the dock. I've been wrong about everything.

"What's happening?" Number One Boy asked urgently.

"Mama never told him about me," Ning said.

His eyes widened, and his mouth formed a circle. "That's bad."

"How could she?" Ning started for the parlor.

"Ning, wait," Number One Boy reached out to grab her sleeve, but the satin tunic was too slippery. Shoving the partition door aside, she heard the rice paper tear, and then she was confronting her mother.

Startled, her father bolted upright. "Is this her?"

Ning ignored him. "You never told him!" she accused her mother in Chinese. For once, Ning wasn't asking a question. "You let me think my father did not care. But it was you! It was your fault that I have no family."

"I did not say you could come in!" Mama's eyes blazed. "What will your father think?"

Ning spared him a glance. He looked bewildered, clearly not understanding a word.

"If you wanted him to like me then you should have told him I was alive."

"I did what I thought was best," Mama said.

How many times had Mama demanded that Ning accept her judgment without question? No more. Ning's whole body trembled. She wanted to hurt Mama. Her breath ragged, her eyes lit on Mama's prize tea set. Not giving herself a moment to think better of it, she heaved the tray onto the floor. The cups went flying and shattered against the wall.

"I will never forgive you," Ning said.

chapter *Fourteen*

Tea pooled across the floor. Mama stared daggers at Ning. "I loved that tea set."

"More than you have ever loved me." The words flew out of Ning's mouth. Mama had always lavished more care on those bits of porcelain than she ever had on her daughter. Didn't she know Ning was just as fragile? A hard knock could destroy her, too.

George leapt to his feet and shouted, "Enough!" His face was red. Was he angry or embarrassed? Which was better for her?

Ning and her mother glared at each other but let him talk.

"First of all, let's speak a language I understand," George said. "Does she know English?"

"Yes," Mama and Ning answered at the same time.

"Good. Sun, tell me what's going on!" George demanded. He spoke to Mama, but he couldn't take his gaze from Ning. "Why is she so angry? Why did she break that tea set I paid a fortune for?"

Mama's eyes flitted, quick as a hummingbird's wings, to the mess on the floor. She inhaled deeply, calming herself. Smoothing her hair, she said, "This is your daughter. Her name is Ning."

"But she's Chinese," he said, tugging at his too-tight collar as though it were a noose.

"So?" Mama asked warily.

"How do I even know that she is mine?"

Ning whirled to glare at her father. "My mother doesn't lie." It was head-spinning to hate Mama with one breath and defend her with the next.

"Be quiet, Ning," Mama said. "You understand nothing." She turned back to George. "You are my husband; of course, she is yours."

He began to pace from one side of the small room to the other, an animal trying to escape a trap. "How old is she?"

Don't ask her. Ask me.

"I am twelve." Ning said quickly.

"I was here in '66," he said, after doing sums in his head. "I suppose it could be true."

"Use your eyes, George." Mama touched his arm and said in a quiet, insistent voice, "Just look at her."

With two strides he was in front of Ning. He grasped her chin and tilted her head up so he could see her face. Ning tried to pull away, but his fingers held firm. He drew in a quick breath and stared. Ning's mouth dropped open. His green eyes were the mirror image of hers.

His hand dropped away. "She has my grandmother's eyes." His voice broke, and he cleared his throat before he spoke again. "I have a child."

"You do." The tension in Mama's body seemed to ease a tiny bit.

"Why didn't you tell me, Sun?"

"You regretted our marriage. I knew you wanted to return home," Mama said in that simple way that allowed no argument. "I knew you would be happier not knowing you had a daughter here."

"It wasn't your decision to make!" he said angrily. "You had no right to keep this from me."

"You would have forced us to go to America," Mama said, "I could never be happy away from China."

"What about my happiness, Mama?" Ning asked in Chinese.

"I did my duty. You have never wanted for anything!" Mama snapped. "Now be quiet. The hardest part is still to come."

Ning's breathing grew shallow.

What could be worse?

"Greet your father properly," Mama said in English.

Ning bowed the slightest, smallest bow that would be acceptable to her mother.

With a twitch of his shoulders the way an ox feels the whip on its back, George nodded. Then he stuck out his hand. "In America, we shake hands."

Ning kept her arms stiffly at her side.

"Take his hand, Ning!" Mama ordered.

Ning shook his pale, callused, foreign-devil hand. Shouldn't there be a spark of recognition when you meet your father for the first time? She felt nothing.

"Now sit down because we must talk." Mama waved George to a chair while she perched on the bench like a doll, the pointed toes of her shoes barely touching the ground.

"I'll stand," he said, looking oversized for the small room.

"Fine." Mama shrugged. "Ning has become a problem."

"What's wrong with her?"

"Yes, Mama, what is wrong with me?" Ning asked rudely. She felt dizzy with the freedom of speaking her mind. Let Mama punish her later!

"*Bu gong!*" Mama snapped. Disrespectful. A deep breath and she went on, "I've tried to raise her as a proper Chinese girl."

George narrowed his eyes. "A proper . . ." Before Ning knew what he was doing, he knelt down and lifted her pants leg to reveal her feet. "At least you didn't mutilate her feet, like yours" he said, sinking into a chair.

122

"I wanted to bind them as mine were bound," Mama said. "But I knew that if I did, you would never accept her as your daughter."

Mama had told the matchmaker that it was George's fault that Ning's feet weren't bound. But he had never even been consulted! Ning glared at her mother, fingers clenching and unclenching like cat claws.

She's betrayed both of us.

"No matter what I do, she will always be the daughter of a foreign devil," Mama said. "Never Chinese. She'll never be part of good society."

Ning edged toward the door. She didn't belong to either of her parents.

"Shanghai has hundreds of kids like her with one Chinese parent," George said.

"But none from a clan as elevated as the Foo-Tais," Mama said. "There are certain expectations . . ."

He grimaced. "You knew when you left that you couldn't expect anything from your family." He pulled a checkbook out of his coat pocket. "I can give you whatever money you and the girl need."

"Money can't buy her a respectable husband."

"Husband?" He sat up in his chair, eyes wide with horror. "She's a little girl."

"She's the age when we start looking for husbands," Mama reminded him. "And the matchmaker says she is unmarriageable."

"Good. It's a barbaric custom!" he muttered. "We'd never stand for it in America."

"It is our way." Mama went on, "I hoped with a large enough dowry, she could still marry. But I was wrong. She will never have a respectable place here. Once I die, she'll have no one to protect her. She might as well be a beggar on the street."

"What do you need from me?"

Make her finally say what she wants.

Instead of answering, Mama beckoned to Ning. Ning shook her head, her long hair swishing about her shoulders.

"Ning, sit with me!" Mama barked.

Slowly, unwillingly, like a kite string being reeled in, Ning came over and sat close enough to Mama that their legs touched. Mama's body was rigid as a board, and Ning braced for the worst.

"She must go to America," Mama said.

"Mama, no! I don't want to go to America!" Her mother pinched her thigh hard, and Ning choked back a cry of pain.

George struggled to speak. "I can't . . . that is impossible."

"She has no future in China," Mama said, as casually as she might criticize Ning's embroidery. "But in America, no one will care about her feet. You are wealthy enough that she can marry well. She will have a good life."

His red face had gone pale. "I travel for my work all the time," he said. "I can't take care of a little girl."

"Once you told me about your father's big house. She can live there."

"How long have you planned this?" he asked.

"It was always a possibility."

"I have to return to America immediately," George said, eyes flitting around the room as if the walls were closing in on him. "She'll never be ready in time."

"Her trunk can be packed in a week."

Was her whole life to be tidied away in just seven days? Ning leaned in and whispered in Chinese in her mother's ear. "Don't make me go. I don't like him. I want to stay with you and Number One Boy. I'll do anything you want. I'll . . ."

"Stop it, Ning!" There was no pity in Mama's words. "He is your father. You belong with him now."

"Sun, look at her," George said pointing at Ning. "She doesn't want to come with me."

"What she wants does not matter. I decide what is best."

"You're not thinking straight!" George pulled up a chair to look at Mama, eye to eye. "America is on the other side of the world. The girl might never come back to China."

"I know." Mama's calm reply brought a chill to the room.

Ning stood up, swaying as though she had lotus blossoms instead of whole feet. Neither of her parents tried to stop her as she ran out of the room. She didn't stop running until she climbed out on her ledge at the top of the house.

She pulled herself into a ball, making herself as small as she could. Despite the heat, she was shivering.

Even this high above the ground, she could still hear them arguing. George thought he could change Mama's mind. Ning knew better. Mama was a puppeteer making everyone dance to her tune. Ning was going to America. Everything she knew was finished.

She covered her face with her hands as she considered the image of her whole childhood, now shattered, trying to reassemble the pieces into a whole that made sense.

It started with her birth. Mama didn't tell George. Instead, she had kept Ning for herself. But why? That decision exiled Mama from her family forever. The Mandarin Foo-Tai might have been persuaded to take his niece back, but he would never accept a half-American child. Mama must have thought she could make a life for them. Maybe she had loved Ning then.

All babies look alike. Mama must have hoped Ning would grow into a miniature Mama—that she could be Chinese in appearance at least. But then Ning's eyes had turned green. Her hair had never quite darkened enough.

And she was taller than other girls. Mama must have started to worry. Was that when America began to look like a solution? Was that why Mama had made sure Ning's English was good?

When Ning was six, Mama must have faced the worst dilemma of all: whether to bind Ning's feet. If she did, George would never bring her to America. No one with lotus blossoms could travel around the world. But if she didn't, she condemned Ning to be a yellowfish.

A baby cried out in the next house. His mother soothed him by singing a lullaby that Ning remembered from her childhood.

> *Without your Mama,*
> *you are like a blade of grass.*
> *Away from your Mama's heart,*
> *Where will you find happiness?*

The words of the song felt like hot oil spattered on her skin. Away from Mama could Ning survive?

Pop. Pop. Pop. The boys were setting off firecrackers in the alley as they often did. A bit of charred red paper floated by her. Holding on with one hand, Ning stretched out her other hand to grab the paper, but the moment she touched it, the fragment disintegrated.

Like my life.

"Come inside," Number One Boy spoke gently, but she still jumped. She could hear him panting from climbing the steep stairs but also from worry.

She half-turned her head in his direction. "Did you know Mama planned to send me to America?"

"I feared it," he said. "Come before you fall to your death."

If I go inside, I'm one step closer to leaving.

"America is too far," she said. "I only wanted to leave our house once in a while. I never wanted to go around the world. I'm afraid."

"You are as brave as a lion. Braver even than the Pirate Queen. Now come in." Number One Boy reached for her sleeve. She slid on her bottom, just out of reach. "Please don't make me go out there and fetch you."

"You couldn't fit even your big head through that window," she said with a sniff.

"Ning!"

She could always tell when she had pushed Number One Boy too far. "All right," she said. As soon as she was within reach, he hauled her inside, depositing her on the floor with a thump.

"You scared me," he said, glaring down at her. "You should be ashamed to treat your friends like that."

"I'm sorry," she whispered. In that instant, she realized she would miss Number One Boy most of all. "You're my only friend! I can't lose you too!" she cried. "Come with me."

"You know I can't." His eyes were watery. "Your father would never allow it. He dislikes me as much as I dislike him. And someone has to look after your mother."

"Who will look after me?" She crossed her arms tightly against her chest to keep from splitting apart.

He pulled her up by her elbows. "Necessity breeds strength. You can do this."

"But I don't want to leave," she cried.

"Maybe this is for the best," he said earnestly. "The problems you have here won't matter there. And think how jealous Hui will be when she hears you've gone all the way to America."

A small laugh started in her throat, but it got lost in a sob. He pulled her close, and she buried her face in his blue robe and let herself cry and cry and cry. She didn't pull away until she had used up all her tears.

"I love you, Number One Boy."

"I love you too, little pirate."

chapter *Fifteen*

Number One Boy dropped the trunk on the floor with a loud thump.

"Finally," Mama said from her cosmetic table. "Her ship leaves in three days. I don't know why it took you so long to buy a simple trunk."

"I had to make sure it was the best for our Ning," he said.

"One trunk is much like another," Mama retorted.

"Only if you don't appreciate what makes it special."

They had been sniping at each other for the past few days. Neither noticed that Ning winced at every jab.

"It is very nice," Ning said, eyeing the wooden box with leather straps and brass fittings.

"Where is the dress I ordered?" Mama asked. "And the coat and boots?"

"They are in the trunk. If you ask me, they are very ugly."

"I did not ask you," Mama said. "Leave us alone."

Ning looked up—something in Mama's voice made

her uneasy. She had sounded the same when she told George Hamill, "Ning has become a problem."

Number One Boy's lips pressed tightly together.

He hears it, too.

"I said . . . go," Mama said, her lacquered fingernail tapping on her sleeve.

"Very well, mistress," he said as he slowly backed out of the room. "I would not think of disobeying you. You might send me away and then I would have no one."

Ning wished he would stay. She preferred their bickering to being alone with her mother.

"What is it, Mama?" Ning asked wearily.

Instead of answering, Mama said, "Aren't you going to look at your new clothes? They were very expensive."

"I want to stay here and wear my old clothes," Ning said sullenly.

"That is not possible." Mama was implacable.

"You decided to send me away. You can change your mind." Even as Ning made the argument, she knew it was useless. They had had a dozen variations of this conversation over the past several days. Ning and Mama were on opposite sides of a wide divide and neither would extend a hand to the other.

Mama let out an exasperated puff of air. Turning to her mirror, she undid her chignon and began brushing her long hair. "Just pack your things."

Ning picked up her tunic. It smelled of garlic and ginger and something harder to identify. Maybe the herbs in Mama's special foot ointment? Definitely the oily soot on the landing of her private attic. There was a hint of rotten egg from an exploded firecracker. And who could mistake the chili on Number One Boy's special prawns? Until that moment, she hadn't known "home" had a smell.

Ning dropped the tunic down to the bottom of the trunk. The interior reeked of new pine and shellac. How long before her clothes did, too?

"Pack your dolls too," Mama instructed. Her cranky voice was like a cat yowling in the night, an unwelcome interruption.

Ning pulled out her favorite Chinese doll, leaving the yellow-haired doll behind.

"Pack all of them," Mama said. "You shouldn't leave anything behind."

"Why?" Ning's hand tightened around the doll's waist. Mama's brush went from the top of her head to the bottom of her hair five times while Ning waited for her answer.

Finally Mama said, "I am selling this house."

I knew there was something more.

"Where will you go?" Ning asked, letting herself hope that Mama was just moving to a smaller house in town.

Her eyes lifted to watch Ning in the mirror. "I am going home. To Suchow," Mama said simply, as if her

132

words weren't shredding what was left of Ning's world. "There is nothing to keep me here."

Because you are sending me away.

"But . . . what will I come back to?" Ning couldn't remember ever living anywhere else.

"Ning, I have never lied to you, and I won't begin now," Mama said, twisting her hair into a new knot on the top of her head. "You won't come back to China. It is a long, expensive journey, and there is nothing here for you."

"I have you. And Number One Boy," Ning said, desperately wishing Mama would turn and really see her. It was too easy to kill Ning's spirit from a mirror.

"America is your future now. It is better to make the break clean," her mother said.

"You just want to get rid of me forever."

Forever.

The word was like acid on Ning's lips. Mama had tidied up the shards of her tea set and tossed them in the rubbish heap. Now she was doing the same to Ning.

Ning threw the doll to the floor as hard as she could. "I don't think I want to take her after all. She would only remind me of you."

Mama stood up and went to the door. "Take the doll or not. It is your choice. But I think you will regret it if you leave her here."

After Mama's painful steps down the stairs had faded,

Ning kicked the doll as hard as she could. It skittered under her bed, out of sight.

"I don't want you either, Mama."

. . .

"Ning!" Number One Boy called from the front door. "We have to go."

It was an hour past dawn. Her father was waiting for her on a ship called the *Dixey*.

Ning was out of time, but she couldn't bring herself to go downstairs just yet. She slipped on her plain cotton tunic. Mama had demanded she wear the new dress so she would look more like a foreign devil. But Ning had shouted, "I am Chinese! I won't pretend I'm not." Mama had shrugged and said, "If you want to make it harder on yourself, that is your choice."

She went to her mother's mirror and considered her reflection. Her green eyes stared back at her, unblinking like a cat's. "No Chinese girl has green eyes," Madame Wu had said. But if she wasn't Chinese, then what was she?

Standing in the center of the room, she couldn't find a single trace of her presence left here. Mama was ruthless. But Ning could be ruthless, too. Before she left, she would take one thing of Mama's—something she prized. She rummaged through Mama's mahjong tiles until she found the luckiest one of all, the red dragon. She slipped it in her pocket. If Mama ever wanted to play with this set again, she would have to let Ning come back.

"Ning!" Number One bellowed.

"I'm coming," she called. She took her time going downstairs.

"Where is she?" Mama's querulous voice floated in from the courtyard.

Then Number One Boy's sad rumble, "Give her a moment."

Ning poked her head in the kitchen. She ran her fingers across the table, remembering hundreds of meals. How she would she miss the way Number One Boy's Szechuan peppers burned her tongue. Or the way Mama had placed her hands over Ning's to roll the dough for dumplings.

"Dumplings are for luck," she whispered past the lump in her throat.

Bright orange kumquats filled a bowl on Number One Boy's workspace. Any day now he would be making a huge pot of his special jam. But Ning would never taste it. She took a handful of the small fruits, stowing them in her trouser pocket for the voyage.

He won't mind if I take a few.

"She will miss the boat," Mama's voice fretted.

"She's coming," Number One Boy said.

The scent of sandalwood incense drew her away from the front door and into the parlor instead. Bowls of dried fruit had been placed in front of the Buddha in the corner.

Number One Boy had been praying for her. Ning hoped his prayers would work across the oceans, but she doubted it. She sneezed loudly; sandalwood always tickled her nose.

Number One Boy's anxious voice at her shoulder startled her. "Are you ready?"

"No," she said. He lifted his eyebrows. "Yes." She followed him outside. Their gate was open to the alley, and Ning saw her trunk strapped to the back of a rickshaw.

Mama waited in the courtyard. She looked so young this morning: her hair was loose around her shoulders, and she wore her housecoat and linen pants. Her face, bare of makeup, looked sweeter. Not at all like a mother who would send her child away forever.

Appearances can be deceiving.

"We must hurry," Number One Boy said, holding out his arm to help Mama walk to the rickshaw.

Mama shook her head. "I am not going."

Number One Boy drew in a breath. Glancing at Ning then Mama, he stepped backward so he wasn't between them.

Ning stared, stunned. "You won't even see me off?"

Mama's eyes narrowed, but she kept her voice level. "Number One Boy will bring you to the ship. It will be easier that way."

Ning had thought she had exhausted all her anger, but now it came flooding back. "For you or for me?"

"I don't want you to make a scene at the dock and disgrace the Foo-Tai family," Mama said.

"I don't have a family," Ning said.

Number One Boy cringed.

"You will have a new one in America," Mama said. "Now it is past time for you to go. Your father will be angry."

"Mama," Ning's voice broke. "Please . . . don't let it end like this."

For a moment, Mama's resolve seemed to falter. "You will never know how much this costs me," she whispered.

"Tell me!" Ning begged. Looking desperately at the rickshaw, she made a final appeal. "This is our last chance." She extended her hand but stopped short of touching her mother.

Mama kept her body stiff. Even without her white powder, her face looked like stone. "This is how it must be. Now go. You are late."

"Yes, you have wasted enough time on me." Ning's spiteful voice reverberated in the courtyard. She could almost feel the neighbors watching and listening. Let them. Soon both Ning and Mama would be beyond the reach of their gossip. "Goodbye, Mama."

Mama's lips were pressed tightly together, but Ning thought she saw them tremble before her mother turned and went back inside the house. The door closed with a loud bang.

Number One Boy came forward to comfort her. Brushing him aside, she lifted her chin so high that the back of her neck hurt. She climbed into the rickshaw. With a grunt, the driver lifted the poles attached to his cart, and they started to move. Number One Boy trotted behind.

Not very long ago, Ning had watched Hui leave to be married. The alley had echoed with her mother's mourning. As the rickshaw left her house behind, there was silence.

Ning didn't look back.

chapter *Sixteen*

The rickshaw lurched to and fro, avoiding pedestrians and other rickshaws on the crowded street. Ning stared unseeing at all the sights that usually fascinated her.

How can I feel so alone when the street is so full of people?

She turned her head to look for Number One Boy. Even at their slow pace, Number One Boy was falling behind.

"Slow down," she told the driver.

"Your mother told me to get you to the boat. If you miss it, I don't get paid," he answered without turning his head. "Your fat servant will have to run faster."

They plunged into the passage leading out of the Old City. She turned in her seat and watched her home fade to a smear of red and gold behind her. The Chinese sounds disappeared except for the flapping of the driver's sandals against the cobblestones. The last time she was here, she had been so excited to reach the river and see her father. A week later, she would happily stay in the dank tunnel forever. Let her father go back to America alone.

But I have nowhere to go if I stay here. Mama is probably already packing for Suchow.

Emerging from the tunnel, the rickshaw driver stopped. He turned and asked her, "Which dock?" Without his weight on both handles to counteract the trunk, the rickshaw tumbled back. Ning was nearly thrown into the air.

"Ai yi yi!" she cried.

Without apologizing, the driver used his weight to balance the rickshaw. "Where is your ship docked?"

Ning glanced down the length of the Bund and saw only one steamer moored at a dock. It was close, too close. But she couldn't go any farther without Number One Boy.

"I don't know," Ning lied. "We'll have to wait for my servant."

The driver fidgeted, but for once Ning was able to sit patiently. If she missed the boat, so be it.

She watched a trio of wizened, old women standing knee deep in the river in front of her. Trousers tied at the knee and their feet bare, they were catching eels in baskets to sell in the Old City for a pittance. It was a backbreaking occupation but their ancestors had done it for centuries.

A hundred feet down the shore was a very different sight. A handful of white men, dressed in white linen pants and straw hats and gathered at the river's edge, were cheering two long boats racing on the river. As pale legs stretched out and long oars pulled in unison, the four-man crews sped over the water, outpacing a Chinese junk coming in at full sail. One boat pulled ahead of the other and crossed some finish line invisible to Ning. One of the watchers groaned and handed the others some paper money.

"Crazy English," the driver said, spitting on the ground.

The men, laughing and confident, swaggered past.

Foreign devils and the eel mongers—Shanghai's future and past were both present on the bank of the Huang Po River. Ning didn't belong to either. To the Chinese, she was a yellowfish and half-foreign devil. To the English, she was as low class as the eel mongers.

Despite the warmth, Ning rubbed goose bumps on her arms. She didn't like or understand the foreign devils who lived in her own city. Now she was going to a country full of them. The weight of all her worries pressed down on her chest making it hard to breathe.

Where is Number One Boy?

Just beyond this dock, she could see the wooden Garden Bridge that spanned the Suchow Canal. A day's sail up the canal would bring Mama to Suchow and the Mandarin Foo-Tai's estate. But Ning would never be welcome there. Dredging the Suchow Canal had brought her father to China, she thought. If the canal had just been a little deeper, George Hamill and her mother would never have met.

She peered anxiously through the passage. *There!* Number One Boy finally stumbled out of the tunnel, his hand pressed to his side, breathing hard.

"I was afraid I'd lost you," she said.

"Never."

The driver was tapping his foot impatiently. "Which ship?" he asked.

Number One Boy pointed, and instantly the rickshaw driver took off. Heaving a sigh, Number One Boy lumbered after them. In moments, they arrived at the dock. A squat steamer waited like an enormous water beetle.

While Number One Boy paid the rickshaw driver and untied the trunk, Ning stared at the small steamer. The *Dixey*'s name was painted in white letters on the black hull. Three red smokestacks were already puffing smoke. An American flag flew from the stern. Was that her flag now, too? The Chinese didn't have a flag, she realized, unless you counted the Emperor's flag. But no one was allowed to use that flag but the Emperor.

"Let's go," Number One Boy said, easily hoisting her trunk to his shoulder.

"It's not as big I thought," she said. She couldn't see how a boat so small could traverse so much ocean.

"It's a mail boat—very fast. It only takes a few passengers and light cargo. The *Dixey* is considered a very sound ship," Number One Boy told her.

Startled, she tore her eyes from the boat and looked at him. "How do you know?"

"I checked," he said, "I wouldn't let Foo-Tai Sun's daughter travel on just any boat."

"Thank you," she said, resting her head on Number One Boy's massive arm. "You always take care of me."

He patted her hair. "It has been my honor."

Who will look after me now?

There were two ramps from the dock to the ship. One was for cargo: a line of coolies carried bales of silk and crates of tea and porcelain on their shoulders into the hold. Judging by the jumble of empty wagons and wheelbarrows left on shore, the loading was almost finished.

In the water, a swarm of flat-bottomed sampan boats converged on the ship like a cloud of gnats. The farmers, wearing patched homespun clothes and conical bamboo hats, were selling their wares to the ship. After inspecting baskets full of fresh vegetables and fruit and crates of live chickens, a crewman exchanged coins for the food. She heard the fierce bargaining in the pidgin English that the foreign devils used to converse with the Chinese. Ning wondered how they would eat for four months at sea. *What if they ran out of food?* Another worry to make her stomach ache.

"That's where you go," Number One Boy said leading her to the second ramp that connected to the main deck. This ramp was narrower and had cleats to aid in the steeper climb. On deck, Ning could see half a dozen passengers leaning on the rail, watching the activity on shore. Her father was nowhere to be seen.

A deep gloomy horn sounded from the ship making Ning feel small and unimportant.

With a grunt, Number One Boy dropped the trunk to the ground. "I have two gifts for you," he said. "One is for today and the other is for America. Which do you want first?"

The gloom lifted just a little. "The one for America," she said.

He pulled a sack from the satchel he wore strapped across his chest. "Only the best Szechuan peppers for you."

She untied the bag and plunged her face inside. They were hot enough to make her skin tingle just from being near them.

"The foreign devils don't understand cooking, I hear. Very, very bland. When you use this . . ."

"I will think of you," she finished, carefully tying a tight knot to keep the peppers in. And for now?"

"Such a greedy little dumpling," he said with a catch in his throat. "Speaking of dumplings." This time he pulled out a handful of sweet *tang yuan* dumplings wrapped in a lettuce leaf. These were still hot. Both she and Number One Boy adored the moon-like treats and couldn't wait until the New Year to eat them. Now she knew what he was doing while she waited for him in the rickshaw.

"Tang yuan . . ." she whispered. The words also meant reunion. But there would be no reunion for them. This trip to America was in one direction only. Her mouth twisted and rather than let a sob escape, she popped a dumpling in her mouth.

"I had them made special because . . ." he choked up and his eyes filled with tears. "Because you won't be here at the New Year."

It was too much. Both of them started to sob loudly, attracting curious stares from the ship's crew busily preparing to depart.

"I'll never have a better friend," Ning cried.

"Don't cry!" he begged. "You are starting a new life. You'll have a new family. And you will find more friends."

"I don't believe you. I don't want to go." She pressed her fists to her eyes to stop the tears.

"A great journey starts with a single step," he said. "Put one foot in front of the other and go up the ramp." He jerked his head toward the deck of the ship. "Your father is waiting."

chapter *Seventeen*

Ning looked up and saw George Hamill standing at the railing. He inspected his pocket watch then scanned the docks. His eyes lit on her, and he scowled.

"You're late!" he yelled down to her. He jabbed his finger at her then gestured toward the gangplank.

"I can't do it," she whispered, backing away. Number One Boy grabbed her arm to hold her still. "I don't like him. He doesn't like me."

"You owe him the first Obedience," he said, taking his satchel from around his neck and giving it to her to hold her gifts. "Besides family does not have to like each other. You have the whole voyage to get to know him. Show him who you are, and he will love you as I do."

"There will be a Number-One-Boy-sized hole in my heart," she cried, flinging her arms around him.

"We will both have a long life to share the light of the moon, even though we are a thousand miles apart."

"I will even miss your stupid proverbs," she said, memorizing every line of his face. How had she never noticed that his left eyebrow was slightly crooked?

He held her tightly for a minute, then gave her a gentle shove toward the gangplank. "Now go, Ning."

Suddenly, she was blocked by a sailor in a white uniform.

"No Chinee on ship," he said.

Her face felt scorching hot, and her words froze in her throat. Ning couldn't think what to do or say. Maybe there was a huge mistake, and she wouldn't be allowed on board.

"No speakee English? No Chinee!" the crewman shouted the words as if that would help her understand.

Ning looked back at Number One Boy. "What do I do?" she mouthed.

He held out his hands helplessly. Then her father strode down the gangplank. "You! What are you doing? Let my daughter pass!" he said loudly, his face purple with anger.

The crewman's bluster disappeared. "I'm sorry, sir. I thought . . . she looks . . ." His voice trailed off in embarrassment.

"Bring my daughter's trunk on board," her father ordered. The crewman scurried to obey.

He said his daughter.

Ning stood up a bit straighter. Even though she had lost everything in Shanghai, she was gaining a father in America. Maybe . . . just maybe, that would be consolation.

George Hamill looked her up and down, frowning

at her loose cotton trousers and embroidered slippers. "What on earth are you wearing?" he demanded. "I told your mother to get you a proper dress."

"These are the clothes I am comfortable wearing." He might as well get used to that from the beginning. He could bring her to America, but she was always going to be Chinese.

"Your comfort is the least of my worries," he said. She tensed as his hand moved toward her face, but he only flicked her long braid back over her shoulder. "You'll have to change that, too. You're American now," he said. He gestured for her to proceed up the gangplank. "Now get on board. I want to introduce you to Mrs. Grand."

"Who is Mrs. Grand, *Baba*?" she asked.

"Don't call me that!" His voice was sharp, slashing her new hopes to bits.

"Then what should I call you?" she asked. Such a simple thing—every child knew what to call her father. Except Ning.

"Call me George." He brushed past her and strode up the gangplank.

Ning followed him slowly. George. It sounded so cold and impersonal.

Her cloth soles slipped and slid on the slick wood, and she had to grab the railing to keep her footing. As soon as she reached the deck, she turned to wave goodbye to Number One Boy.

He was gone. Her eyes swept the dock which was emptying of people now that the ship was about to embark. She pressed her knuckles to her lips to keep from moaning.

"Where is Mrs. Grand?" George said to himself.

Who is Mrs. Grand? Does he have a new wife?

"Ah, there she is." His hand at Ning's elbow, he marched her to the prow of the ship. "Mrs. Grand has been teaching here and now she is going home. She's agreed to work with you."

Mrs. Grand was an elderly white woman. Her violet dress was buttoned to her neck, and she wore a fussy hat with feathers. She turned when Ning's father called her name.

"Mr. Hamill, is this the young lady?" she asked, smiling. She had pale blonde hair and a complexion like chalk.

"Mrs. Grand, this is my daughter." He paused, and she saw him swallow hard. "Her name is Neenah."

Ning's chin shot up, and her eyes met her father's. "That's not my name," she whispered urgently.

"You're an American now, Neenah." He emphasized the new syllable added to her name. "A new country. A new name."

"But what does it mean?" she asked, bewildered. After all, "Ning" had a special significance. It meant "Peace."

"It doesn't mean anything," he said. "It's just a name."

Mrs. Grand extended a pale hand. "Neenah, pleased to meet you."

Still stunned, Ning shook it.

"I'm sure we will get along beautifully," Mrs. Grand said. "We'll have plenty of time to practice your English. Your father wants me to teach you all about America."

"Are you coming with us?" Ning asked.

Mrs. Grand took in a quick breath "Mr. Hamill, haven't you told her?"

He cleared his throat. "I was about to."

A memory flashed in Ning's mind: Mama telling her she was to go to America. Her father, despite being a man and an American, had the exact same expression on his face. Something terrible was about to happen.

Mrs. Grand's light blue eyes moved from Ning to her father and back again. "I'll leave you two alone." She moved several steps away and stood at the railing, her back to them. Ning was sure she could still overhear their conversation.

Arms folded across her chest, Ning demanded, "What haven't you told me?"

He avoided looking at her. "I won't be joining you. The company I work for wants me to do an urgent dredging project in Wuzhen."

Ning swayed as if the ship were already moving, and she would lose her balance at any moment. "I don't understand," Ning said.

"The Peking to Hangzhou Canal is silting up. We need to dig it out so Western boats can make the trip," he explained.

"I don't care about the canal," Ning cried. She grabbed his sleeve. "You are putting me on a ship to America by myself?" Her voice sounded shrill, and she was happy to see him wince.

"Mrs. Grand has agreed to look after you during the voyage." He spoke quickly as though he was racing to the end of the conversation. "I'll follow when I can. It won't be long, probably only a few weeks." Despite the cool morning breeze, sweat dotted his brow. He carefully wiped his forehead with a white handkerchief. "Maybe longer."

"I can wait here at home with Mama," Ning said. "And then we can go together."

"I've already booked your passage. It would be too expensive to change," he answered.

"You changed your ticket, though."

He looked confused, then nodded. "Yes, but they wouldn't change two fares."

All at once Ning knew that he was lying to her. He had never intended to travel with her. "You just don't want to be stuck on a ship with me for months," she accused.

"I told your mother I wasn't cut out to be a father," he said, finally looking her in the face. "My work is important to me and will always take precedence over

151

personal considerations. I've wasted four months to come here at your mother's request. At least now I'll be paid for my trouble."

From the railing, Ning thought she heard Mrs. Grand make a little dismayed mewing sound. If Ning's heart could speak, that was the sound it would make.

She meant nothing to him.

"Did you tell Mama you are sending me alone?" she asked. Surely Mama hadn't approved.

Number One Boy would have warned me.

"She made it clear that you are my responsibility," he said. "I didn't have to consult her."

"What happens when I get to New York?" she said slowly, trying to grasp the huge distance between here and there.

"I've arranged to have someone meet the ship."

"Who?" Ning asked.

"I won't be questioned by a child. I make the decisions and you obey." He shoved his handkerchief back in his pocket. "Mrs. Grand has all the documents and informa- tion. All right?"

The ship blasted its horn.

"Do I have a choice?" she spoke more to herself than to him. Number One Boy was gone. No one would help her if she refused to go. As her father intended, she was stuck.

George made an awkward half step toward her as

though he might embrace her but thought better of it. "Mrs. Grand?"

She hurried back. "Are we all squared away?" she asked. She didn't try to hide her curiosity, but her face was full of sympathy.

"Thank you for your help, Mrs. Grand. Neenah, I expect you to take this time to learn how to be an American girl." He tipped his hat. "I must disembark. Bon voyage." He turned on his heel and headed off the ship.

Mrs. Grand looked startled by his abrupt departure. "Goodbyes are hard for some people," she said. "I remember how my dear husband, he's been dead for seven years, used to hide in his cabin rather than say goodbye to our friends . . ."

Ignoring Mrs. Grand's babbling, Ning watched her father hurry down the gangplank and out of view. She was an orphan now.

The horn blew again two times. At this signal, the sailors started to pull up the wooden ramp. Without any thought or plan, Ning started toward the gangplank. Mrs. Grand grabbed her hand and pulled her back.

"Neenah, it's too late. You have to stay."

The sailors threw off the lines and, with a jerk, the ship began to move away from the dock. Ning stumbled, but Mrs. Grand kept her from falling.

"Are you all right?" Mrs. Grand asked.

"No!" The wind on the river might have made her

eyes water if she was not already cried out. *What's the use of crying*, she wondered. No one cared about her. This was the loneliest she'd ever felt in her life.

Mrs. Grand stood with her silently as the ship moved slowly to the center of the river, the prow pointing toward the grassy empty marshes on the far side of the Huang Po. Then the ship straightened its course and started heading out to sea. The Bund was to her right. The Customs House appeared and then fell behind. Ning's gaze rested longest on the opening in the great wall that encircled the Old City.

When the *Dixey* reached the place where the sea met the river, Ning shrunk back from the railing. The sky was too wide here. And the horizon was endless. Ning reached into one pocket and gripped the dragon mahjong tile tightly. Would the dragon's good luck stretch as far as America?

"Don't be frightened." Mrs. Grand patted her on the back. "Your father hired me to take care of you, Neenah."

Ning was bound by the rules of Obedience to do as her father said. And Mrs. Grand was only trying to be nice. But Ning didn't have to let them take the last thing that was hers.

"Thank you, Mrs. Grand." She took a deep breath. "But my name is Ning."

Part
Two

New York, October 1878

chapter *Eighteen*

Ning took a bite of her chicken breast and made a face. Flavorless and dry, like every single meal aboard the *Dixey*. At the other end of the table, the Captain and the only other passengers—a quartet of businessmen who wore dark suits and kept to themselves—gobbled the food like little boys shoving sweets in their mouths. Ning's belly hadn't been satisfied in months. What she would do for Number One Boy's spicy Szechuan peppers or his prawns and garlic! It would kill him to know Ning was so hungry. At least this was the last meal she would have to suffer through.

She hated everything about these dinners. The food, the company, and, most especially, the conversation. The foreign devils talked only of money and business. And the disrespectful way they spoke of China made her angry enough to spit. When they said how stupid and lazy the Chinese were, only Mrs. Grand noted Ning's white knuckles gripped tightly around her fork.

In the beginning, Ning had spoken up. She had angrily defended China. Not to the gentlemen, of course, but

157

privately to Mrs. Grand. She had bragged about Chinese poetry and Confucius. How hard the people in the Old City worked to make a living. The grandeur of the Longhua Pagoda and the teahouses and the theaters.

"Don't be ridiculous, Neenah. America has all that and more," Mrs. Grand had said smugly. "Isn't that why your father is sending you there?" She had tried to change Ning's clothes, hair, and manners, and she had judged Ning to be an inferior product of China as well.

Ning pushed herself away from the polished oak dining room table. That it was bolted to the floor had astonished her on the first day aboard the *Dixey,* but now she took it for granted.

"What do you think you're doing? Sit still," hissed Mrs. Grand, grabbing Ning's arm to pull her back down. "You haven't cleaned your plate." She gestured at the hard pellets the cook called potatoes. "The Captain said there is going to be a special dessert because this is our last night."

Desperate to escape from dinner and from Mrs. Grand's constant carping, Ning said, "I don't feel well."

"Again?" Mrs. Grand asked.

Seasickness had been unknown to her before she left Shanghai, but now Ning understood it from the bottom of her sour stomach. It had taken weeks before she found her "sea legs" and could bear the motion of the waves. Only then, when she could keep food down, did she discover how bland American food was.

"I'm going to be sick," she lied.

"Then go." Mrs. Grand glanced at the Captain who was still eating. "Be discreet, and the Captain won't notice."

Ning snorted. The very first night the Captain had looked her over, scowling. "I usually don't take Chinese passengers, but since you are a child, I agreed to make an exception," he said. Then he made clear that he would tolerate no mischief on his ship. Ning was not to speak to his crew nor get in their way. "Do you understand, young lady?" he asked.

Cheeks tear-stained, Ning nodded mutely. The Captain was just another person who wished she wasn't there. He had never spoken to her again.

"Go to the cabin," Mrs. Grand said. "And if you do get sick, please do it over the railing and not in our water closet. The smell is quite disagreeable."

Hand over her mouth to keep up the fiction, Ning bolted out of the dining room through the swinging door to the empty lounge. The lounge was where the male passengers spent their time smoking and reading (and rereading) weeks'-old newspapers. Ning hated the stale air that reeked of cigars and whiskey. It smelled like foreign devils.

Mrs. Grand and Ning had a tiny "Ladies" Parlor to themselves where they practiced conversation and worked on their embroidery. There were no papers there. At the

159

start of the voyage, Mrs. Grand had told Ning that it wasn't appropriate for a young lady to read the newspapers. Hiding a bitter smile, Ning had not told her guardian she had learned English reading the *The North China Daily News* with Mama.

One day on her way into breakfast, a headline in a month-old *New York Tribune* had caught her attention. "No Chinese Need Apply." Intrigued, she'd smuggled the newspaper out of the lounge to read in her favorite hiding spot, a sheltered niche on deck between the lifeboats.

The article was brief. It was about a Chinese gentleman who had lived in the United States for 28 years and called himself Charles Miller. He had asked the court to say he was American. The judge said only a white person could be naturalized. Mr. Miller was not white, the judge decided. Therefore he was not eligible for American citizenship.

Scanning the rest of the paper she found a report of a riot in California. A mob had burned down a Chinese store and beat a Chinese man almost to death while chanting "Chinese Go Home!" Clutching the newspaper in her hand, she ran to find Mrs. Grand in their cabin.

"You told me that America was a place where everyone was welcome," she said angrily, waving the newspaper. "The Chinese aren't welcome!"

"There have been troubles," Mrs. Grand looked

everywhere but at Ning. "Jobs are scarce, and people have blamed the Chinese. Don't worry, it will come to nothing."

Ning jabbed her finger at the article. "This says I can never be American. So why are you trying to so hard to make me one?"

Maybe she'll leave me alone now.

"This has nothing to do with you." Mrs. Grand snatched the paper away. "Your father is American, so you are too. It's the law."

"I decide if I am Chinese or American," Ning muttered. "I have a choice."

"Not really, dear."

"Good evening, miss." The cheerful voice of the dining room steward pulled her out of her memories. He had wavy, floppy brown hair and wore a jacket with shiny buttons. "You aren't leaving before I serve dessert, are you?"

"I'm not hungry," she said, eying the cake he carried. It was seven layers and covered with chocolate frosting with red flourishes. If Ning squinted, it looked a little like the Longhua Pagoda. She braced herself for a wave of homesickness as she remembered her first view of the temple. The bells had spoken to her. That was the day Mama prayed for the ancestors to safeguard Ning. And Ning had begged the dragons to grant her wish to belong to a family. So much joy and sadness woven together in a single memory.

"Never knew a kid who didn't want cake," he said cheerfully.

"We don't eat chocolate in China."

"It's your loss," he said.

"When will we get to New York?" Ning asked, dreading the answer. While she was at sea, she could still be either Ning the Chinese girl or Neenah the American. But once she landed, she would have to choose and she wasn't ready.

"I think we've already arrived," the steward said. "Can't you hear?"

Ning listened. Yes, the engines were slowing.

"We can't land soon enough for me," he said. "It's been almost a year since I saw my family."

"You must miss them," Ning said. "I miss mine." The familiar tears sprang to her eyes; she blinked them away.

"I do," he agreed. "While I've been gone, my Pa got sick. They need me."

Would I know if Mama needed help?

"The Captain must be wondering where his cake is," the steward said. He disappeared through the swinging door.

Before the door creaked closed, Ning moved to the enormous map of the world mounted on the wall between two portholes. She placed one finger unerringly on Shanghai and traced the route they had taken: the Huang Po River, the China Sea, the Pacific Ocean, then the Indian Ocean, the Arabian Sea, the Red Sea, the Suez Canal, the Mediterranean Sea, and finally the Atlantic Ocean. But once she hit land, the United States of America, her finger hovered uncertainly over New York City. Where was Baldwinsville, New York, her father's home? The map wasn't detailed enough to show her.

Once I fall off the map, can I find my way back home?

She heard the shouts of the crew as they dropped anchor. She hurried out to the railing. Lanterns had been placed at the prow and stern to warn off other ships in the night. Above her, the stars disappeared in a greenish glow flooding the sky. It reminded her of something, the color of the sky. But what? She caught her breath as she remembered. The milky green was the exact shade of the lustrous jade dragons twined around the Buddha's feet at Longhua. A color of home.

The anchor must have taken hold on the sea bottom because now the *Dixey* was slowly swinging around. Ning gasped as the city came into view. Aimed like an arrow at the ship, the city started at a narrow point of land, then spread wide in a tapestry of gas lamps. Hundreds of lamps. Maybe thousands. At home, only the International Settlement had gas, but here there were so many gaslights Ning couldn't tell where they ended. There must be tens of thousands of people to need so much light. She wrapped her arms around her body as if she could wall herself away from so many foreign devils.

Waves buffeted the ship, and she nearly lost her footing. She grabbed the railing tightly with both hands to steady herself. Her thoughts were racing as she reexamined every conversation with Mrs. Grand. She had tried to tell Ning that Shanghai was tiny compared to New York City and how America was so much more civilized than China. Ning had scoffed because China was thousands of years old and America had only just celebrated its 100th birthday. Nothing could compare with home, she assured herself.

Her heart thudded as she realized she had been mistaken. A city as big as New York could swallow her whole. What else had she been wrong about? So intent on staying loyal to her Chinese life, Ning had wasted the months when she could have been learning about America.

"There you are," Mrs. Grand said, joining Ning at the railing. "Wonderful, isn't it?"

Her voice sounding thin in the night air, Ning said, "It's bigger than I thought."

Mrs. Grand looked at her sidelong, a gratified expression on her face. "I did try to tell you, but you wouldn't listen."

"Do the lights go across the country?" Ning asked.

Mrs. Grand looked startled. "Of course not. There are only a few cities as large as New York. Most of America is much less populated. Your new country still has plenty of room to grow."

"America is not my country," Ning protested weakly.

Here, I am the foreign devil.

chapter *Nineteen*

The steward's tap on the door woke them when it was still dark. She hated this room, but now she wouldn't mind staying a little longer. Anything to postpone setting foot in America. Ning reached in her nightdress pocket and clutched her dragon tile for comfort; if anything could protect her here, it was a Chinese dragon.

"Don't forget to pack your sewing," Mrs. Grand said.

"I already did," Ning answered. The unfinished embroidery was the first thing she had packed. Mrs. Grand had insisted they sew together to pass time on the long voyage. Ning had chosen to embroider a scene of the Longhua Pagoda. At first the project had only made her sad, but soon it had begun to soothe her homesickness.

"We have to be on deck soon," Mrs. Grand said.

"I'm almost finished," Ning said. "Just one more thing . . ."

From its place of honor on her pillow, Ning picked up her old doll who she had renamed "Sun." She smoothed out the doll's hair and let the tip of her finger rest on her polished wooden cheek.

I couldn't have come this far without her.

As Shanghai disappeared from her horizon, Ning's grief had been so thick she choked on it. She had refused to get out of her bunk. Her last memory of Mama was full of pain and anger. And because Ning had been so vicious, she didn't have anything to remember Mama by except a stolen tile. Her memories always spiraled to the saddest place and ended with more tears.

At the end of the first full day at sea, Mrs. Grand had unpacked their trunks. "I found this at the bottom of your trunk," she said, handing Ning a package of red tissue paper tied with string. There was a white card on which was written a single character, painted in Mama's distinctive calligraphy.

"It's my name," Ning whispered.

Ning, not Neenah.

She opened the package carefully and stared. "My doll!" Mama must have found it and secretly packed it in her trunk. How did she know that Ning would need a talisman from home so badly? She hugged the doll to her chest, caressing her black hair.

Coiled around the doll's body was a necklace of green and red jade stones with gold beads. Ning had seen it only once before, in her mother's strongbox. Green and red jade were lucky stones and gold always signified good fortune. Without saying a word, Mama had blessed her. She clasped the necklace around her neck; she promised herself she would never take it off.

Drawn back to the present, Mrs. Grand's voice was an unpleasant reminder that time was passing.

"Stop your woolgathering and help me." Mrs. Grand tightened her corset on top of her chemise then pulled her dark wool dress over her body. Ning moved to fasten the line of buttons on the back. After four months, Ning still marveled that American women chose to wear such impractical clothes. No one had to help Ning get into her trousers and tunic.

"Now it's your turn," Mrs. Grand said. "Where is that plaid dress?"

Bracing for another argument, Ning said, "I'd rather wear my own clothes."

"Absolutely not," Mrs. Grand said firmly. "You aren't going to meet your grandparents wearing mended pants and slippers." She found the red-and-black striped dress and held it up. The clashing pattern made Ning's eyes hurt.

"Will it still fit?" Mrs. Grand asked, frowning. "You've grown these past months—I don't know how since you don't eat anything. Let's see." She unbuttoned the dress and indicated Ning should step inside.

The fabric was stiff and hard against her skin. "It's itchy," she complained.

"You'll get used to it," Mrs. Grand said, measuring the distance between the bottom hem and the floor. "I hope it's not too short."

Ning put her arms through the sleeves, but the dress pulled so tightly across her chest she couldn't breathe. She pulled her shoulders back with a jerk and a seam ripped apart.

"You did that on purpose!" Mrs. Grand accused as she examined the sleeve hanging by only a few threads.

"I did not," Ning protested, but she was secretly pleased that she had to wear her old clothes after all. She pulled on her tunic and trousers and touched the necklace at her throat. At the last minute, she slipped the dragon tile in her pocket. She would need all her luck today.

"Sooner or later you'll have to dress like the American girls," Mrs. Grand warned. "Especially in a small town. You will already be so different from them, why make it worse?"

Ning had never had much luck with other girls. Number One Boy had told her that her problems would disappear in America, but Mrs. Grand was more honest. Ning would still be different. This was a fight she couldn't win.

"I'm sure your grandparents will care what you wear. Don't you want them to like you?"

Of course, Ning wanted them to like her! But she wanted them to like the real Ning—not a girl pretending to be someone she wasn't.

"I shouldn't have to wear a costume," she insisted.

"It's not a costume. It's a dress." Mrs. Grand sighed.

"Why do you have to be so stubborn, Neenah?"

"For the thousandth time, my name is Ning."

"Your father is paying me, and he said your name is Neenah," Mrs. Grand replied, exasperated. She jerked her head toward shore. "A Customs Officer is going to ask your name. Your answer had better match your papers."

"My name is Ning." Ning glowered at Mrs. Grand. If she repeated it often enough, it would still be true . . . in Shanghai or New York.

chapter *Twenty*

The harbor was just waking up under a bright blue sky. Ships moved purposely to and from the city on water that sparkled in the sunlight. A tugboat had met their ship to pull it to shore. Ning willed the tug to go just a little slower and let her postpone meeting her grandparents for just a little longer.

A shiver ran down her back.

Her breath frosting, Mrs. Grand asked, "Are you cold?"

"A little," Ning pulled her wool coat tighter.

"At least that still fits," Mrs. Grand said. "What would your grandparents think if you didn't have a proper coat?"

Ning had no idea what would please her grandparents since they had only just learned of Ning's existence. "What if they don't like me?" Ning asked so quietly that Mrs. Grand asked her to repeat herself.

Mrs. Grand lifted her eyebrows. "They're your family."

What had Number One Boy told her? "Family doesn't have to like each other."

"Cheer up, dear. I'm sure your grandparents will be delighted to meet you." Mrs. Grand shielded her eyes against the sun. "It's too nice a day for you to sulk."

Number One Boy liked to say that "good beginnings meant good endings." Maybe Ning should take heart: she was arriving in fine weather. Her grandparents would rush to embrace her and offer her flavorful food. Baldwinsville would be a fine city to rival Shanghai. And a dozen girls would fight to be her friend.

Stop dreaming!

Mrs. Grand nudged her out of her reverie. "This is New York Harbor," she said. "And that is the island of Manhattan. To the right, the East River."

Ning's eyes followed her pointing finger. "Is that a temple?" she asked looking at a stone structure that towered over all the other buildings.

Mrs. Grand chuckled. "That is one end of a bridge that will connect Manhattan to Brooklyn," she said with local pride. "We started it almost a decade ago and it should be finished in five more years."

Ning's jaw dropped. A bridge? The river was so wide; it would be like trying to span the Huang Po River. She squinted to see the tower on the far side of the river.

"Who would be brave enough to cross it?" Ning asked, thinking that she never would.

"They say it will be the eighth wonder of the world."

The tug pulled them toward the rounded point she had

172

seen the night before. In daylight, she could see it was a park, with walking paths and gas lamps. The foreign devils had made a park like this in Shanghai, too. She wondered if this park had the same sign: No Chinese Allowed.

To the left, separated from the park by a tall fence, was a large round building made of brick, with tiny windows looking in all directions.

"That's Castle Garden," Mrs. Grand said. "Long ago it was a military fort, but when I was a girl, it was a theater. My mother took me there to see Jenny Lind, the famous opera singer."

"I went to an opera once with my mother," Ning said. Even though she had been very young, she had never forgotten the elaborate costumes and the haunting music.

"Don't talk to me about your Chinese operas!" Mrs. Grand grimaced. "The caterwauling hurt my ears."

Ning's memory of the opera was too sweet to ruin by discussing it with Mrs. Grand.

The tug pulled the *Dixey* round the point. Now that she had a better view, Ning saw that Castle Garden was enormous.

"Is it still a theater?" she asked.

Mrs. Grand pointed to a painted sign that faced the water, Emigrant Landing Depot. "Castle Garden is used to process immigrants now."

Even though the sun was just barely up, there was already a line of people snaked outside the building.

The immigrants, laden down with children and their belongings, looked frightened and tired. Official men shepherded them through a wide door.

"It's overcrowded and dirty in there," Mrs. Grand said, lowering her voice as though the newcomers in line might hear. "Sometimes they have to wait for days. It's an embarrassment that this is the first thing immigrants see in America."

I'm an immigrant.

Nervously, Ning asked, "Do we have to go there?"

Mrs. Grand shook her head. "Everyone on this ship is American. An official will come here and ask us a few questions. There's nothing to worry about."

Her gaze fixed on the darkness behind the door, Ning asked, "But what happens to them in there?"

"The government collects each family's information. Then a doctor examines each person individually. Poor things. After months in steerage, with the terrible food they get, it would be a miracle if they weren't ill." Mrs. Grand touched the cameo pinned to her bosom to show how affected she was.

"What if they are sick?" Ning asked, worried now for them, especially the children.

"We don't want any diseases to come into the country. They're sent back," Mrs. Grand said.

"If I were sick, would I have to go back to China?" Even as she asked the question, Ning knew better than to hope for such a thing. Mama and Number One Boy were gone, and there was nothing to return to.

"Firstly, you are American and they can't turn you away," Mrs. Grand said. "Secondly, the steerage passengers can't afford doctors and your father can. So even if you were sick, they would let you in."

The tug changed course to bring the *Dixey* closer to shore. Now Ning could see the line began at a large steamer docked at the first pier.

"Where are they from?" Ning asked.

"That's a Norwegian ship," Mrs. Grand told her, pointing at the red flag with a blue and white cross flying from the top mast. "My grandparents came here from Norway, too."

In all her studying of the world map, Ning had never noticed Norway. She craned her neck to see past the Norwegian steamer but it was too big. "Where are the Chinese boats?"

"There aren't any," Mrs. Grand said. "Most ships from China go to the West Coast. Most Chinese live there, too. I'd be very surprised if there are any Chinese in the town where you are going."

"Oh," Ning said, startled and disappointed. She had just assumed there would be others like her in America— just as the British and Americans had settlements of their own in Shanghai. What would it be like to be the only Chinese?

Lonely.

The Norwegian ship had two gangplanks, one coming from the bowels of the ship and the other from the top deck. Down the lower gangplank came an endless line of passengers, blinking at the bright light. The men wore dark shapeless coats and hats, while the women wrapped shawls tightly around their shoulders and covered their hair with colored handkerchiefs. There were just as many children as adults: babies in their mother's arms, boys looking like miniatures of their fathers, and girls with gold hair, shyly clutching their mother's skirts. Ning wondered if their skin was always so pale or was it from being trapped belowdecks for the entire journey? She glanced down at her hand, slightly bronzed from the sun. Her voyage had been very different than theirs. She felt ashamed for complaining so much.

Mrs. Grand's eyes were fixed on a family just stepping onto the dock. The father had a trunk hoisted on his shoulder, his other arm draped protectively around his pregnant wife. A little girl followed close behind lugging a basket that was almost as big as she was. "They are carrying everything they own," Mrs. Grand said softly. They risked everything to come here for a better life for their children."

"They are brave" Ning said.

"Very brave, indeed," Mrs. Grand said.

Now the first-class passengers began disembarking

from the ship's upper gangplank. Their gangplank was installed past the steerage exit, so that first and third classes did not have to cross paths. They came at their own pace; no official herding. The men were warm in wool coats and felt hats, and the ladies navigated the ramp gingerly in their bustled skirts. An army of stewards delivered their luggage to the waiting carriages.

"You can tell the first-class passengers by what they wear." Mrs. Grand glanced at Ning's trousers and slippers.

"They don't have to go into that building?"

"They aren't immigrants; they're citizens."

Suddenly Ning understood why Mrs. Grand had tried so hard to teach her how to be an American. America had one rule for citizens and another for immigrants, but Ning was both. Glancing at the pitiful line of people waiting to enter Castle Garden, Ning's choice was obvious.

chapter *Twenty-One*

The tug took them past the bulk of the Norwegian ship to their own pier. Ning's eyes widened as the rest of the river port came into view. A forest of masts and smokestacks, piled three-deep against the shore, made Ning feel tiny. The *Dixey* shared the pier with a small sloop and a large cargo steamer. The wooden dock was swarming with stevedores moving crates from the ships to wagons waiting in the road.

"I didn't know there could be so many ships," Ning murmured.

"New York is one of the biggest ports in the world," Mrs. Grand said. "You didn't think it would be like Shanghai, did you?"

The crew tied up the ship's mooring lines and lowered the passenger gangplank.

"Do we leave the ship now?" Ning asked.

"Not yet," Mrs. Grand replied.

Relieved but curious, Ning asked, "What are we waiting for?"

"Him." A man wearing a round hat with a golden badge was boarding the ship. The Captain waited at the top of the gangplank to greet him. "That's the customs inspector," Mrs. Grand said.

The inspector's blue coat was exactly the same color as a Shanghai magistrate; he carried himself with the same official swagger. Number One Boy's voice sounded in her head, "Bureaucrat. Stay away!"

"Don't look so worried!" Mrs. Grand said. "Just follow my lead, and you'll be fine."

Glancing back at the Castle Garden Emigrant Depot Center, Ning decided she was willing to do anything Mrs. Grand asked.

With so few passengers, they didn't have to wait very long to see the inspector in the dining room. He seemed friendly enough, giving Mrs. Grand's papers a cursory glance before handing them back. Then he turned to Ning. "Who is this young lady?"

Nerves jangling, Ning forgot Mrs. Grand's instructions. "My name is Ning Hamill."

"Ning is a pet name," Mrs. Grand interrupted smoothly. "She is Neenah Hamill. Her father hired me to accompany her on the voyage." She took a folder from her black leather pocketbook. "Here is her passport."

The inspector unfolded Ning's long paper passport with its large, red wax seals and stamps from the American

179

consulate in Shanghai. He read them carefully. His smile disappeared, and he puffed up like a cat that's spied a mouse. "Your mother is Chinese?" he asked,

"Yes," Ning said.

"By the order of the Page Act of 1875," the Inspector said, full of his authority, "I've been instructed to give Chinese female immigrants extra scrutiny."

"Just Chinese women?" Ning asked.

"The United States is not concerned with any other race," the inspector said.

Scowling, Ning demanded, "What is wrong with being Chinese?"

Mrs. Grand elbowed her hard. The message was clear: Ning had better be quiet. To the inspector, she said, "There should be no problem. Neenah's father is American. Neenah is an American citizen."

"I have to enforce the law," he insisted. "It's just a few additional questions."

Ning edged closer to Mrs. Grand. What if she gave the wrong answers?

"The law doesn't apply to Neenah. Perhaps I should inform your superiors that you are harassing a twelve-year-old United States citizen?" Mrs. Grand hadn't raised her voice, but it cracked like a whip.

The Inspector shrank in his chair like a cowed school-boy. "Ma'am, that won't be necessary. Her papers appear to be in order. Welcome home, Miss Hamill."

Back outside Mrs. Grand was pleased with herself and unhappy with Ning. "I showed him what was what, even though you tried to wreck your own chances."

Feeling hollow with relief, Ning thanked her.

"I won't be there the next time you make things more difficult for yourself," Mrs. Grand said. She handed Ning the envelope with her documents and warned her not to lose them.

While they waited for the signal to disembark, Mrs. Grand scanned the dock. "I don't see anyone waiting for the *Dixey*. Your father's colleague, Mr. Stemple, should be here already."

This was the first time Ning had heard the name of her escort. What kind of person was he? Mrs. Grand, for all her faults, had protected Ning when it counted. Could she count on this Mr. Stemple to do the same?

"What if he doesn't come?" Ning asked, her eyes resting on one stranger, then another.

"I'm sure he will," Mrs. Grand said. "Your father made all the arrangements."

Ning paced back and forth, clutching her dragon tile so tightly the carving made a mark on her hand. So many things could have gone wrong between here and Shanghai. Maybe her father's messages had gone astray. Maybe he hadn't sent them. She didn't trust George Hamill at all.

"You won't leave me, will you?" Ning asked.

"I won't leave until your escort comes," Mrs. Grand

181

said, "but then I have to go to my home in Hoboken. Your father only paid me to accompany you to New York."

I'm only a job to her.

Turning away from Mrs. Grand, Ning leaned against the railing to watch the dock. The men unloading the next ship over were wearing loose cotton shirts and pants. They had short hair and often thick mustaches. Not a queue in sight. She reached behind her and touched the tip of her own long braid. It was so common at home, but here it looked odd. Foreign.

Finally, a *Dixey* crewman beckoned them to disembark.

"It's about time," Mrs. Grand said. She signaled him to precede them down the gangplank with their trunks. As Mrs. Grand picked her way down the slippery wooden ramp, Ning kept a sharp eye on her trunk. Like the immigrants, she was carrying everything she owned.

Distracted, Ning stubbed her toe on the cleat meant to keep her from slipping. Arms flailing, she tried to keep her balance. The mahjong tile went flying. Clinging to the gangplank's rope railing, she watched, helpless, as it arced through the air and bounced on the wooden dock. It would have tumbled into the water if a crewman hadn't caught it neatly in one hand. Ning scrambled the rest of the way down to get it back.

"Thank you, thank you," she babbled to the crewman.

How could she have been so careless? She pressed the tile to her lips.

Dragon, don't even think of abandoning me when I need you most.

"Neenah, stop making a spectacle of yourself," Mrs. Grand snapped. They struggled to keep their place on the pier as the crowd swarmed around them. It was cold in the shadow of the other ships. Looking up past the flags on the topmasts snapping in the breeze, she could see gulls sweeping across the blue sky.

The *Dixey* was being unloaded, too, in a parade of wooden boxes stamped with the mark of Shanghai's finest porcelains, followed by bolts of silk and crates of tea. *How odd*, Ning thought, that she had traveled with all these luxuries from China. Someone in America must value fine Chinese things.

Maybe they will value me, too.

"Excuse me, miss." The rough voice at her elbow made Ning jump. A stocky crewman shoved her to one side, his face hidden by the huge bunches of red bananas on his shoulder. Behind him was a long line of sailors with more bananas and crates full of oranges and lemons. As they passed, Ning inhaled the sweet smell of fresh fruit, and her stomach grumbled loudly enough that Mrs. Grand noticed.

"So now your appetite returns," Mrs. Grand said sourly.

The steward cleared a path for them and their luggage. When they reached the street, he stopped. "Do you need a carriage?" he asked.

"No, we're meeting someone," Mrs. Grand said, sliding a bank note into his hand. He tipped his hat and returned to the ship at a jog. The river to their backs, they faced a row of warehouses where wagons were being loaded and unloaded. Everyone in sight moved purposefully about their own business; no one appeared to be waiting for them.

"Where is that man?" Mrs. Grand asked. "Perhaps he's waiting for us in the shipping office across the street." She crossed the road, nimbly avoiding the carriages and wagons as though she could see in every direction. Scurrying to keep up, Ning tripped on a groove. She stopped, looking down to examine the steel tracks embedded in the stone trenches. What were they for?

Clack thunk. Clack thunk. The sound was far away but growing louder. Now it was interspersed with the clopping of hooves. She glanced up to see two enormous horses barreling toward her. They were pulling a box on wheels along the steel tracks. She froze.

"Get out of the way!" A driver frantically waved at her from his seat behind the horses.

With a jerk, Mrs. Grand pulled her to safety. "I didn't bring you all the way here for you to be squashed by a streetcar!"

Short on breath, Ning tried to thank her. As she panted, the streetcar passed. Two dozen people stood inside, looking bored—as though this way of getting around was perfectly normal.

Suddenly a man was at their side. "Are you Mrs. Grand?" he asked.

"Mr. Stemple, I presume?"

Ning stepped back to see what kind of person her father had arranged to meet her. He was short with gray sideburns and rounded black-rimmed glasses. He ignored Ning, speaking only to Mrs. Grand.

"I'm to escort the girl to Baldwinsville." He paused and looked around, eyes passing over Ning as though she were invisible. "Where is she?"

"She's right here," Mrs. Grand said, nudging Ning who moved forward reluctantly. She hated how he called her the "girl" as if she didn't have a name.

Lifting his eyebrows so they popped up over his black-rimmed spectacles, he said, "I thought this was your servant."

"As if I'd bring a servant all the way from Shanghai," Mrs. Grand said with a grimace. "This is Miss Hamill." In her teacher's voice, she said, "Neenah, say hello."

"Hello, Mr. Stemple," she said warily.

"Miss Hamill." He pulled out a pocket watch. "We have to go immediately, or we'll miss the Albany Day Liner. We only have thirty minutes before it departs."

Mrs. Grand turned to Ning. "Well, dear, I wish you well."

Already?

"Can't *you* take me to my grandparents?" Ning whispered, clutching at Mrs. Grand.

"Don't be silly," Mrs. Grand said, peeling Ning's fingers off her forearm. "My job is done. Goodbye, my dear."

"Goodbye," Ning said faintly.

"It's time to go, Miss Hamill," Mr. Stemple said. "Tick tock."

chapter *Twenty-Two*

Everything had happened too quickly. First, Mr. Stemple had rushed her to catch a riverboat up the Hudson River to Albany. Instead of enjoying the majestic scenery, Mr. Stemple had chafed at the slow pace set by the mighty waterwheel. No sooner had they arrived in Albany then he chivvied her into a "cab" to the Albany Train Depot.

If only they could just slow down for a moment so Ning could catch her breath. When Mama had taken her to Longhua they had traveled leisurely in a small boat. There had been time to admire the pagoda rising out of the marshes. Americans were in such a hurry that Ning wondered how they even knew where they were.

The depot was a large room with wooden benches and a vaulted ceiling. In the late afternoon, the gas lamps were already lit.

"Please hurry, Miss Hamill," Mr. Stemple said.

"Where are the trains?" Ning asked, panting as she ran to keep up with him. At least she was wearing her comfortable slippers.

A porter in a crisp uniform and shiny black shoes answered her question as he hoisted her trunk on his shoulder. "The trains are through that door, Miss."

Mr. Stemple shoved a boxed lunch in her hands and beckoned for her to follow the porter outside to the empty track. She looked up and down the tracks eager to see a train up close.

"Where is it?" she asked.

"It will be here soon enough," the porter assured her. "We're running on time today."

"How far is it to Baldwinsville?" she asked.

"About four hours," he said. "It used to take a full day by horse or even by canal."

Four hours until she met her grandparents. She would have preferred four months. If only she had listened to Mrs. Grand a little more . . . her worries were cut short by a gleaming machine rolling into the station like a black serpent. The engine, belching billows of white smoke, pulled four additional cars. She covered her ears at the awful squeal of metal scraping against metal as the train slowed. With a groan and long sigh, the metal beast came to a halt.

Ning gulped. It was bigger and heavier and louder than she had imagined. The front wheels were almost as tall as she was. Ning touched the side of the engine and quickly pulled her hand back from the hot surface.

An attendant slid open the door to the first car. An

ingenious set of stairs unfolded from the train to the platform. Mr. Stemple climbed aboard without a backward glance.

Ning held back. Wasn't it crazy to put herself into a metal box that moved so fast? But then she thought of Number One Boy telling her how brave she was. She couldn't disappoint him.

"There you are, Miss Hamill!" Mr. Stemple's irritated voice grated as she climbed the stairs. The car was hot and steamy, reminding her of summer in Shanghai. "Sit there," he said, pointing at an empty leather bench. She sat, scooting over to be next to the window. The porter secured her trunk in the cubby at the entrance to the car and gave her a cheerful wave goodbye. Mr. Stemple sat on the opposite side of the aisle. Lighting his pipe, he prepared to read his newspaper. If this trip was like the riverboat one that morning, he would ignore her until they arrived.

Ning fidgeted in her seat, longing for the train to start. At the same time, she wanted to savor every detail. She heard a whistle, then the train jerked forward. It moved slowly, wheels creaking in protest. Then faster and faster. Gripping her seat, Ning wondered how the train didn't fly off the tracks. At home, there were always rumors of a train being built in Shanghai, but Number One Boy had always been doubtful. She wished he could be here now to see that trains were real. When the tears came, as they often did when she thought of home, she squeezed her eyes tightly until the tears stopped.

Pressing her forehead against the cold glass, she saw small shops and houses clustered around the station. Soon the train left the town behind to travel through fields marked with wooden fences or stone walls. White splotches turned out to be sheep who ignored the metal monster roaring by. Placid cows looked up briefly as the train passed, then returned to chewing their grass.

Farmhouses and barns painted a lucky red color were scattered through wide swathes of cropland. She tried to remember the day when she went to Longhua; she couldn't recall a single painted barn. The people who lived here must be rich to decorate buildings meant only for animals.

Outside, it grew darker. It was harder to make out the details of the landscape. The conductor lit the lamps in the train. She leaned back in her seat, feeling the motion of the train vibrating through her body. Each click and clack of the metal wheels brought her a little closer to her grandparents. Uncertainty gnawed at her insides. If only her father had come with her to introduce them. *Why hadn't he?* she wondered. Did he know something she didn't?

Ning let herself breathe deeply. One breath. Another. She was tired of wondering about her grandparents. With George or without him, she was ready to find out the truth about her grandparents. She hoped the train would arrive before her courage faded.

. . .

The conductor passed through the corridor announcing "Baldwinsville. Next is Baldwinsville."

Mr. Stemple startled awake. "That's our stop," he said unnecessarily.

The last stop for me.

With a giant hissing noise, the brakes started the work of slowing the great train. It creaked to a halt. Staring out the window, Ning saw only blackness.

Shrugging into his wool coat, Mr. Stemple said, "Let's go."

Ning followed slowly, half longing to stay in the warm rail car and half eager to finally get to her destination.

The station was really only a covered platform and a small office that was closed for the night. New York City had been so crowded and busy it had overwhelmed her. But here there was nothing. It was also much colder than it had been in New York City. She pulled her collar up around her ears.

Mr. Stemple went to find the driver. Moments later, the train glided away. Its forlorn whistle sounded like a warning. Ning had to keep herself from running after it.

"I'm not ready after all," she whispered. Her jaw began to tremble; she clenched her teeth to make it stop.

Number One Boy would be ashamed of me!

She closed her eyes and thought of her friend. What

would he tell her to do? He would remind her that he didn't call her little pirate for nothing. The Pirate Queen would square her shoulders and face her fears. Ning must do the same.

"Come, Miss Hamill!" Mr. Stemple called out suddenly. "Don't keep me waiting."

She was out of time.

chapter *Twenty-Three*

"There's her luggage," Mr. Stemple said to a gaunt man who doffed his cap to Ning before hefting the trunk with both hands and carrying it easily to his wagon. Ning followed him, giving wide berth to his horse which was even larger than the ones pulling the streetcar in New York. Ning hopped up and sat in the middle of the rough wooden bench.

"Hurry up, old man," Mr. Stemple said, settling himself next to her. "I need to deliver her to Hillside Farm and then catch the last train back to Albany."

"You're cutting it awfully close," the driver warned as he adjusted the lantern that hung on a pole next to him.

"Then you had best get moving," Mr. Stemple snapped.

He couldn't wait to get rid of Ning and disappear. Just like Mrs. Grand. And her father. And Mama.

Shivering, Ning blew on her hands to warm them.

The driver frowned. "You're shivering, Miss." From under his seat, he pulled out a rough-woven wool blanket and draped it over her shoulders.

"Thank you," she said.

"I'm Joe Arthur," he said. His breath hung like a cloud in air that smelled of horses, tobacco, and frost. "Call me Joe."

"My name is Ning."

"That's a funny name," he said, taking a closer look at her. "Where are you from?"

"China," she said.

"That's far away," Joe said, letting out a long whistle.

Ning stiffened.

"Did I say something wrong?" he asked.

She shook her head, reminding herself that whistling wasn't an insult in America the way it was at home. The Americans on the *Dixey* had done it all the time.

"So you're staying with the Hamills?" he asked.

"That's none of your business," Mr. Stemple said.

Ning was determined to be courteous, if only to annoy Mr. Stemple. And it occurred to her that the driver might know something about her grandparents. "Do you know them?" Ning asked.

"It's a small town. Everyone knows everyone. They're nice people."

Mr. Stemple bristled. "Perhaps you could mind the road instead of the young lady's affairs?"

"Of course, sir." With a grin at Ning, Joe jiggled the reins and they moved away from the station.

Theirs was the only wagon on the hard-packed dirt

road. The silence filled Ning's ears. It was never quiet like this in Shanghai. Even the clopping of the horse's hooves was muffled. No lights shone from the scattered brick factories. Not a person could be seen anywhere. If it weren't for the scratchy blanket around her shoulders and the hard bench beneath her, Ning would have thought she was in a bad dream. She'd had plenty of those since she left home.

As they left the train station behind, Ning perked up at the sight of a row of shops and offices. But she was disappointed to see their plain storefronts. Simple signs described their purpose: Barber. Lawyer. Hardware Store. In the Old City, every business bragged about themselves with bold signs in red and gold. Didn't these proprietors want to attract customers?

"Everything's closed," Joe said. "Around here, we roll up the sidewalks after seven o'clock." Ning looked closely at the front of the storefronts and saw wooden paths lining the road. Built a few inches off the ground, they were far superior to the sewage-filled streets of the Old City. You could walk here without soiling your shoes. But she didn't see how they could be rolled up.

Joe's lantern and the glint of light off his horse's harness were reflected in the wide panes of the closed shops' glass windows. Ning leaned forward and noticed that she couldn't see herself or Mr. Stemple in the wavery reflection. They might as well be ghosts roaming a town with no living creatures in it. Already anxious, Ning felt a lump of sadness settle in her belly.

Mrs. Grand had said that Americans were spread out—but this was supposed to be a town. Surely someone lived here. "Joe, where is everyone?" she asked.

"Most people have houses off the main road," Joe answered, pointing down a side street. She could make out small houses with tiny squares of light at the windows. All the houses were separate from each other and had their own small yards. Used to neighborhoods crammed with people, she wondered if the people who lived here were lonely.

"Now you'll see some Baldwinsville folks," Joe offered as they turned left onto a larger road. The intersection was a perfect cross. Two brick buildings, each three stories high, faced each other across the street. Both were brightly lit inside and crowded. On the left was a tavern, filled with patrons, almost all men, talking and laughing. Despite the chill, the door was wide open and customers holding tankards spilled out into the street. Opposite the tavern was a restaurant. Through the glass window, she could see half a dozen people dining together at tables. Unlike Shanghai restaurants which were narrow and deep, there was plenty of room between the tables for the servers to move about. An appetizing smell of roasted pork wafted from the kitchen, and her stomach growled. Maybe the ache in her belly was not worry but hunger; it had been hours since she had eaten the dry sandwich from the Albany depot.

Mr. Stemple's voice interrupted her thoughts of hunger. "Can't this nag go any faster?"

Joe shook the reins. His horse quickened the pace for a few steps, then settled back to a plod. They lumbered across a bridge over a small river and turned right. Ning twisted in her seat to look back at the lights behind them. It hadn't been much of a town, but there were people there. What was waiting for her out here?

The road followed the river. That at least felt familiar. Picturing herself standing at the edge of the Huang Po River, she took a deep breath and tasted the mineral tang of river on her tongue. But the air was different here. After a moment, she realized that it was missing salt. The Huang Po emptied into the sea, and the river air was always tinged with ocean.

An open expanse of ground separated the road and the glistening water. The blue-black sky was full of wispy clouds drifting in front of a half-moon. She could make out enormous trees silhouetted against the sky. If Mama could see this, she would use it as the inspiration for one of her silkscreens. Ning wished she had the same skill so she could show her mother what America looked like.

Gusts of wind chilled her face and hands. And it was only autumn. Winter here must be brutal. A wave of longing for the mild weather of Shanghai swept over her.

She spied small stone rectangles in rows. "Is that a cemetery?" she asked.

Joe nodded. "Hope you aren't superstitious."

"All Chinese are superstitious," she said without paying much attention. She was more interested in the people buried here. Madame Wu had said her father's ancestors were useless because they were so distant. But maybe now they were just a stone's throw away. Perhaps they would take pity on their descendent from China. She fumbled in her pocket for her dragon tile.

Dragon, can you put in a good word for me?

Joe made a turn and they began to climb. Joe's horse took the incline as easily as if they were still on a flat road. They passed only a few dark farmhouses with long empty fields in between.

"We're almost there, miss," Joe said.

"It's about time," Mr. Stemple said under his breath.

Almost there? Where? There's nothing here.

The road leveled out and, all at once, Ning could see an enormous barn on the left.

"This is the Hamill's place," Joe said as he turned into the graveled drive fronting a pale brick house. Facing them was a long open porch with two wooden rocking chairs. A tall tree loomed over the house. A stained glass window over the front door glowed red and orange like embers. Was it to welcome visitors or warn them?

Joe pulled back on the reins. "It looks like they waited up for you."

"Get her trunk," Mr. Stemple said as he climbed down. "I'm in a . . ."

"A hurry, I know," Joe said.

Ning didn't move a muscle. Her hand gripped the wooden bench, and she ignored the splinters that drove into her fingers. When she left this wagon, she was officially starting her new life. She had no choice, but still she waited. As if Number One Boy were sitting beside her, she heard his voice whispering in her ear, *Necessity breeds strength.*

She peeled her fingers from the bench and staggered down from the wagon. Stiff from the journey, she stretched her arms wide while her head swiveled around trying to see everything. She could hear neighing from the barn; there must be horses in there. The house looked sturdy and well-kept. They'd passed so many fields, some of them must belong to the Hamills. How ironic that the only life she had been sure she didn't want was one on a farm. She hadn't been interested in breaking her back in the rice paddies. But the chairs on the front porch said the Hamills had the means and time to be idle.

Did Mama know that the Hamills were rich?

The front door swung open. A tall man stepped out. His silhouette was illuminated by the light from the house, but Ning couldn't make out his face. She had the impression of a crown of white hair sticking up around his head. A tiny woman popped out from behind him. Ning was glad to take their measure from the shadows.

"Mr. Stemple?" The deep voice suited his height. "I'm Erastus Hamill. My wife, Sarah."

"Pleased to meet you," Mr. Stemple said.

"Where is she?" Sarah demanded. "Where's this girl who claims to be George's daughter?"

Claims?

Ning couldn't speak. The sound of her own breathing, fast and panicked, filled her ears. She was glad that Mr. Stemple blocked their view of her.

Mr. Stemple stepped to one side. "She's right here."

"Come closer, child, we won't bite," Erastus said. "I want to see my granddaughter."

Behind her, Ning heard Joe's startled voice, "Grand-daughter?" With a thump, the trunk landed on the ground. "Wait until Martha hears about this."

"Miss Hamill, your grandfather wants to meet you," Mr. Stemple said, taking her arm and propelling her forward. "As you can see, sir, she's in perfect condition. Should Mr. Hamill ask, I hope you will give him a good report. If you'll excuse me, I have to go."

"Now wait a moment, Mr. Stemple." Sarah held up her hand. "We have some questions."

"I know nothing of Mr. Hamill's business. I have a

train to catch." Mr. Stemple hurriedly climbed back into the wagon. "Good night."

"Good night, miss." Joe tipped his cap to Ning. "Welcome to Baldwinsville."

Quickly, the wagon was gone. Staring at her grand-parents, Ning wanted to run and hide in the darkness, but her feet seemed to have taken root in the gravel. What would Mama tell her to do in this situation? The answer was so simple and based in the Virtues. Be modest. Ning bowed so deep she felt she might tip over.

"What's she doing, Erastus?" Sarah asked. "Is she ill?"

"The girl's just shy," Erastus said. "Come closer. Let us look at you."

Swallowing her fear, she lifted her chin and stepped into the light.

Sarah's hand went to her mouth. "Erastus, she's Chinese!"

chapter *Twenty-Four*

I'm not welcome here.

Her feet started to back away of their own accord.

"Don't worry, we don't bite." Erastus said, sounding more amused than angry.

Ning took hold of herself and stood still. She tried to say "hello" but somehow it came out in Chinese. "*Ni hao.*"

"She doesn't even speak English," Sarah said. "This is a disaster."

"I do speak English." Ning could barely hear her own voice, but at least she was speaking the right language.

"It's freezing," Erastus said. "Let's go inside and talk."

"What about my trunk?" she asked, wishing she could curl up and hide inside it.

"I will bring that in," he said lifting it easily. He gestured for her and Sarah to precede him into the house.

In the foyer, Sarah pointed to a row of hooks. "You can hang your coat there."

Ning obeyed then followed her grandmother down the hall to the farthest door. Ning stopped short as she stepped inside, marveling at a room fit for a Mandarin. A thick rug the color of ripe cherries protected the wood floor. Paper with a floral pattern of peonies against a deep forest green covered the walls. Above the fireplace, a large gilded mirror made the room brighter.

They heard thumping as Erastus brought her trunk upstairs. Silently, Sarah and Ning stared warily at each other. Sarah was a handsome woman. Her silver hair was pulled back from her face in a tight bun. She looked like she might be ill-tempered, but that might have been because she disapproved of Ning's appearance. Glancing at the mirror, Ning saw that her plain tunic and patched trousers were out of place in this fine room. No wonder Sarah seemed so disappointed.

Mrs. Grand tried to warn me.

Erastus finally returned. "Do you want to sit down?" he asked.

"No, thank you," Ning said.

He cleared his throat with a cough. "We only know what George told us in his telegram. Your name is Neenah?"

Sarah's suspicious face told her that this was the time to use the name her father had chosen.

"I'm Neenah Hamill," she said, nodding. Then in a small defiance for Mama's sake, she added, "That is my name in America."

"But you aren't American," Sarah accused. "You're Chinese."

"Only half-Chinese." Neenah could almost hear the foundations of her life crumbling. She had defended China across three oceans, four seas, two rivers, and one canal. Five minutes in her father's house and she was "only half-Chinese."

"How do we know you're really who you say you are?" Sarah demanded.

Neenah's back stiffened. "I'm not a liar."

"Sarah didn't say that," Erastus said quickly. "You've just taken us by surprise. Let me take a look at you." He squatted so their faces would be level.

His bronzed face was weathered, and he squinted as though he was used to being outside. The lines around his mouth told Neenah he smiled often.

Please smile at me.

"Sarah, her coloring may be a little peculiar," he said, "but she has George's eyes."

Sarah kept her distance.

"Unfortunately, you inherited the bump on my nose." Erastus tapped the tip of Neenah's nose with his finger.

When his calloused finger touched her skin, she felt a spark that warmed the rest of her. She let out a nervous giggle. "Hello, Grandfather," she whispered.

He looked startled, then he smiled.

I think he might like me.

"Don't call him your grandfather." Sarah's shrill voice shattered the fragile moment. "Not yet. We don't know if it's true."

"Be reasonable, Sarah." Erastus straightened up with a grunt. "George telegraphed us to expect his daughter and here she is." He pulled a creased, onion-skin telegram from his pocket and read it aloud:

JUST DISCOVERED I HAVE DAUGHTER NEENAH.
ARRIVES BALDWINSVILLE EVENING OCT 10.
LETTER TO FOLLOW.
GEORGE

Every word is true, but it doesn't tell the whole story. Not even close.

"I'm not in the mood to take George's word on anything at the moment," Sarah said in a sour voice.

"Well, I'm satisfied," he said, carefully replacing the telegram in his pocket. "But of course, we need to know more. Neenah, how old are you?"

"I'm twelve."

"And George was in China in '65," Erastus said. "She's the right age."

"That doesn't mean anything," Sarah insisted. "We have no way of knowing when she was born."

"I have papers," Neenah offered.

"Sarah, she has papers," he said, almost pleading with his wife.

"They're in my coat. I'll get them," Neenah said, eager to escape the thick atmosphere in the drawing room. She quickly retrieved the envelope with her passport, but she lingered at the door to listen.

"Sarah, you could be nicer to the girl," Erastus said. "She's family."

"She's not my family," Sarah snapped. "And maybe not yours either. We know nothing about her. She might be a swindler or a thief. You're too trusting."

"You're just angry at George," Erastus said. "Don't take it out on the child."

Slumping against the wall, Neenah felt tired, both in body and spirit. This was worse than she had imagined. She didn't want to go back in there, not with Sarah calling her names. But she had nowhere else to go. To face Sarah, Neenah would have to be as fearless as the Pirate Queen. Touching Mama's necklace for good fortune, she took a deep breath and opened the door.

"I am who I say I am," she said, offering the envelope to Erastus.

"I believe you." Erastus gestured to an upright chair. "Warm yourself while we sort everything out."

Neenah brushed the dust from traveling off her pants

and sat next to the fireplace. She held her hands out to the fire. Sarah took a seat in an overstuffed velvet chair opposite Neenah, her expression ice-cold.

"Sarah, she's telling the truth." He held up a piece of paper. "George married her mother in 1865."

"Why did he hide her from us?" Sarah demanded. "What is he ashamed of?"

Another wave of anger swept over Neenah. "My mother is nothing to be ashamed of! She is very well-born. The Foo-Tai family is very important in China."

More important than yours.

"This says her name is . . . Foo-Tai Sun." The quizzical look on Erastus's face lightened Neenah's mood for an instant.

"Her first name is Sun," Neenah said. "In China, we say the family name first."

"What kind of foolish name is Sun," Sarah asked irritably.

"Sarah, let the girl talk," Erastus begged. "Neenah, where is George?"

"My father is still in Shanghai."

"He sent you here alone?"

Shaking her head, Neenah explained. "He paid a woman to accompany me on the ship because he had to work. He said he would follow in a few weeks. I'm sorry but I don't know anything more."

"Sending a little girl around the world by herself," Erastus muttered through a clenched jaw. "I taught him better. When he gets home, I'll . . ."

"If he bothers to come home at all!" Sarah burst out.

Neenah's head jerked up. "What do you mean?"

"He's gone away before," Sarah said. "Sometimes for years."

Years? Her father had said a few weeks . . . but she already knew he wasn't to be relied upon.

Erastus tried to calm Sarah. "Be fair; he always lets us know where he is."

"A letter from Shanghai or Brazil or India every six months or so! And now he's sent us a child—like a package to be claimed at the post office!"

What if he doesn't claim me?

"She's not a package, Sarah," Erastus said patiently. "She's a girl."

"Look at her, Erastus." Sarah ranted on. "What am I supposed to do with a twelve-year-old Chinese girl who looks like that?" With her gray hair and her dark blue dress, Sarah looked like a magistrate pronouncing judgment. Guilty. No Chinese Allowed.

Faintly, Neenah said, "Half-Chinese."

"Half won't make a difference to people in town." Her words felt like drops of melted wax on Neenah's skin.

"Sarah, the girl's here now. What else can we do but keep her until George returns?" Erastus asked.

"But what if he doesn't come back for months?" Sarah demanded.

"We'll cross that bridge when we come to it." Erastus had the air of a man who liked postponing difficult questions. "In the meantime, we should feed the girl. Are you hungry, Neenah?" he asked. "Sarah can give you some dinner."

"No," Neenah lied. She was starving, but she wouldn't ask Sarah for anything.

His brown eyes watched her carefully. "Are you sure?" he asked.

She nodded.

"Sarah, why don't you show Neenah to her room?" Erastus suggested.

For a moment, Neenah feared that Sarah might refuse. But after a long moment, she nodded. "Come with me," Sarah said heading out of the room.

"Can you come, too?" she asked Erastus.

"Don't worry Neenah, Sarah will treat you right," he assured her. But the troubled look on his face said he wasn't so sure. He ran his fingers through his crown of white hair. With a flash of recognition, Neenah remembered George had done the same thing. It must be a family habit whenever the Hamill men had a problem.

What are they to do with me?

chapter *Twenty-Five*

A lamp in her hand, Sarah led Neenah through a cavernous, shadowy kitchen. The aroma of roasted chicken hung in the air. Neenah hoped that Sarah might insist on feeding her, but instead she brought her outside to an outhouse.

Neenah stared at the seat built into a wooden shelf. Even in the dim light, she could see it was polished and immaculate. "Is it a toilet?" she asked.

"Yes. Do you need to use it now?" Sarah asked, embarrassed.

Neenah had used the toilet on the train; she shook her head.

After a moment, Sarah's curiosity got the better of her. "What kind of facilities do you have in China?"

"None as nice as this one," Neenah answered. "There was one 'facility' for a dozen houses. And it smelled terrible."

"Disgusting." Sarah wrinkled her nose. She looked satisfied as though Neenah had confirmed her suspicions.

"The rest of your house is as beautiful as your toilet,"

Neenah said, thinking that flattery would win Sarah over.

Sarah raised her eyebrows. "Er . . . thank you."

That wasn't the right thing to say.

Back inside, they climbed the sturdy wooden stairs to the third floor where the roof came to a point above their heads. Unlike home, these stairs didn't squeak.

"George's room is there," Sarah pointed to the right. "And this is yours." She opened the door for Neenah to go inside.

"This room is just for me?" she asked, turning her head to see every corner.

"Who else would share it with you?" Sarah asked.

"I have never had a room to myself."

Sarah shot her an inquisitive look but said only, "I had the window open earlier to air out the room, but it will warm up."

Her jaw locked to keep her teeth from chattering, Neenah nodded.

"There are extra blankets." Sarah tilted her head toward the bed in the corner, wedged under the sloped roof.

The top blanket was made of patches of different colored cloths sewn together. Although Neenah couldn't decipher a pattern to the blocks, it was still harmonious. And it was expertly sewn. "Did you make this?" she asked, touching the fabric with the tips of her fingers.

"I did."

"It's very well-done. Even Mama couldn't do better."

Sarah seemed to be torn between accepting the compliment and not wanting to be reminded of Neenah's mother. "Thank you," she said hurriedly. "There's a chamber pot in the corner behind the screen. Tomorrow you can empty it in the outhouse." She used the lantern to ignite a match and light the candle on the nightstand. "If you need anything, my room is at the top of the stairs on the second floor."

I wouldn't think of asking for your help.

Sarah paused in the doorway as if she wanted to say something—maybe something reassuring to a girl far from home in a strange house—then thought better of it.

"Good night."

Neenah listened to the clacking of her shoes descending the stairs. She was alone. She looked around the large room. She went to the corner where there was a small table with a washbasin and an ewer of water. Eyes closed, she scrubbed the grime from her face. She heard a rustling noise, and her hands stilled.

Face dripping, Neenah opened her eyes warily. She heard the sound again. It was coming from the ceiling. She held up the candle and listened. Nothing. But something might be there . . . waiting for her to go sleep. Her hand shook and the flame danced, throwing fantastic shadows on the walls. Like demons waiting to pounce.

Take hold of yourself Foo-Tai Ning! Number One Boy would be ashamed of you.

She pulled the extra quilt off the bed and wrapped herself in it. Her hands clumsy with the cold, she fumbled open the latch on her trunk and found her doll. Clutching it to her chest, she sat on the stool and started to weep. She cried until her eyes ached, and the quilt was damp with tears. Putting the doll aside, she wiped her face with her sleeve.

She was startled again by a tapping sound. This one had an easy explanation. There was a branch outside the window knocking against the glass. Plate glass was precious in Shanghai and she didn't have much experience with it. Afraid it would break, she hurried to open the window very gingerly. The cold air rushed in, smelling of manure and wood smoke.

Sticking her head out, she examined the large tree that towered over the house. One of its long branches just reached her window. Suddenly an enormous bird with white and brown feathers landed in front of her. Its round face was crowned with tufted ears, and it stared at her with eyes that were much too intelligent for a bird.

Hoo. Hoo.

"Go away!" she whispered. "*Zou kai! Zou kai!*" The bird flapped his great wings and swooped away.

What other wild animals are out there?

The half-moon cast enough light for her to see a good distance. Besides the house, the only building she could see was the barn. There were no other lights, no close neighbors. It reminded her of the nights when the *Dixey* floated in the middle of the ocean, totally alone.

Footsteps on the gravel caught her attention, and she watched as Erastus slipped into the enormous barn like a thief. A moment later he emerged, holding something under his coat. Was he stealing from himself? *Maybe he was sneaking around to avoid his ill-tempered wife*, Neenah thought. She wouldn't blame him if he was.

Sarah. *What could she do about Sarah?* Erastus liked her and wanted her to stay, but if Sarah refused . . . Neenah didn't know what would happen. Neenah had foolishly assumed that the family would accept her for George's sake. But Sarah had no love for her son. And it was her decision. Having grown up with Mama, Neenah knew what a woman who got her own way looked like.

She broke off the end of the branch to protect the glass and closed the window. Opening her trunk, she pulled out a nightdress and prepared for sleep. But first she had to figure out how to get into the massive bed. She found a wooden step stool under the bed and used it to climb into the bed. She had to be careful to duck her head to avoid hitting the steep sloped ceiling. Snuggling deep under her blankets, only her nose and eyes were left exposed.

Although she was exhausted, she couldn't get comfortable on the feather mattress. She tried lying on her stomach, then her side. Finally, she settled onto her back. Staring at the ceiling, Neenah realized that this was the first time in months that her bed had not been tossed and turned by ocean waves. She missed the rocking motion. And she missed being on the *Dixey* when she could still hope her grandparents would greet her with open arms.

She held the doll in front of her and whispered, "What do I do now? No one wants me. I can't go home but I'm not welcome here."

The doll, so like Mama, stared back at her. Mama would be practical. She would tell her daughter to make the best of her situation. After all, this place, Hillside Farm, was not terrible. She had her own room. The Hamills could clearly afford to keep her. Even if it was far from town, the house was comfortable and sanitary. And Erastus liked her. When—if—George came back, he might take her anywhere. She had to find a way to change Sarah's mind so she could stay here.

The key is Sarah.

Why didn't Sarah like her? She didn't even know of Neenah's many faults yet. Sarah hadn't seen how disobedient Neenah could be, or how disappointing her embroidery and calligraphy were. Her new grandmother had no idea that Neenah fought with girls at school or broke into strongboxes. Or that she had smashed Mama's tea set.

215

Sarah was judging Neenah on the one thing she could see: Neenah was Chinese. Hadn't those been the first words out of her mouth? Chinese marked Neenah as different. And it seemed Sarah could not abide different.

Neenah understood Sarah's point of view. Hadn't Neenah tried her whole life to look more Chinese so she could fit in? She would have changed her feet, her hair, her eyes if only that made her more acceptable. But that had never worked. At home, her old home, she couldn't change her physical body to fit in. But in America, she could do better. Here, not everyone had the same color hair or eyes. Maybe if she tried hard, she could fit in here. That might please Sarah. She must try. It was the only way.

I'll bury all the Chinese in me. I'll be whoever, whatever will make Sarah happy. Then maybe she will let me stay.

A light rapping at the door interrupted her thoughts.

"Hello?" she called out.

"Neenah, it's me." She could barely make out Erastus's voice.

She clambered out of bed and opened the door.

"Your candle was still lit," he said. "I wondered if you might be hungry."

"I'm starving," she admitted.

"I thought so." He chuckled as he patted his left pocket. There was a mewing sound. "Not that pocket." He reached into the other and pulled out a napkin bundle. "I

216

could see you didn't want to impose on Sarah," he said. "But I couldn't have you go to bed hungry."

She unwrapped it to find a large chicken drumstick and two hunks of fresh bread. Pulling up the stool, she sat down and tore into the chicken meat. Roasted with herbs, it was more flavorful than anything on the *Dixey* had been. The bread was light and airy. Sarah was almost as good a cook as Number One Boy.

"Thank you," she said, speaking around the food in her mouth.

"I have something else for you," he said, reaching into his left pocket.

With a pang, she remembered Number One Boy's farewell gifts. He'd given her dumplings and spices. What would Erastus's present be?

"I thought you could use some company." Erastus pulled out a tiny yellow kitten. Struggling to stand on Erastus's outstretched hand, it mewed at Neenah.

"A kitten!" Charmed, she rubbed its head with the tip of her finger. "He is so soft," she murmured.

"We got the cats to keep the mice out of the barn. He's not supposed to be inside, so don't tell Sarah." He looked shame-faced like a little boy sneaking a treat.

"It will be our secret," she promised. How many times had she said that to Number One Boy? "I've always wanted a cat, but they make Mama sneeze. What's its name?"

"You can choose," he said.

Neenah scratched between the kitten's ears until he purred, a rumble that seemed too loud for his tiny body. "I'll call him Jin Mao; it means golden cat. Golden cats are very lucky."

"We can all use some luck," Erastus said.

The kitten jumped to her shoulder and started to lick her face.

"Thank you for everything . . ." She paused, then added, "Grandfather."

He smiled wide, exposing a full mouth of straight, gray teeth. "Get some rest. Granddaughter. And don't worry about Sarah."

Eyes fixed on Jin Mao's ears, Neenah said, "She doesn't want me here."

"She's angrier with George than with you," he said sadly. "Sarah wants everything in the house to be orderly and stable, but George is the opposite. He's always happiest when he's leaving for someplace new. Like oil and water, they never understood each other."

Like me and Mama.

"And now we find out he's kept a huge secret from us," Erastus said. "Her feelings are hurt."

Neenah didn't want to defend George in any way, but Erastus deserved the truth. "Mama never told him about me," she said. "I was born after he left Shanghai."

"Why tell him now after all these years?"

"The matchmaker told Mama I would never find a good husband because I was half-American," she explained, omitting any mention of her feet. Erastus wouldn't understand. "Mama thought I would do better here."

"Matchmaker?" He frowned, his bushy eyebrows bulging. "You're a little girl! Wait until I tell Sarah what we are saving you from . . . that will help sway her to our side."

From downstairs they heard Sarah's fretful voice. "Erastus?"

"Speak of the devil!" He winked to show he was joking. "I have to go down," he said, resting his hand on top of her head for a brief moment. He hurried to the door. "Good night, Neenah."

"Good night."

She slipped back into bed and blew out the candle. With Jin Mao purring under the blankets, she wasn't afraid.

chapter *Twenty-Six*

The smell of frying pork lured her from a lovely dream of a hazy spring day in Shanghai. She was floating down the canal, and Mama's back was to Neenah while her high voice sang of lost love. If only she could stay asleep a few minutes more, Mama might turn and smile at her daughter. Neenah rolled over and buried her face in the pillow. Just a little longer!

Her nose started to itch from the feather pillow. Neenah sneezed hard. And just like that, Mama was gone. The present came flooding back.

Jin Mao mewed in protest as she disturbed his sleeping place under the heavy quilts. "I'm sorry, little friend," she said in Chinese, stroking his head. He stretched out his front paws, and then toppled on his side, asleep again.

She slipped out of bed, bracing herself for the cold. But she was pleasantly surprised; the sun flooding through the window had warmed the room. Outside, the blue sky was bright enough to make her eyes hurt. Maybe the sky was newer in America and not faded and tired like it was in Shanghai.

In the light of morning, she still liked her idea to please Sarah. They needed a new beginning. First her clothes. She rummaged in her trunk to find the plaid dress. Yesterday—*could it really only be yesterday?*—she'd refused to wear it. But today the same dress would prove to Sarah that Neenah could change her ways.

Shaking out the dress, she stared in dismay at the ripped sleeve. How could she have forgotten that? She pulled out her embroidery needle and thread and quickly sewed it back on. The dress was still too tight; she had to exhale all her breath to button it.

Neenah looked down at her feet and groaned. The dress was far too short. Either Mama had bought something too small or Neenah had grown half a foot since Shanghai! Mrs. Grand had told her a young lady should never display her knees, so Neenah pulled on a pair of trousers under the skirt. It was better than Sarah thinking her immodest.

She exchanged her comfortable slippers for the leather boots Mama had bought, lacing them up over her ankles. They were also too small and pinched her toes, but they looked like Sarah's shoes. That had to count in Neenah's favor.

She picked up the hand mirror that was next to her basin. Examining her hair, she tried to see it with Sarah's eyes. The braid was Chinese and had to go. Hanging loose about her shoulders, Neenah's hair reached almost to her waist.

She tilted the mirror to see her whole body. She definitely didn't look Chinese, but she suspected she didn't look quite American, either.

I tried.

"Neenah! Breakfast."

Sarah's call startled her, and she nearly dropped the mirror. Gently, Neenah placed it back on the dresser and hurried out to the landing. She stopped in front of her father's room and tried the door. It was locked. What secrets was he keeping behind that door? In Shanghai, she'd picked a lock to discover her mother's mysteries. Thank goodness, Number One Boy had packed her metal chopsticks.

How did he know I would need them?

Neenah sniffed the air. There was the smell of bacon again! Would it be soft and chewy like Mama preferred or crispy the way Neenah liked? Number One Boy always made both. She was starving, and Sarah was becoming impatient. She hurried down the stairs.

The house looked so different this morning. The sun streamed through a stained glass window over the front door, bathing the foyer in jeweled reds and oranges. Now she could see that the hallway to the kitchen was lined with family paintings and photographs. Her family. Last night, she had walked past her ancestors and hadn't even known it. Hopefully, they would understand she had not intended to be rude.

The first painting was a portrait in cracked oils of a solemn-looking woman with dark hair and light eyes. Perhaps she was Erastus's mother? Her great-grandmother. She reached out to touch the stern face with her fingertips. What would she think of her newly arrived descendent?

"That's my mother, Eugenie," Erastus said from behind her.

She pulled her hand back. "I'm sorry," she said.

"For what?" he asked. "You're curious about your great-grandmother, that's to be expected."

"You must miss her," Neenah said.

"She passed a long time ago," Erastus said. "But she was a tough lady."

"Do you visit her grave?" she asked, seeing a way to get the information she wanted. "Is it near here?"

"What an odd question."

Neenah felt her face heat up. "In China, we often visit our ancestors. But I never knew where my father's ancestors were buried."

"How could you?" he asked. "The family has a nice plot under a red maple tree at the cemetery down by the river. We visit sometimes, probably not often enough for Mother's tastes."

Neenah stored that fact away for the future; you never knew when you would need an ancestor. She hoped Eugenie would not hold it against her that she was so late to honor her.

An oil painting of a young man was next. "What do you think of this handsome fellow?" Erastus asked.

"How old were you when this was painted?" Neenah asked, smiling.

"Twenty-one and ready to conquer the world."

Neenah moved down to look at a group of photographs clustered together.

"This is George's mother." He pointed to a stern woman with a strong chin and a disapproving expression on her face.

Neenah leaned in closer, confused. "That isn't Sarah, is it?"

"No, of course not." Glancing at the kitchen, he lowered his voice. "Sarah is my second wife. Helen was my first. She died not long after George was born."

Neenah stared, stunned. No wonder Sarah didn't treat Neenah like a granddaughter. There was no blood linking them at all.

"This is me and Sarah on our wedding day," Erastus said, not noticing Neenah's consternation. They both looked directly into the camera without smiling. *Sarah hasn't changed much*, Neenah thought.

"And you know him," Erastus said, pointing to a photograph of George.

Neenah gasped. "Mama has this picture, too." She didn't tell Erastus she had stolen it from her mother's strongbox. Or that she had torn the photograph into pieces after her first disastrous meeting with her father. This picture brought only bad memories.

"George sent it to me from China . . . it must have been about twelve to thirteen years ago," Erastus said.

"He was with my mother then," Neenah murmured. "I wonder if she had her picture taken, too?" It wasn't fair that she had to look at George's face but didn't have a single picture of Mama.

"He never showed me one. Remember, we didn't know about her until last night," Erastus said, his mouth twisted with bitterness.

"If you did have Mama's picture, would you put it on the wall, too?" Neenah asked with a sideways look at Erastus.

"Your mother?" Erastus coughed in surprise. He tugged at his collar as though it was suddenly too tight, just like his son did. "I suppose we might."

"A Chinese woman goes on that wall over my dead body," Sarah said, sticking her head out of the kitchen doorway. "Where have you been, Neenah? I've been calling you."

Neenah whirled to face her. She knew the sudden movement was a mistake the moment she felt a button pop off the front of her dress. It fell to the floor and rolled toward the kitchen. Three sets of eyes followed it until it stopped at Sarah's feet.

"I didn't think it could get any worse than what you wore yesterday," Sarah said, stooping to pick it up. "The rest of those buttons won't last long."

"It's too small," Neenah said apologetically.

"You're wearing trousers!" Sarah accused. "Ladies do not wear trousers!"

"I'm sorry. The dress was too short." Sarah didn't seem to appreciate the effort Neenah had made at all.

"Sarah, the girl looks fine."

His wife ignored him. "You need some new clothes." Her own dress was shirt-waisted with buttons up the front and, when she turned, Neenah saw it was gathered in a small bustle in the back. She hoped that Sarah wasn't planning on buying her a dress like that—who wanted to be squeezed in the middle and puffed out in the back like a peacock?

"I have to go," Erastus said. "I'm visiting one of my other farms today."

"Now? What about breakfast?" Neenah asked, dismayed. She had assumed Erastus would eat with them.

"I already ate."

Neenah steeled herself. "Before you leave, can I tell you both something?"

Sarah dusted flour off her skirt and glanced back toward the kitchen. "Be quick about it."

"I will be." Neenah's tongue darted out to wet her lips. "I don't want you to lose face because of me."

"Face?" Sarah asked, irritably touching her cheek.

"It means . . . how you are looked at by your neighbors," Neenah explained. "My mother says, 'Trees can't live without bark, men can't live without face.'"

"Hamills don't care what other people think," Erastus declared.

"Yes, we do," Sarah snapped. "The ladies at the church can be quite vicious when they want to be."

Although Neenah was shaken at the thought of a church filled with vicious ladies, she didn't let Sarah fluster her. What she had to say was too important. "I don't want to embarrass you," Neenah said meeting Sarah's eyes. "If you don't want me to be Chinese, I can change. I'll do anything you want."

chapter *Twenty-Seven*

"Anything?" Sarah asked, the irritation in her face easing a little.

"She's fine as she is," Erastus protested.

"Anything," Neenah said at the same time.

"We'll start with your hair," Sarah said, looking at Neenah thoughtfully. "You'll have to put it up like American girls."

"Sarah!" Erastus spluttered. "Leave her hair alone."

"Erastus, she can't be Chinese and American! She has to pick one or the other."

I owe Mrs. Grand an apology; she was right.

"I'll do what you want, Sarah." To prove her sincerity, Neenah bowed.

"First—stop bowing, it's irritating," Sarah said, grabbing Neenah's chin and lifting her head. "We have some pride in America."

Pressing her nails into her palms, Neenah agreed, "No more bowing."

"Good. Now come to breakfast before the bacon is charred to a crisp," Sarah said, returning to the kitchen.

Erastus turned to Neenah. "Are you sure about this?" he asked in a whisper. "There's nothing wrong with you."

If only Erastus was the one I had to please.

"I thought about this all last night," she whispered back. "I want Sarah to like me."

"It would be a relief if Sarah was happy," he admitted. "Now, while she's busy, I'll put the kitten in the barn."

"He's sleeping next to my pillow."

"I'll see you for dinner," he called to Sarah as he gave Neenah a push into the kitchen.

Last night, she had been too tired and hungry to notice this room properly. Her eye was drawn first to the massive iron stove. A fire was burning inside—she could see the flames flickering through the vents—and the heat took her breath away. Neenah hated being warm, and she wondered if Sarah was prickly because her kitchen was so hot.

The corner of the room where the stove lived was lined with bricks. Neenah recognized a sensible precaution. She'd grown up with the threat of fire in the Old City. That was why Mama's house had only a small kitchen fire and Number One Boy did his baking at a communal stove shared by all the houses on the block. Out here in the wilderness, there wouldn't be any neighbors to help put out a fire.

The rest of the floor was covered in wide, wooden planks. They were immaculate. She could see her reflection in the gleaming copper pans and pots hanging from hooks on the wall. Sarah's servants must scrub hard to keep them so clean.

The sizzle of bacon in the pan made Neenah's mouth water, reminding her of Number One Boy's special fried rice with strips of pork. Maybe Sarah's breakfast would be just as tasty. The roast chicken from the night before boded well.

Sarah shifted the bacon to a towel so the fat could drain, then moved a few feet toward a wooden worktable. She measured white flour and water into a bowl, added an egg from a basketful on the table, and began to stir.

"Can I help you?" Neenah asked.

"You can get the plates," Sarah said, pointing to a half-open door. Inside were shelves with neatly stacked plates, big ones and smaller ones. And bowls. And glasses. And cups. At least a dozen of them. Neenah glanced out at the enormous stove that could handle ten meals.

"How many people live here?" Neenah asked.

"Only me and Erastus," Sarah said. "And now you . . . for the time being."

At home, there were only three plates and three bowls. Why would they need more?

Collecting two plates, Neenah brought them to a small eating table in the corner. She picked her dress away from her body to get a little cooler.

"Fill the teapot," Sarah ordered.

The teapot was easy to find on the edge of the stove away from the flames. But Neenah didn't see a water bucket. "Where can I find water?" she asked.

"In the scullery. I'll show you" The scullery was a small room off the kitchen; a slate sink took up the entire back wall. Sarah tugged on an iron lever above the sink, forward and back. Suddenly water gushed from a spout below.

Neenah's mouth dropped open. "Where does it come from?"

"We have a deep well."

She put her hand under the cold water and let it pour over her skin until her fingers were numb. The flow slowed to a trickle and then nothing. "Where did it go?" she cried. "Bring it back!"

"Just pull on the lever until you fill up the teakettle halfway." A tight smile appeared on Sarah's face. "I suppose you've never seen indoor plumbing before?"

Neenah shook her head.

"America is much more advanced than China," Sarah said. "In town, they have water piped almost to every house. Out here, we have to rely on the well."

Neenah thought of the water sellers who dipped their buckets into the Huang Po River, and then brought the water to the Old City to sell. The Hamills owned their own water.

They must be very rich.

The stovetop was big enough to fit a kettle and another flat pan that glistened with melted butter. "I'm making hotcakes," Sarah said. "They're George's favorite." She poured batter from her bowl into the pan. "Do you like to cook?"

Neenah found herself lost in a memory that felt as real as Sarah's kitchen. Mama's small manicured hands gently touching Neenah's as they rolled out dough together.

"Neenah? I asked you a question," Sarah said.

"Number One Boy does most of the cooking for us," Neenah answered quickly.

"Number One Boy?" Even standing next to the hot stove, Sarah's face paled. "Don't tell me you have a brother, too?"

"No, he is . . . was our manservant."

Sarah exhaled with relief. "Thank goodness."

"Where are your servants?" Neenah asked.

"We have no servants here. I take pride in doing everything myself."

There was that word again. *Pride*. At home "face" was about how people saw you from the outside. But Sarah's pride seemed to come from both the outside and the inside. There was no one to know that Sarah did all her chores herself, but she valued the fact that she did. Neenah wondered how you learned to be proud of yourself—no one had ever taught her.

Once the hotcakes had sizzled and risen in the pan,

Sarah flipped them in one smooth motion.

Neenah wandered about the room. She reached up to touch a gleaming brass bell on a shelf by the back door.

Although Sarah pretended to focus entirely on her cooking, Neenah saw that she was watching her closely. "It's from a train," Sarah said. "Erastus loves it. I use it to call him to dinner when he's in the fields."

"The Buddhist temples at home all have bells," Neenah offered.

Sarah grimaced. "We call them churches here."

"I won't forget," Neenah assured her.

Whatever you want, Sarah.

"I think it would be best if you don't mention the word 'Buddhist' either," Sarah said. "Or anything heathen. Do you understand?"

Neenah nodded.

"You probably can't avoid questions about where you're from—not if I know the ladies in town—but you don't have to call China 'home.' And don't volunteer anything that's too Chinese. Like 'face.' And definitely don't talk about a matchmaker—Erastus told me about that last night. People will think the worst if you let them."

For Sarah, the worst is being from China.

"I'll try," Neenah muttered. When she had offered to change to please Sarah, she hadn't realized how much deception would be involved.

I hope it will be worth it.

Sarah made up two plates with hotcakes and bacon and brought them to the table. On the *Dixey*, Mrs. Grand had been offended when Neenah had complained about American food. She wouldn't make the same mistake with Sarah. Neenah would eat everything. She cut a piece of hotcake and popped it in her mouth.

"Oh," she said in surprise. "It's sweet." *Too sweet*, she thought.

"Not yet." Sarah placed a bottle of syrup on the table. "Pour this on top."

Neenah tasted a bit of syrup, but it made the hotcake more like a dessert than breakfast. She forced herself to keep eating even though it made her stomach ache. If the cake was too sweet, the bacon was crispy and delicious just the way she liked it. She ate the hotcake without syrup, chasing every bite with bacon.

They ate quietly for a bit, the silence broken only by the bubbling of water heating on the stove. Finally, Sarah spoke, "Do you have hotcakes in China?"

"A different kind. They are salty, not sweet." For an instant Neenah was transported home, watching Number One Boy fry his special scallion pancakes. She would eat her fill of the crispy dough and lick her fingers afterward. If she closed her eyes, she could hear Number One Boy bickering with her mother. She felt her bottom lip start to tremble and hurriedly said, "Maybe I could make them for you?"

"I don't think I would care for salty pancakes."

Well, I don't care for your too-sweet hotcakes.

The kettle screamed. As Sarah made the tea, she said, "Don't worry. Once you get used to the way we eat, you won't miss the food in China."

Neenah knew she'd never stop missing her favorite foods; she'd never be so disloyal to Number One Boy. But she forced herself to smile and nod at her step-grandmother as if she agreed completely. Anything to ensure that Sarah liked her.

chapter *Twenty-Eight*

After breakfast, one of Erastus's farmhands harnessed a buggy. In the back, he loaded a small box full of preserves and breads that Sarah had prepared. Neenah eagerly followed Sarah into the buggy; she was looking forward to seeing the countryside properly. Slowly.

"Mrs. van der Smith's shop, please, and then we have to stop by the church to drop off some supplies," Sarah said to the farmhand. She turned to Neenah. "I would prefer to drive myself, but my arthritis makes it difficult for me to hold the reins." She held up her hands so Neenah could see her swollen knuckles.

"Number One Boy has the same problem, especially when it's damp," Neenah said, hoping to make herself useful. "Master Li, the apothecary, gives him a salve made of willow bark."

"My ointment is good enough for me," Sarah said. "Doctor Clemson would think I was crazy if I started using tree bark. In America, we have real medicines."

Neenah was offended on Master Li's behalf, but

she thought it worth another try. "Master Li also gave Number One Boy green tea to help with the swelling."

"George brought me back some green tea once. It tasted like dishwater. Black tea is good enough for me."

Neenah didn't say anything. Sarah had served black tea this morning laden with sugar. Neenah had choked it down. She wished she had paid more attention the last time Mama had served her chrysanthemum tea. That would be a good memory to balance out the bad ones.

The carriage started down the steep slope, jolting Neenah away from her maudlin thoughts. From up here, she could see farmland rolling out in all directions like an enormous carpet. The dirt had been plowed into furrows and was waiting for winter.

"Is this all my grandfather's farm?" she asked.

Sarah nodded.

"He must be very wealthy."

"We don't say things like that," Sarah said sharply. "It's crass. Let's just say that Erastus has worked hard and he has prospered."

"I'm sorry," Neenah said. "At home . . ." At Sarah's lifted eyebrows, she corrected herself. "In China, if you are rich, you let people know it."

"Here it is considered very bad manners to talk about money."

"I won't say anything," Neenah promised.

"See that you don't," Sarah warned.

In the distance, Neenah could see a small forest on the side of a hill. The leaves of the trees were ablaze in an undisciplined display of red and yellow and gold. At home, the yellow-leafed gingko trees were planted in neat rows. She inhaled a deep breath of fresh air . . . and tasted fruit.

"I smell apples," she said. She missed fresh fruit. The *Dixey*'s chef had only served it stewed or dried.

"Our orchard is behind the barn," Sarah said. "We've picked most of the apples, but there are a few left. I daresay Erastus will enlist your help to bring in the last of them."

At the bottom of the hill, they turned right. Neenah remembered this part of the trip from last night. The scattered farmhouses soon gave way to smaller lots with neat little houses and white fences. They must be getting closer to town. Yes, there was the water. By daylight, she could see it was a sleepy, slow-moving river. Tall willow trees lined the banks, their long arms dangling into the water. Neenah smiled to see how they danced on the river's surface when the wind gusted.

The buggy rattled past the cemetery. Neenah looked for the tree Erastus had mentioned. One tree with brilliant red leaves towered above the others. An auspicious color. Sarah confirmed it was a red maple. Neenah marked the place in her memory: her ancestors were there, waiting for her.

A few houseboats and barges were moored near the

riverbank, but the water was otherwise deserted. "Where are all the ships?" she asked Sarah.

"There's nowhere for a boat to go," Sarah said. "The river ends at a dam just past town. It provides power for all the factories. But we do have an outlet to the Erie Canal." She pointed to a manmade channel parallel to the river. A metal barge, the size of a train car, was docked there. Beyond it was a gate across the canal. "That's the lock that raises the boats up to a higher water level. You can take a boat all the way from Albany to Buffalo."

Albany to Buffalo. Sarah might as well have said from the moon to the farthest star. But Neenah did know about canals—Shanghai was full of them. "It's very nice," she said politely.

"Your father went to China to teach them about canals," Sarah said.

The apothecary. The tea. Neenah had let those slights pass, but this was too much. "China has had canals and locks for thousands of years," she pointed out. "Maybe my father went to China to learn about canals from us?"

Sarah stiffened. "I doubt that very much," she said. "Your father's company had a very profitable contract to go to China and dredge the waterways. They needed American know-how, not the other way around!"

From her seat next to Sarah, Neenah could see her nostrils flaring.

Stupid. I can't offend Sarah.

239

"I'm sure you're right," Neenah said quickly. "I'm sorry."

Grudgingly, Sarah accepted Neenah's apology. "People here are proud of our canal. You should be careful what you say."

Neenah swallowed hard. "Yes, Sarah. I will be."

The carriage stopped at a row of shops just short of the bridge into Baldwinsville.

"We're here," Sarah announced.

"Aren't we going into town?" Neenah asked, disappointed.

"Not until you have something to wear," Sarah said. "People are going to ask enough questions as it is."

The dress shop occupied the center of the row. The sign over the door read Dressmaker and Ladies Apparel. In the window, mother and child mannequins wore identical dark velvet dresses. Neenah averted her eyes from their blank faces; they were too much like ghosts for her.

As they entered the shop, a bell jangled over the door. Inside, a polished wood table took up most of the space. The walls were lined with bolts of fabric in a rainbow of colors. An elegant woman with fiery gold hair appeared in the doorway at the back of the store. She wore a well-tailored dress in dove-gray taffeta. She greeted Sarah warmly. "Mrs. Hamill!"

"Hello, Lucy," Sarah replied. "Neenah, this is Mrs. van der Smith."

Over Sarah's shoulder, the woman stared at Neenah. "So this is George's daughter from China?" she asked. Her eyes glinted with curiosity and maybe a little malice.

The smile on Sarah's face became fixed. "News travels fast in a small town. However did you hear so quickly?"

"Joe Arthur." Mrs. van der Smith said. "He drove her from the station. And you know what a gossip his wife is. Half the town knew before breakfast."

Sarah lifted her chin. "Well, it's not a secret. Neenah, this is Mrs. van der Smith."

"She doesn't look so foreign . . ." Mrs. van der Smith said. "If I didn't know better, I would think she was just a little jaundiced."

"Neenah just finished sailing around the world, of course she got sunburnt," Sarah said dismissively. "But that's neither here nor there. She needs some proper clothes."

"Is Neenah's mother visiting too?" Mrs. van der Smith asked casually.

Sarah's sudden tension told Neenah that the question wasn't offhanded at all. "No. George's *wife* was unable to come to America."

"That's a shame," Mrs. van der Smith said. "Neenah, take off your coat." When she saw Neenah's dress, her eyes bulged a little. "Oh my. I see why you came to me."

"Obviously, she needs an entire wardrobe—at least three day dresses, something for church, and a coat that fits. And we'll have to buy underthings, shoes . . . everything. And quickly."

Mrs. van der Smith reached into an ingenious hidden pocket to pull out a notebook and scribble down Sarah's requirements.

"Can I get pockets, too?" Neenah asked. It was the first useful thing she'd seen on an American dress.

"Neenah, the pockets are not important," Sarah said severely.

"They are my own design," Mrs. van der Smith said beaming. "I can add them to any dress." Looking over the list she said, "I can make everything here in the shop."

"We'll need some things quickly. Perhaps we can order some ready-to-wear from McCarthy's in Syracuse too."

"For you, Mrs. Hamill, I will put all my other work aside."

Watching Mrs. van der Smith, Neenah felt a flash of the familiar. How often had she seen merchants angling for her mother's business in Shanghai?

"The sooner we can throw these rags away, the better," Sarah said.

Neenah didn't say anything, but she felt a pang of loss when she thought about disposing of her old clothes.

Mrs. van der Smith pulled out a tape and noted Neenah's measurements in her notebook.

"Don't slouch," Sarah ordered. Neenah was startled; she was used to pretending she was shorter.

"Let's look at some patterns." Raising her voice slightly, Mrs. van der Smith called, "Letty! Bring me the latest Butterick's."

The door opened and a girl emerged struggling with an enormous book. She was the first American girl of her own age that Neenah had seen up close. Her purple dress was tailored to fit perfectly with only the barest hint of a bustle in the back. With her long gold ringlets pulled back from her face and hanging down her back, Letty looked just like Neenah's doll, Abigail. Neenah told herself that the resemblance did not mean that Letty would be an enemy too.

Maybe we can be friends.

Letty's bold eyes met Neenah's, taking in every detail of her appearance. Madame Wu had looked at her like a horse for sale, too. As a knot of hurt feelings formed in her stomach, Neenah regretted the comparison.

"Hello, Letty," Sarah said, nodding at the girl. "I'd like you to meet Neenah. As you can see, she desperately needs some proper clothes."

Neenah's fingers went to the buttons on the front of her dress that were barely holding the fabric together.

"Hello, Mrs. Hamill," Letty said with a sly look as though she was enjoying Neenah's chagrin.

"Hello," Neenah said, starting to bow. Sarah shook her head ever so slightly. Instead Neenah bent at the knees in a halfhearted curtsy.

"Are you really from China?" Letty asked.

Looking to Sarah first for permission, Neenah said she was.

"Will you go to our school?"

Sarah's face went blank. "She just arrived; we haven't made any arrangements yet."

"I would like to go to school," Neenah said. "There is so much I don't know about America."

"Don't get your hopes up, Neenah," Sarah warned. "We don't know how long you are staying."

"No one likes going to school," Letty said. "It's boring." She plopped the book on the table. It fell open, and Neenah could see it was full of dress patterns.

"Mrs. Hamill, let's look through the latest styles and fabrics," Mrs. van der Smith said. "That canary yellow wool would make a nice spring coat."

"Not yellow!" Neenah said before she could help herself.

"Why not?" Sarah asked.

"Only the Emperor wears yellow. It's the law."

"Anyone can wear it here." Sarah took off her coat and sighed. "Obviously Neenah won't be much help." She offered Letty a coin. "Why don't you and Neenah get a treat at the drugstore?"

Neenah couldn't quite believe her ears. "There are opium dens in America?"

"Opium?" Sarah exclaimed, shocked.

"Of course not!" Mrs. van der Smith cried.

"But you said it was a store for drugs."

Sarah explained a drugstore sold medicines and sometimes, like the one next door, served sweet drinks. Pointing at Neenah, Letty laughed until she had to hold her stomach.

Neenah's hopes for Letty shriveled away. She was just like every other girl who didn't like her. After all, how many friendships started with one girl mocking the other?

chapter *Twenty-Nine*

"L etty, hush," her mother hissed. "You are being rude to our best customer."

Letty abruptly stopped laughing. "Why don't we stay here. I don't want soda right now," she said, glancing at Neenah's dress. "Neenah's not dressed to go out."

Glaring at the other girl, Neenah agreed.

Mrs. van der Smith moved closer to Letty and hissed in her ear, "You heard Mrs. Hamill . . . she would like you to bring Neenah next door."

"But, Mama . . ."

Mrs. van der Smith's eyes were like daggers.

"Fine, I'll go." Letty pocketed Sarah's money in a quick motion that made Neenah remember pickpockets in the Old City. "Here's your coat." Letty tossed it to Neenah.

Shrugging into her coat, Neenah noticed that Letty didn't put one on. She followed Letty to a shop two doors down called Lord's Drug Store. A half-dozen glass globes, striped bright green and orange, hung in the window. At first Neenah thought the glass was colored or painted—

but when she looked closer, she saw the design was created from different colors of liquid trapped inside the globe. Somehow the liquids stayed separate. The apothecary must be very talented.

Letty held the door open. "Come in," she said impatiently.

Just inside the entrance was a display case filled with all sorts of soaps and creams. A young man with slicked-back hair waited on a customer. Behind him were dark wooden shelves with glass doors containing bottles full of pills and potions. Master Li's shop had a thousand tiny drawers built into the wall and, without looking, the apothecary could tell you the contents of each one. His shop smelled of the herbs he used to make his powders and ointments. This drugstore smelled of sugar and soap. Neenah didn't trust it at all.

"We're not here for soap," Letty said. "Come to the back." As she walked to the rear of the shop, her image was reflected in a huge mirror on the far wall. Letty's spun-gold hair caught the lamplight, and her pale skin seemed to glow. Neenah's hair, braided and loosely pinned up, looked lifeless in comparison.

They were the only customers in this part of the drugstore. Letty took a seat on a round stool bolted to the floor in front of the counter.

Neenah started to unbutton her coat.

Letty held up her hand. "Leave your coat on."

"But it's warm in here," Neenah protested.

"Your dress is ridiculous," Letty said. "Keep your coat on or we're leaving."

Sarah's warnings echoing in her head, Neenah bit her tongue.

"Were you poor in China?" Letty asked.

Taken aback by the suddenness of the question, Neenah shook her head. "We weren't poor at all."

"My Pa says that the Chinese are all coming here and taking jobs from real Americans."

Neenah remembered the newspaper articles that Mrs. Grand had tried to keep from her. "That isn't why I'm here," she said taking the stool next to Letty. "I came to live with my American family."

A smiling young man, wearing a red-and-white striped jacket, popped up from behind the counter. "Hello, Miss Letty," he said. "Who's your friend?"

"She's not my . . . this is Neenah. She's visiting Mrs. Hamill."

"Oh, the Chink, I heard about you," he said. His well-scrubbed face looked too innocent to say such things. Neenah felt her face grow hot.

"That isn't a real word," Neenah said, staring down at the white marble counter.

Glancing toward the front of the store, the waiter said, "Did I say something wrong?"

Remembering the promises she'd made to herself

and Sarah, Neenah managed to get out the words, "I'm American now."

"Fair enough." He shrugged. "What can I get for you young ladies?"

"Two hot chocolates," Letty said.

"I don't care for chocolate," Neenah said quickly.

"Everyone likes chocolate."

"Well, I don't." Neenah heard the edge in her voice and reminded herself that she wanted Letty to like her.

"What about soda? Do you like that?" Letty asked.

"What is it?"

"It's carbonated water. You get to pick your flavor."

Neenah didn't know what carbonated water meant. But she could read the sign listing her choices: candy cane, coffee, cherry, vanilla, peach, chocolate, sarsaparilla, and more. Neenah's eyes went up and down the list. *How could they stock so many flavors? And what was 'candy cane' or 'sarsaparilla'?*

Letty twirled in a circle on her stool. After three revolutions, she burst out, "Neenah, just choose!"

"I'll have the . . . peach." At least that was a familiar flavor.

"I'll have a hot chocolate, and she'll have a peach soda," Letty told the waiter.

First, he served Letty a steaming cup of chocolate with a large dollop of whipped cream on top. Then he placed a glass under the spout on a silver machine. A clear liquid gushed out. He pressed a button and a bright orange syrup oozed into her glass. He mixed the two, stuck a straw in the liquid, and slid the drink across the counter to Neenah.

Neenah leaned back as far as she could on the stool. "It's boiling!"

Letty smirked. "Is it though?"

Neenah cautiously dipped a fingertip in the glass. It was cold. She sniffed. It smelt like peaches, but not like peaches. Remembering the orchards at Longhua, Neenah knew what peaches were supposed to smell like.

"It's got fizz," Letty said. "Try it. You suck through the straw."

Neenah took a large swallow and started coughing.

Letty laughed out loud. "Slower, silly."

Neenah tried again. The flavor, like so much else in America, was too sweet, but the hundreds of tiny cold bubbles dancing on her tongue made up for it. Smiling shyly, she glanced at Letty. "It's strange."

"Do you like it?" Letty asked.

"I think so." Taking very small sips of her bubbly drink, she felt herself relax a little. This was fun. Maybe Letty wasn't as bad as she seemed.

"You really don't have chocolate in China?" Letty asked.

"The English brought it to Shanghai," Neenah said. "But we Chinese don't like it."

"Everyone or just you?"

Neenah thought back. Her mother, who did enjoy sweet food, had not cared for chocolate either. "Everyone." She heard the straw slurp at the bottom of the glass and felt a bubble of gas in her stomach. She opened her mouth and let out a long burp.

"Neenah!" Letty's pale face had gone scarlet. "That is so unladylike!"

The waiter burst out laughing, a loud guffaw that attracted the attention of the customers at the front of the store.

Slapping her hand over her mouth, Neenah mumbled an apology. "In China, it is considered a compliment."

"Not here!"

"I'm sorry," she mumbled. She wanted to sink through the black-and-white parquet floor and disappear. "Our manners are very different."

Any goodwill she had collected from Letty seemed to have disappeared with the belch. Letty's expression turned mean as she dropped her voice to a loud whisper. "I've heard all about Chinese manners. My father says Chinese always lie to your face. About everything."

Neenah's shame was erased by a surge of anger. "That's not true!"

"How can I believe you?" Letty asked in a lilting voice that seemed purposefully annoying. "He also told me there are too many Chinese people and not enough food. They're so poor they eat rats. Do you eat rats?"

"I've never eaten a rat," Neenah said, struggling to keep her temper. "Only the poorest peasants eat rats."

"So, Chinese *do* eat rats! Pa was right!"

Neenah put her hands flat on the marble countertop to find some balance before she answered. Why was Letty being so nasty? "I'm not a peasant!"

"But you are Chinese. Chinese eat rats. So you eat rats."

"Miss Letty, do you think you can possibly stop saying 'rat'?" the waiter asked, looking uncomfortably about the shop.

"I don't eat rats, you stupid girl!" Neenah's voice got louder in spite of her resolution to stay calm. "Your father doesn't know what he is talking about!"

Letty jumped to her feet. "Are you calling my Pa a liar?" she demanded.

"Neenah!" Sarah's voice was like a bucket of icy water tossed over Neenah's head. She looked up in the mirror to see Sarah standing behind them, shaking with fury. When Number One Boy caught her being naughty, he said "Ning" in that warning way, too. But he said it with love. No one had ever said "Neenah" with love.

"Be quiet, Neenah." Sarah spat the words. "Letty, I apologize for my . . . for Neenah's poor manners."

"That's all right, Mrs. Hamill," Letty said, taking her seat again. "I guess Chinese people don't learn how to be polite like we do."

"But you were rude to me!" Neenah cried.

"That is quite enough from you, young lady," Sarah said, marching her across the checkered floor. Glancing back, Neenah saw Letty smugly sipping her cocoa, like a cat lapping at her milk.

Sarah didn't release Neenah until they were back in the buggy. "You obviously aren't ready to go out in public," she said.

"She said I was a peasant."

"So? You're the stranger here. It's up to you to keep your temper."

Mama had said the same when Neenah fought at school. It was never the other girl's fault. Neither Mama nor Sarah would ever take Neenah's side. Neenah turned her head away and stared at their distorted reflection in Lucy van der Smith's store window. Even the mannequins were laughing at her. "You will never belong," they seemed to say.

In the distance, she heard the mournful sound of a train horn. She wished she were speeding away on that train, heading anywhere but here.

"Remember, you promised to behave." Sarah reminded her. "That means you can't argue with everyone who has an opinion about China."

A stupid opinion!

"I would prefer to go straight home, but I must stop at the church," Sarah said, tugging her gloves onto her swollen fingers. "Usually, I make a full morning of a trip into town, but you've ruined this outing for me. I hope you are happy."

Neenah was not happy at all.

Sarah stared stonily ahead as they clattered over the iron bridge onto the same gravel road that Neenah remembered from the night before. The shops were just opening. Neenah wanted to ask what a Dry Goods Emporium was or what was sold at a Hardware Store, but she didn't dare break the silence. A handful of shoppers waved to Sarah; she leaned forward and told the driver to go faster.

She doesn't want to introduce me to anyone.

Midway up a tree-lined hill, they pulled in front of a stone church with buttresses on each side. Craning her neck to see the slate roof topped off by a tall spire, Neenah thought it might be as tall as the temple at Longhua. She was certain there wouldn't be any dragons or Buddhas here. Sarah told Neenah to carry the box full of provisions and follow her.

Happy that Sarah was talking to her again, Neenah gladly brought the box inside.

"The Ladies' Benevolent Society feeds less fortunate families," Sarah said as she brought Neenah through the double doors to a long, elegantly proportioned room filled with polished wooden pews. On both sides were high colorful windows. At first Neenah thought the glass itself was stained, but then she realized it was painted.

Sarah didn't pause to let Neenah admire the church; she hurried down the aisle to a door in the corner. Before they could reach it, an intimidating woman stepped through. Neenah had never seen anyone like her. A large-bosomed lady, she was encased in a maroon taffeta dress. Her hair was coiled around her head tightly and piled in a bun.

"Eva," Sarah said, stopping short. "What a nice surprise to see you here." She did not sound as though it were a nice surprise.

"Good morning, Sarah. I was just taking inventory of our foodstuffs for the needy. I know this is your responsibility now, but I want to be helpful." She looked past Sarah's shoulder to examine Neenah from the tip of her untidy hair to her too small shoes. Neenah pulled her coat closer about her body to hide her short dress and trousers. "Is this the girl from China?"

With a little sigh, Sarah said, "This is Erastus's granddaughter. Neenah, say hello to Mrs. Rushbridger."

Neenah mumbled a greeting.

"When I heard, I said that Sarah Hamill couldn't possibly have a granddaughter that I didn't know about."

Neenah wondered which she found more unlikely: the granddaughter or that Sarah hadn't told her.

"Step-granddaughter," Sarah corrected.

"Why did you never tell me that George had married?" Mrs. Rushbridger waited for the answer like a dog salivating for a bone. "He did marry, didn't he?"

Neenah opened her mouth to defend Mama, but was forestalled by a flick of Sarah's hand. How often had Mama done the same thing to keep her outspoken daughter quiet?

Sarah folded her arms and said very clearly, "George's wife stayed behind in Shanghai. Neenah is staying with us until George can make other arrangements for her."

Sarah still wants me gone. I've made things worse.

"That is a relief," Mrs. Rushbridger said. At Sarah's raised eyebrows, she quickly added, "As the newly elected President of the Ladies' Benevolent Society, you don't have time to raise a child. Particularly one who will require as much guidance as Neenah."

Sarah's fingers drummed on her forearm. "I assure you I am perfectly capable of doing both. I would never shirk my responsibilities. Actually, I've just come from Lucy van der Smith's shop. Neenah will soon have everything she needs."

Mrs. Rushbridger's eyes shifted from Neenah to Sarah as though she was choosing which tidbit to chase. Settling on one, she dropped her voice confidingly, "It's such a shame about Lucy's husband. I wonder that you brought Neenah there, considering everything."

"Eva, it's been lovely to see you, but I'll thank you not to question my judgment again," Sarah said abruptly. "Neenah, give Mrs. Rushbridger the box." Bemused, Neenah handed over the provisions to the speechless woman. "I will see you at our next meeting. Goodbye." Sarah turned on her heel and headed for the door.

Neenah stared. When Sarah was disrespected, she stood up for herself like the Queen of the Pirates. If only she would take Neenah's side like that. But she wouldn't even let Neenah defend herself.

This is going to be harder than I thought.

• • •

That night at dinner Erastus asked about the visit to the dressmaker. Sarah said nothing, but continued to drop spoonfuls of mashed potatoes on each plate as if they were cannon balls. Neenah concentrated on folding and refolding the napkin in her lap.

"Did something happen today?" he asked finally.

"I had a small argument," Neenah told him.

"With Letty van der Smith," Sarah interjected. "So the story was all over town before we even got home."

"Is Letty the one with the blonde curls that are always bouncing?" Erastus asked.

Neenah smiled sourly at his apt description. "That's her."

"She came here with her mother once. She talked a lot of poppycock!"

"Neenah was very impolite," Sarah said cutting her meat into tiny pieces.

Erastus asked quietly, "I hope you didn't make a fuss, Sarah."

"What if I did?" Sarah said. "She humiliated us."

"You mean *you* were humiliated. I couldn't care less what the van der Smiths think."

"I haven't told you the half of it. We went to church and just happened to meet Eva Rushbridger."

"Oh, no," Erastus hooted. "Is she still angry that you became President of the Society instead of her?"

"Of course," Sarah said. "And she was extremely inquisitive about Neenah."

He leaned back in his chair and shrugged. "She would be."

"I told her Neenah was only here for a short time." She threw out the words like a challenge to Erastus. He harrumphed but said nothing.

Even though I knew Sarah's opinion mattered most, I did everything wrong today.

The three ate in silence until their plates were clean.

"Letty asked if I would go to school," Neenah ventured.

"Everyone goes to school," Erastus said. "It's the law now."

"Not just the boys?" Neenah asked, puzzled.

"Everyone," Erastus said firmly.

If that happened in China, it would change everything, she thought. Education was one of the few ways a poor man could advance and improve the social position of his family.

"Don't girls go to school in China?" Sarah asked.

Neenah shrugged. "Girls aren't worth educating. Everyone knows that. 'One lame boy is worth a dozen girls.'"

"That's absurd," Sarah exclaimed. "A girl's education is just as important, if not more so. She is the one who will be responsible for the children."

Erastus nudged Neenah with his elbow. "Now you've set her off."

Sarah ranted for a few minutes about the situation of women in America. She told Neenah that in America all men were supposed to be equal, but women had fewer rights than men. Her particular interest was getting women the right to vote. And not just wealthy women, but all women.

"I wouldn't want to vote," Neenah said, dismayed. "I'm just a girl. I don't know anything." But even as she said it, she wondered. After all, Mama made all the decisions for the family. And Madame Wu and Mrs. van der Smith had their own businesses. Even Ching Shih, the Pirate Queen, who had no schooling at all, could hold her own against the Emperor and his armies. Maybe women could learn to be just as informed as men.

"You go to school so you can become a responsible citizen!" Sarah finished triumphantly.

"So will I go to school?" Neenah asked again. She waited for Sarah's answer on pins and needles. If Sarah said yes, then she intended to let Neenah stay.

"You won't be here long enough to make it worthwhile," Sarah said.

Neenah slumped back in her chair.

"Nothing's been decided yet," Erastus said, scowling at Sarah. "Neenah, did you have any schooling in Shanghai?"

Neenah nodded. "My mother sent me to the Presbyterian Mission School for Girls. And then I had tutors."

I won't mention I was thrown out for fighting.

Erastus glanced at Sarah. "Hear that, Sarah? She went to a Presbyterian school."

"Why does that matter?" Neenah asked.

"Your mother sent you to a school run by our church," Erastus explained.

It couldn't be a coincidence that Mama had sent Neenah to a school run by a church that would be acceptable to her father's family. On the other hand, Mama had also brought Neenah to the Buddhist temple. A good gambler, Mama knew how to hedge her bets.

"If she's not a Christian, it makes no difference," Sarah said. "Were you baptized Neenah?"

Neenah lifted her shoulders. "I don't know."

"That minister of yours can take care of it," Erastus said.

"What will Eva Rushbridger and the other ladies in the Society say?"

Erastus made a motion as if to sweep away all the ladies and their gossip. "You worry too much."

Neenah thought of all the people she had met that day. Mrs. van der Smith had been appalled by Neenah's clothes. Letty had said awful things about China. Mrs. Rushbridger used Neenah to attack Sarah's position in society. They all had an opinion about Neenah. *Erastus is wrong*, she thought. *Sarah might not be worried enough.*

chapter *Thirty*

The next morning, Neenah discovered that American life was remarkably similar to life in Shanghai. There was a daily routine. Meals, washing up, gardening, sewing, baking—each had their appointed time. But unlike at home where Neenah would begrudge any task, here she tried to make Sarah happy. She willingly tackled chores, no matter how dirty. For the first time, Neenah appreciated all that Number One Boy had done for her.

Someday I'll thank him.

As if she could read Neenah's mind, Sarah had said, "There are no Number One Boys here. In this house, everyone works."

"Yes, Sarah," Neenah answered.

The second morning, Neenah scraped and rubbed the surface of a frying pan to clean off the burnt egg. Once the pan was spotless, she showed it to Sarah.

"Excellent," Sarah said with satisfaction. "I know you aren't used to doing such labor, but it's good for your character. We have a saying, 'Idleness is the parent of many vices.'"

Neenah's hands stilled in the cold water. Scraps of a hundred proverbs, heard since birth, reverberated in her head.

"What's wrong?" Sarah demanded. "You look like you've seen a ghost."

Startled, Neenah pulled her hands, numb with cold, out of the dishwater. "Nothing's wrong," she said, splashing the water as she started to wipe the remaining plates.

"Child, stop scrubbing," Sarah said. "For the life of me, I don't know what I said to upset you."

"Mama and Number One Boy like proverbs, too," she said with a sniff. "They had whole arguments only in proverbs. Number One Boy usually won." Gripping the scrubbing brush hard enough to crease her palm, she said, "I miss them."

"It's natural to miss your mother," Sarah said, "You're far from home."

"Close in spirit though far away," Neenah recited. Number One Boy really did have a proverb for every occasion.

"That's pretty."

"Number One Boy used to say that."

Sarah's eyes watered with tears, but she quickly blinked away any sympathy for Neenah. "As they say, 'Absence makes the heart grow fonder.'"

"Do you think that Mama's heart is fonder now that I'm far away?" Neenah asked, combining the Chinese and American proverbs.

"I don't know your mother," Sarah said taking a wet dish from Neenah. "But I'm sure she made the right choice for you. An American girl should be raised here, not China."

"Why?" No one had convinced her that this was true yet.

"For one thing, we would never force you to marry," Sarah said. She polished the dish until it shone.

"Don't I have to get married?"

"Most young women do. But only when you are older and to a man you choose. We are more advanced here. Even without the vote, girls have more rights than you are used to," Sarah answered. "Your mother was very wrong to try and force you to marry so young."

"She was doing her best for me," Neenah protested. "It is not easy to marry off an ugly daughter."

"Don't be ridiculous," Sarah said. "Once we get you some clothes, you will be perfectly presentable. You won't need a matchmaker."

As Neenah dried the rest of the dishes and put them away, she pictured a meeting between Mama and Sarah ten years from now. Neenah would still be a spinster and Mama would shake her head, purse her lips, and say, "I told you so."

• • •

The next morning Erastus enlisted her help in the orchard; the last of the apples were ready for picking. The trees

264

weren't very tall, and Neenah easily climbed to the highest branches. The tree swayed under her weight and she imagined she was the Pirate Queen, clinging to a mast as she surveyed her fleet of seven hundred ships.

"Does everything I see belong to you?" she asked.

"Just about," he said with satisfaction. "Whenever some land comes on the market, I buy it."

The Pirate Queen must have been just as pleased with her domain.

Neenah twisted and pulled the last few apples off the branches then tossed them down to Erastus.

"You aren't afraid of heights," he said approvingly.

"Not at all," she assured him. "At home, I used to climb out on our roof. This isn't nearly as high."

"That's good. I can't abide the girls in this town who are fearful of everything." He threw up his hands and let out a high-pitched scream. "Oh no, I'll fall! Eek, a mouse! Oh, the horror, I've got a stain on my dress!"

Neenah laughed, then stopped. "Should I be more afraid? Is that what Sarah wants?"

"Child, even if she does . . . it's not what I want. I like that you're brave. I knew it from the first instant I saw you." He held out his hand to steady her as she worked her way back to the ground. "It took guts to get out of that wagon and face us."

"I was ready to run . . ." She landed on the ground with a thud. "But I didn't have anywhere to go."

"But you didn't run. That took courage." With a grunt, he stooped to pick up the bucket full of apples. "These go in the cold room." He brought her to a door leading from the outside to a stone room in the basement of the house.

Neenah rubbed her arms. "Brrr."

"It's good for the apples. They'll last for months at this temperature," he said. "You'll be glad to have something fresh to eat in February. The winters are hard here."

Shivering, she said, "It's cold enough now."

"This is nothing! George told us that winters in Shanghai are mild. Do you get snow?"

"Sometimes," she said. "Once we got this much." She held up her finger and thumb, spaced slightly apart. "It was beautiful—like one of Mama's paintings. But it didn't last."

"Last year we had snow up to here." He indicated a spot in the middle of his chest.

"That's impossible!" Neenah said.

"You'll see. But we'll be snug as a bee in a box. I lay in plenty of firewood. And Sarah bakes pies—her apple cranberry pie with walnuts wins the prize every year at the Ladies' Benevolent Society picnic."

Placing the last apple on the rack, Neenah said, "I've never had an apple pie."

"But you've had apples before, haven't you?" he asked. "Because if not, you have to eat one now."

She nodded. "We fry them with sugar." It was one

266

of the few sweet treats she liked. Thinking of the sweet oily smell made her stomach feel empty and homesick. "Apples are very lucky because the word for 'apple' in Chinese sounds like 'peace.'"

Ning means 'peace,' too.

"Peace? Hmm, I like a nation that is thoughtful about its food," Erastus rubbed an apple on his waistcoat until it shined. "Now, when I eat an apple I think of temptation. Do you know the story of the Garden of Eden?"

Neenah remembered a long-ago lesson at the Mission School. "But you eat them anyway?"

"I grow them myself." Erastus handed her the apple. "I know there's no evil in them."

He gave her a small basket of red and green apples. "Bring these to Sarah. Fridays are pie-baking day. You're in for a treat." He licked his lips.

Neenah grinned. She liked Erastus so much. Unlike Sarah, he never judged her. She never had to worry about saying the wrong thing. He was a simple man who just wanted peace in his house. Peace and apple pie.

"Go on," he said shoving her gently. "She'll be glad you saved her a trip."

That afternoon, Sarah had Neenah peel dozens of apples. Not just for pie, she explained, but also to make applesauce and apple butter. Neenah didn't mind the work because Sarah showed her how to use a machine—or as Sarah called it "a labor-saving contraption." Neenah stuck thc apple onto sharp prongs, then turned a crank. An ingenious roller with sharp edges not only peeled the fruit, but also sliced it into rounds, then pushed out the core. At first Sarah had watched matter-of-factly, but soon she caught Neenah's excitement. They were both grinning by the time Neenah pared the last apple.

"Can I do some more?" Neenah asked as she wiped her forehead; the room was hot from the stoked oven.

"Later. First, we'll make our pies," Sarah said, sprinkling the cut apples with vinegar to keep them from turning brown.

Haltingly at first, as if she was used to being alone in the kitchen, Sarah soon was explaining every step of making pie dough. The correct ratio of lard to flour. How the water to moisten the dough must be cold. The secret amount of salt to add. Neenah listened hard, but she was distracted by memories of Mama teaching Neenah her secret dumpling recipe.

Sarah let her have a taste of the first pie when it came out of the oven. Having put two whole cups of sugar into the filling, Neenah had been afraid it would be too sweet. But to her delight, the tartness of the apples was a perfect balance to the sugar.

"It's good," she said.

"Well, of course," Sarah had huffed. "I've noticed you're not fond of sugar, but you'll learn to like it."

That evening Neenah was on edge watching Erastus

as he took his first bite. He smiled broadly. "Well done, Neenah," he said. "Your first pie is a big success."

"Neenah has a deft hand with dough," Sarah said a little grudgingly.

"My mama taught me how when we made ginger pork dumplings," Neenah said shyly.

"Dumplings? Do you put them in stew?" Sarah was always curious about food.

"You dip them in soy sauce and pop them right in your mouth." Letting a note of pride come into her voice, Neenah added, "They're very lucky."

"Whoever heard of food being lucky?" Sarah complained.

Erastus let out a bark of laughter. "And who makes pot roast before every meeting of the Ladies' Benevolent Society. That roast is your good luck charm."

Neenah glanced at Sarah and was relieved to see her smiling sheepishly.

"Someday, Neenah, you can make those auspicious dumplings for us," Erastus said. "I'd like to taste some Chinese food. It only seems fair since Neenah is eating our food all the time."

Glancing at Sarah, Neenah said, "I would be happy to."

"I don't know even know what soy sauce is," Sarah said. "And how would I get fresh ginger?"

"Bunkum!" Erastus said. "We can order soy sauce."

"You have powdered ginger," Neenah said eagerly. "We have everything else you need."

They waited as Sarah slowly ate the last bit of her pie. Finally she said, "It might be interesting to try something new."

Neenah wondered if this was how families were formed. *One slice of pie, one dumpling at a time.*

chapter *Thirty-One*

The locked door opposite her bedroom was a constant mystery gnawing away at Neenah's peace of mind. What was George hiding in there? Neenah's chopsticks had proved useless—American locks were evidently more complex than the lock on her mother's strongbox.

She tried another approach: a stratagem designed to appeal to Sarah's housekeeping instincts. "Sarah, I'd be happy to keep dusting upstairs," Neenah offered. "I'm sure my father's room needs cleaning."

"George said the things in his room were private." Sarah looked up from the potatoes she was mashing. "As if I would pry into his business!"

"But it must be quite dusty by now." Neenah noted Sarah's dismay and quickly prodded further. "I can lock it up when I finish."

"No," Sarah said with a grimace. "If he won't let me clean it, then he can do it himself when he comes home."

"There's been no news?" Neenah asked, as she returned the broom and dustpan to the scullery.

"Not yet," Sarah said, her expression tight with disapproval.

Two weeks had passed and still no word from George.

To her surprise, Neenah was is no hurry to see her father again. Slowly, she was making a place for herself at Hillside Farm. Without other children, Neenah had learned to make friends with the animals about the farm. She found them much more satisfying than her dolls back home. The kitten, Jin Mao, was still her favorite. Sarah had discovered him in Neenah's room before the first week was over. Neenah suspected that Erastus had worked hard to persuade Sarah to allow the cat inside the house during the day. Outside, Erastus was teaching her to care for the horses. Grooming his bay mare, Star, was Neenah's special task in the evenings. She couldn't believe how quickly this life had begun to feel normal.

Every day, she and Sarah got along a little bit better. Neenah had learned not to talk too much about China, and Sarah admitted to some curiosity about Shanghi. Since Sarah kept her so busy in the house, there had been few excursions to town. But even then Neenah had been polite and quiet; Sarah hadn't lost face again. They were in a good place.

But each night she went to sleep fearing that the next day her father would return and ruin everything. After all, the last time the dragons had brought George back into Neenah's life, her whole world had been upended. As far as she was concerned, he could take his time returning. In fact, would it be such a terrible thing if George never came back?

Sorry, Dragons, but if you try to give me my father again, I will say no.

"We'll hear from him eventually," Sarah said in a resigned tone.

"What can I do now?" Neenah asked.

Looking about the spotless parlor, Sarah suggested, "Well, the chicken coop needs cleaning."

In exchange for Sarah's goodwill, Neenah told herself there was no chore too smelly or difficult, but the chicken coop came close. Hiding her dismay, Neenah said, "Of course."

Wrapped in a horse blanket Sarah kept for such dirty chores, Neenah trudged out to the coop. As she did almost every day, she sent a message on the winds all the way to China. "You would be so happy, Mama. I'm being very obedient. I take care of these awful creatures, and I don't complain at all."

The chickens were the only animals on the farm that scared her. They, however, were fearless as they pecked at her feet with their sharp beaks. The wooden hut had a low ceiling and she had to stoop inside, feeling at any moment the roof would crush her.

The white rooster with a bright red crest, the ruler of the coop, nearly bowled her over when she opened the door. He didn't lay eggs, and Sarah said he was too tough to cook. Useless. Sometimes he even forgot to crow at dawn, so he was unreliable too. When she was alone, she called him George.

"Good afternoon, George," she said to the rooster. Crowing, he pushed past her, eager for his freedom. "I hope you get eaten by a fox!" she called after him.

As she scraped the chicken droppings into a metal bucket, she wondered if there was another way to get into her father's room undetected. Neenah had been sure the dusting plan would work. Maybe she should "borrow" Sarah's keys?

She was still worrying about the problem one afternoon a few days later. The weather was dreadful; sleet and a cold wind pelted the house. Erastus was at a meeting in town, and Sarah and Neenah were sitting companionably in the parlor. Jin Mao napped on Neenah's feet and there was a cheerful blaze in the fireplace. While Sarah knitted, Neenah pulled out her embroidery for the first time. It had stayed at the bottom of her trunk until now because Neenah hadn't been ready to show Sarah something so personal. But as the days passed, that worry had melted away.

She laid out her skeins of colored threads on the table in front of her, each color representing part of her design. *But also my life,* she thought. The crimson silk for the railings looked like the jade beads around her neck.

Red for good fortune. Yellow for the sun and the color of mourning. Blue for Number One Boy's robes. Gold for the Buddha at the pagoda and dark green for his favorite dragons. Erastus must be a deep brown, like his pipe tobacco. And Sarah? Orange for the fire in her kitchen. In the background, hardly visible but always there, was the color white. That thread represented her father, the ghost, the man she did not know.

"What you are working on?" Sarah asked, looking up from her wool. She drew in a surprised breath when Neenah showed her the embroidery square. "It's exquisite."

"My mama taught me," Neenah said wistfully. How many times had she seen something beautiful and compared it to her mother's work?

"She must be very talented to teach you so well," Sarah said.

Neenah's eyes went to the plain sampler hung on the wall. "Home is where the heart is" had been embroidered on the white background and decorated with simple hearts. Like Sarah, it was plain and no-nonsense.

It is good for Sarah to know there are worthy Chinese skills.

"Mama is from Suchow," Neenah said. "The city is famous for its fine embroidery and lotus blossoms." Neenah's mouth clamped shut—she hadn't meant to say anything about lotus blossoms. Sarah, whose feet were naturally tiny, would never understand.

Sarah didn't notice Neenah's dismay as she traced the thread design with the tip of her finger. "What kind of building is that? A tower?"

"A pagoda," Neenah answered. Sarah still looked puzzled. "It's a sacred building." She hesitated, but Sarah had asked. "A temple. The Buddha's bones are buried there, and the dragons have guarded them for a thousand years."

Sarah's brow furrowed. "Like a tomb at a cemetery?"

"It's more like a church. My mother's family has an altar there."

"Did you visit often?"

"Only once. Mama brought me there on a festival day." This was the most they had ever talked about Neenah's past. She would be careful to keep her answers short and pleasing. "It was a special occasion. In China, women don't leave the house very often."

"That is why your father sent you to America," Sarah said smugly. "A girl can go anywhere here."

Staring down at her sewing, Neenah let the dragons in her embroidery encourage a little mischief. "But Sarah, I've barely left Hillside Farm since the day after I first arrived. You don't even take me to church."

Sarah blushed. "About church," she started to say then looked relieved when she heard the wagon wheels crunching gravel. "Erastus is back."

When Erastus came in, Neenah knew immediately

something was wrong. His hair was damp and his lips were blueish with cold. But more than the bad weather, he stooped as though he was carrying a great burden.

"Hello, dear," Sarah said. "How was your meeting?"

"Fine," he said. He pulled out his pipe and tried to light it with hands that trembled slightly. "Neenah, please bring an apple out to Star."

"What's wrong?" Sarah asked sharply.

"Nothing," he said. But his eyes were sending his wife a silent appeal that Neenah didn't miss. "I'm just tired, and I'd be obliged if Star didn't have to wait for her apple."

"Yes, Grandfather." Neenah gently nudged the kitten off her feet, put aside her work, and left the room. In the hall, she opened and closed the front door loudly enough to be heard, then tiptoed back to put her ear to the parlor door.

Some things never change. I have to eavesdrop to know what's happening in my own life.

"Jeff Dickens, the postmaster, was at the meeting," Erastus was saying. "He gave me a letter from George."

"Finally!" Sarah exclaimed. "When is he coming home?"

"He's not sure," Erastus said. "But he did apologize for not telling us about Neenah's mother."

"Twelve years too late." Neenah could picture that

pinched look on Sarah's face. The one that looked like she had bitten into a wormy apple. "What are his plans for Neenah?"

"He doesn't want her to be a burden on us. But he's not going to settle down, either."

"How does he expect to manage both of those things?" Sarah demanded crossly.

There was a heavy sigh from Erastus. "He's found a boarding school in Boston where they take foreign students. He's made all the arrangements to send Neenah there."

There was a silence. What was Sarah thinking?

"When?" Sarah asked finally.

"As soon as we can put her on a train."

Neenah put her hand on the doorjamb to steady herself. Just as she was beginning to make progress with Sarah, George wanted to tear her away. The life she was building here at Hillside Farm was as fragile as the mahjong-tile walls she used to construct at home. A careless gesture could wreck them both. She could count on her father for the careless gesture.

"Does he expect us to pay for this fancy school?" Sarah asked.

"How can you think of money," Erastus reproached her, "when he wants to ship my granddaughter off to a boarding school?"

"Neenah is George's daughter and his responsibility," Sarah pointed out. "Not ours."

Neenah stumbled outside, gulping huge breaths of cold air until her chest hurt. She went to Star's stall and pressed her forehead against the horse's silky neck searching in vain for any comfort.

I thought Sarah was beginning to like me.

Erastus found her there. "You were listening, weren't you?" he asked.

Neenah nodded miserably, wiping her nose with the back of her hand. "I'm sorry."

"Sarah says eavesdroppers rarely hear good of themselves."

"She's right."

He lifted her chin with the tip of his finger. "You should have listened longer," he said. "I told Sarah we couldn't let you go."

"Really?" Neenah asked. "You said no to Sarah?"

Erastus hemmed and hawed until he finally confessed. "I told her I couldn't send you to a school that I hadn't seen personally. And I'm much too busy to go to Boston right now."

As she stroked Star's neck, Neenah wished Erastus had been braver instead of making an excuse.

That's disappointing.

"So I just wait here?" Neenah asked. The harshness in

her voice made Star jerk her head and toss her mane.

"Whoa, girl," Erastus soothed the mare. "You don't need to worry about anything for a few months. George won't be back before spring."

"Spring?" Neenah repeated.

So much for following me in a few weeks.

"What did Sarah say?" she asked, her fingers teasing out a knot in Star's mane as she waited for the answer. She felt helpless.

"She thinks you should start school on Monday." He waited for her reaction "Neenah, she thinks you're ready for school. That's good news."

"But I'm not ready," Neenah protested. "I've only met one girl my own age, and we quarreled." Neenah thought back to when Mama pulled her out of school for fighting. Mama had never forgiven her. Nor would Sarah if Neenah brought such shame to the family.

Always an optimist, Erastus asked, "What are the odds of that happening again?"

Neenah had already lost Mama and Number One Boy. She did not want to lose Erastus and Jin Mao and Star.

I didn't have a choice when Mama sent me away. Or when George left me on the ship. But I can choose now.

"I will be perfect," she promised. "Sarah will be very pleased."

chapter *Thirty-Two*

"Now, Neenah, don't forget your manners. Say 'Yes, sir' or 'No, sir' to your teacher." Sarah added, "And don't mention China!"

"Sarah, everyone knows where Neenah's from," Erastus said patiently. He'd been sitting in the wagon in the cold for ten minutes while Sarah went over the rules. Again.

"But she doesn't have to flaunt it," Sarah said firmly.

Neenah huddled miserably next to Erastus on the wooden seat. It was freezing, and she couldn't stop shivering. Neenah knew what Sarah wanted; she just wasn't sure if she could do it. *What if the past repeated itself?*

"We're leaving now," Erastus said, shaking the reins.

"Good luck, Neenah," Sarah said. The blessing sounded more like a warning.

Erastus turned the wagon left onto the road, away from the hill leading to Baldwinsville.

"Isn't the school in town?" Neenah asked her grandfather in a raspy voice. She had awakened with a sore throat as if even her body knew that today was a test.

"There is a town school," he answered, "but it would be too far for all the farming kids to walk every morning. Once you know the way, you'll walk, too."

He turned onto a road that looked exactly like the first one, flat and bordered by fields. *The whole landscape is a maze of huge dirt squares,* she thought.

Her stiff new pantalettes rustled as she shifted in her seat, trying to get comfortable. Mrs. van der Smith and Sarah had been pleased with the fit of Neenah's new wardrobe, but Neenah found that the clothes constricted in all the wrong places. Even her lace-up boots felt as though they were crushing the tops of her feet. *Why did American girls do this to themselves?*

"You should feel lucky you are too young to wear a corset," Sarah had said. "Then you would know what suffering is."

Mrs. Grand had told her that a tight corset could rearrange a woman's internal organs. Neenah thought American women were crazy to put themselves in such torture devices. What would Mama say? Then she realized that foot-binding, a hundred times more painful, broke a foot many times over until it became a lotus blossom. Mama would laugh at the mild discomfort of a corset. It was hard for Neenah to remember now that she used to envy Mama's feet.

Women everywhere are just crazy.

Wriggling her back so the wool coat would not rub against her neck, she jostled Erastus's arm.

"Neenah, sit still," he said easily.

"These clothes are so . . ." Her mind went through her English vocabulary: *ugly, prickly, scratchy*. "Awful," she finished. Neenah felt through the layers of cloth for Mama's necklace—the only thing she was wearing that was her own.

Erastus chuckled. "Sarah spent a lot of money to show up that Rushbridger woman. No one will dare say that you are wearing the wrong clothes."

"Do you think I look American?" Neenah asked. She knew the clothes were right—Sarah wouldn't make a mistake—but Neenah felt like she was in a costume. Like the foreign devils at the Shanghai Club who wore Chinese robes for masquerade parties, she was pretending to be American.

"You look fine." His callused hand patted hers. "Be yourself, and the other children will like you."

"Will Letty be there?" Neenah asked.

"Sure to be. Her mother lives out here on her family's farm."

"Letty doesn't like me."

"Letty van der Smith is a foolish girl," he exclaimed. "She takes after her father."

He patted her knee. "These boys and girls have never

283

met anyone like you. Tell them about your life in China. It's really interesting."

"Being Chinese makes me stand out," Neenah said with a groan. "I'm tired of always being . . . different."

"Sometimes different is good," he offered.

"Sarah wants me to be like the others."

"I suppose she does." They were both silent, sure in their knowledge that Sarah was the boss. Erastus patted her knee. "Then do exactly as Sarah told you," he said.

She buried her face in her hands. She didn't want to be sent away because she hadn't tried hard enough. "I'll try," she mumbled.

"We're here."

She peeked through her fingers to see a modest, one-story clapboard building. A dozen kids were playing outside. There were more boys than girls, ranging in age from young children to a boy who looked a few years older than Neenah.

"Are we late?" Neenah asked. "I don't want to be late on my first day."

"The teacher hasn't called them in yet," he reassured her. The children all stopped their games to look at her. High up on the wagon's seat, Neenah felt as exposed as a bird on a bare branch.

"This is for your nooning," Erastus said, reaching beneath his feet to pull out a tin pail. "Sarah put in some of her fresh bread and that apple butter. She'll pick you up at the end of the day."

"Why not you?" she asked.

"Don't you remember? I'm going to Syracuse for a few days for business."

She had forgotten. So it would be just Sarah and Neenah alone.

Lovely.

Neenah spied Letty by the corner of the building, whispering with another girl. Their eyes met Neenah's and both girls started to whisper behind their hands. Neenah leaned closer to Erastus. "They're making fun of me."

"Neenah, you've traveled around the world, surely you can face two silly girls? They don't have to be your best friends; you just have to get along."

Maybe I don't always have to fight. If I've learned any-thing from Sarah, it's that I can think one way and act another.

"Go on," he said, shooing her away like a fly.

After he drove off, Neenah stood alone in the yard. She decided to face her fears head on and talk to the only person she knew. As she approached, Letty turned her back deliberately. Gritting her teeth, Neenah tapped her on the shoulder.

"Hello, Letty."

Letty turned and pretended to be startled. "Oh, Neenah, what a surprise."

"You watched me drive up," Neenah said. "I saw you."

Letty's shrug made her yellow curls bounce.

"This is the girl I told you about from China," she said to her friend, a tiny girl with a face like a ferret and brown eyes and hair to match. "They don't have very good manners there."

Determined to prove her wrong, Neenah held out her hand. "Hello, I'm Neenah Hamill," she said. "What is your name?"

Glancing nervously at Letty, the other girl held out a delicate hand "I . . . I'm Abigail," she said.

Abigail was Neenah's least favorite doll, named for a foreign devil she didn't like. What were the chances that this Abigail would be any kinder than the one in China? Neenah pasted on a smile and used the words Mrs. Grand and Sarah had taught her. "It is nice to meet you," she lied.

"It's nice to meet you." With a high-pitched giggle, Abigail added, "I've heard all about you."

Neenah shot a glance at Letty who looked smug. Almost as if she knew that Neenah was under strict orders to behave like a young lady. "Abigail, I hope we can be friends," Neenah said.

Even if Letty has poisoned you against me.

Before Abigail could answer, a young man came out of the school ringing a handbell. The children quickly fell into two lines, one for the boys and the other for the girls. The younger girls bobbed a quick curtsy to the teacher.

Neenah wished that Letty was in front of her so she could see how the older girls did it. When it was her turn, she hesitated.

"Mind your manners, Neenah." Letty jabbed her in the back. "Curtsy!"

The Obediences called for a teacher to be treated with the deference of a father. Neenah wanted to be very respectful so she sank almost to the floor. She heard tittering behind her. Too deep.

Letty did that on purpose.

"Get up!" the teacher said pulling at her arm. "You must be Neenah Hamill."

Rising so quickly she felt dizzy, she said, "Yes, sir."

"Your grandmother insisted that you were ready for an American school," he said, eyeing her doubtfully.

"I am, sir," she said.

"We'll see."

Just inside the door was a cloakroom for coats and lunch pails. The rest of the students swarmed around her, jostling and shoving. For a moment Neenah felt as though she couldn't stay on her feet. Then, suddenly, she was by herself. She hurriedly put her coat and pail on an empty hook and scurried after Letty and Abigail.

All the children were in the same large room; boys sat on the right and girls on the left. Letty and Abigail took their seats in the second row of desks. The only other girls were younger, and they sat in the front. Each desk and chair was one wooden piece; the back of the chairs in the front row provided a writing surface for the second row. The room was bone cold, like Erastus's apple cellar. The potbelly stove in the corner wasn't lit.

"Why isn't there a fire?" she asked Letty, shivering.

"When the water barrel freezes, we'll have the stove on, not before," Letty whispered as if everyone knew that. The goose bumps on Letty's skin told Neenah that the other girl was cold too; she just didn't want to admit it.

The teacher stood in the front of the room watching her. "That's yours," he said, pointing to the desk next to Letty. "Your grandmother bought your slate and chalk." Next to the wooden framed slate and chalk were a notebook, a bottle of ink, and a quill pen.

She sat down and discovered the desk was screwed into the floor. It reminded Neenah of the furniture on the *Dixey.*

"Good morning, class," the teacher intoned.

In unison, the class chanted, "Good morning, Mr. Chapman."

chapter *Thirty-Three*

Mr. Chapman read out a list of students. "Ambler, Samuel."

A boy answered, "Present."

It took Neenah a moment to realize he was reading the names in the Chinese way, surname first. When he got to "Hamill, Neenah," there was a low hiss of whispers among the other children.

"Present." Neenah stared straight ahead, chin high. Naturally they were curious, she told herself. She would be, too.

"Van der Smith, Leticia" Letty practically bounded out of her chair as she put her hand up.

"Van der Smith, William" The boy who answered was several years younger than Letty. He had the same reddish blond hair and pale skin.

Next was the Lord's Prayer. "Our father, who art in heaven, hallowed be thy name," Neenah chanted the words with the rest, grateful that the Mission School had started its school day in the same way.

"Neenah, every day we study a maxim," Mr. Chapman

said. "I will write it on the board and you will recite it."
With a new piece of chalk, he wrote on the blackboard:

Be kind and gentle to those who are old,
For kindness is dearer and better than gold.

At first, he misspelled "gentle" and had to erase it with
a clump of sheep's wool before starting again.

Neenah stared at the board with a mixture of disap-
pointment and relief. "Maxim" was just a fancy word for
a proverb. If this was American school, she would be able
to do the work easily.

Mr. Chapman pointed to an older boy in the back
row. "Mr. Ferguson, please stand and recite." The oldest boy stood up and mumbled his way through the
recitation.

"Watch your elocution," Mr. Chapman said. "It does
you no good to say something if people can't understand
you." He repeated the exercise with each student, going
from oldest to youngest.

When it was Neenah's turn, she was shy and spoke too
quietly to be heard.

"Miss Hamill, speak up," Mr. Chapman said, drawing
his brows into a triangle above his eyes. "I can't hear you."

She cleared her throat and tried again.

"That wasn't bad," he said. "Can you really read the
words or are you parroting the others?"

He's just asking for information. He doesn't mean to shame me.

"I can read English . . . sir," she answered respectfully.

"Hmm," he said. "We'll see."

Letty read the words loudly and with heart. Mr. Chapman beamed at her. On the other hand, Billy was sullen and read the words in a monotone as though there was no meaning to them at all.

Once everyone had finished, Mr. Chapman said, "Take your slate and copy out the maxim. Your neatest penmanship, please."

The chalk felt awkward in Neenah's hand. Pressing too hard against the slate, the chalk snapped in half. She heard a snicker and looked up to see Letty smirking. What a crude way to write, Neenah thought, longing for the easy swoosh of an ink-dipped brush on smooth paper.

Don't think of China. You're American now.

Wiping the slate clean with her sleeve, Neenah started again. Just as she got used to the chalk, she realized her letters were too big for all the words to fit on the slate. Once Mr. Chapman finished helping the youngest students in the front row, he came to her. He frowned when he examined her slate.

"Miss Hamill," he said. "I was told you knew English." His aggrieved tone said that he had been misinformed.

"I do, sir," Neenah said.

"You just aren't at the same level as the other girls

your age." Looking down his long nose, he said, "You'll have to move to the front row."

I'm not a baby!

"Sir, I never learned how to write in English. Chinese calligraphy is much different and . . ."

"I am not interested in what you did in China." He cut her off. "You are in an American school now. Move your things."

Neenah felt the stares of the other students. She carefully did not look at Letty and Abigail as she shifted her seat.

When he handed out the reading books, Neenah was assigned the second level McGuffey Reader. Glancing behind her, she saw that Abigail and Letty were reading at the fifth level.

"Mr. Chapman, I can read very well," she said. It felt odd to brag about herself, but she couldn't let Letty think she was superior to Neenah in any way.

"Don't interrupt the class," he said, looming over her. "Learning cannot take place without discipline. If you are disruptive again, you will be punished." She followed his gaze to a rod hanging on the wall.

Behind her, Letty whispered, "Neenah, just be quiet." She sounded sincere, but Neenah didn't trust her.

Mathematics was better. China had its own characters for numbers, but since there was so much foreign business in Shanghai, Neenah had learned the Western way, too. The recitation of the multiplication tables was easy. She was surprised—and secretly pleased—to hear Letty get so many wrong.

Finally, it was time for a meal and recess. The boys were out the door first. Before the girls were excused, Mr. Chapman called her up. "You have a lot of work to do to catch up to even the youngest children in writing. I want you to practice lesson one tonight." He showed her the passage in her reader. "Copy the exercise five times in your notebook."

"Yes, Mr. Chapman," she said.

The boys were roughhousing outside the classroom. "What are they up to now?" Mr. Chapman frowned irritably. "Miss Hamill, you may go."

As she entered the cloakroom, Billy van der Smith and one of the other boys were just leaving, smothering giggles as they went. Lunch pail in hand, she went outside. She looked for someone to eat with. Letty and Abigail were walking together arm in arm, deliberately excluding Neenah. With a sigh, she sat by herself on a stone not too far from the door. Her stomach felt empty, and she was ready for her apple butter. She opened her pail eagerly.

"Ai yi yi!" She screamed, shoving the pail away from her. Someone had replaced Sarah's fresh baked bread with a mouse. A loud guffaw made her look up to see Billy doubled over with laughter. She took a closer look and discovered the mouse was not real. It was a knitted toy—like she might make for Jin Mao. She tossed it away.

She slowly got to her feet and confronted Billy. "Was this your doing?" she demanded.

"We wanted to make you feel welcome," Billy mocked. "Don't they eat rats in China?"

Not this again!

"No, we don't." Her hands clenched. "Say you're sorry!" she said in a low voice.

"Won't!" he cried. "Go back where you came from!" he shouted. "We don't want your kind here!"

The boys fanned out, surrounding her. From behind, one boy shoved her. She whirled around to confront him. Another boy poked her in the back. Her red-hot anger was laced through with cold fear. They wouldn't dare hurt her . . . would they?

The boys began chanting.

> *Chink, Chink Chinaman*
> *Eats dead rats. Eats them up.*
> *Like Gingersnaps.*

Billy wanted to shout his song in her ear. He made the mistake of getting too close, and she grabbed him by his shirtfront.

294

"Stop saying that," she shouted, shaking him as hard as she could.

"Lemme go!" He swung his fist at her, hitting her shoulder.

"Ow!" Putting all her weight behind her closed fist, Neenah struck him back hard on the nose. He stumbled and fell to the ground. His nose gushed blood, splotches of red staining his white shirt. Letty ran up to kneel at his side.

"Stay away from him, Neenah Hamill!" Letty tried to staunch the blood with a handkerchief.

"Leave me alone, Letty!" he said, pushing her away.

Mr. Chapman hurried over. "What's going on here?"

"She started it!" Billy honked, his hand holding his swelling nose.

"No, he did!" Turning to Letty, Neenah cried, "Letty, you saw the whole thing. Tell him who started it!"

Letty looked at her brother, then Neenah, then at the ground. "I didn't see anything, sir," she mumbled.

Neenah wondered why she had thought, even for a moment, that Letty would do the decent thing.

Mr. Chapman hauled Billy to his feet. "We had better get you cleaned up. I wouldn't be surprised if that nose is broken." As he led Billy away, he looked over his shoulder, "Miss Hamill, I will deal with you presently. I don't approve of lying or fighting."

Neenah looked around at all the other children. None of them were on her side. Without witnesses, Sarah would believe the worst. She'd never forgive Neenah.

I've lost everything because I couldn't control my temper.

Fighting back tears, she ran out of the yard.

"Neenah! You can't just leave!" Letty called. "Do you even know where you are going?"

chapter *Thirty-Four*

Letty's voice trailed after her, but Neenah didn't stop. She had to get away; she wouldn't let any of them see her cry. It was so unfair.

Why did they hate China so much? Billy and Letty acted like the Chinese had hurt them personally, and they blamed Neenah for it. The things they said, that song he sang, were meant to make her feel ashamed of where she came from.

I won't do it. China is a part of me, and they are just stupid.

Mrs. Grand had tried to warn her that day on the *Dixey* when Neenah saw "Chinese go home!" in the newspaper. She had said that times were hard in America and people blamed the Chinese for taking their jobs. But what did that have to do with her? No matter how hard she tried to fit in, people in America couldn't seem to forget where she came from.

But however satisfying it had been to smash Billy's nose, it wasn't worth the consequences. Sarah was going to send her away.

She trudged on and on, wishing she had paid closer attention when Erastus had driven her to school. Surely if she just turned right at the next road, then right again, she would get back to the farm. But the fields never seemed to end. She glanced back. The schoolhouse was out of sight. But she wasn't home. It seemed like she was always between places, in the empty spaces where no one wanted to be.

Eventually, the road started sloping downhill. With a sinking heart, she realized she was heading toward town and not to Hillside Farm. Was there another way back? Because retracing her steps meant facing Mr. Chapman and the others.

I can't.

Number One Boy's great journey might begin with a single step, but what if your new shoes blistered your feet? Her toes, despite her thick stockings, were rubbed raw. Neenah sat on a rock and loosened the laces. Mama would faint if she saw how big her feet looked in these patent leather boots.

On the other hand, if she had lotus blossoms like Mama, Neenah couldn't have stormed away from school. She had always thought her problems began with Mama's decision not to bind her feet. That more than anything else had marked her as an outsider, not Chinese enough. Today, with normal feet and the right clothes, she was still a stranger. In fact, she was too Chinese and not American enough.

"A person attempting to travel two roads at once, will get nowhere." Number One Boy had said to her once. Why did his proverbs always make her feel worse?

She saw a figure in the distance. Finally—someone to ask for directions. She broke into a run, gasping from the stabbing pain in her feet. But it turned out to be a man of straw dressed in old clothes, a pair of crows perched on his shoulders. Half a dozen more swooped above the field searching for food. They reminded her of the seagulls fighting for eels along the Huang Po River. The gulls hadn't cared about Neenah and neither did the crows.

If only she had someone to talk to—someone she could trust. But Number One Boy was far away and Erastus was out of town.

As she walked, it began to drizzle. Soon her hair was soaked through with freezing rain. Shivers racked her body. Why wasn't anyone on this road? At last, she glimpsed the glint of the river at the base of the hill and the white gravestones of the cemetery. Maybe she hadn't been lost at all. Her ancestors must have brought her here to offer their guidance.

Ignoring her blisters, she hurried to the graveyard. There were dozens of stones and even more granite markers embedded in the ground. She looked for the red tree she'd marked in her memory a few weeks earlier, but the trees had all lost their leaves. She spied a large tree at the center of the cemetery. Purple flowers grew at its base. Too stubborn to give into winter, the flower's petals were intact and felt papery to the touch. She picked a few, tucking them in her pocket.

Purple is for immortality, perfect for a cemetery.

Searching every stone near the tree, at last she found Eugenie Hamill, Neenah's great-grandmother. Finally, an ancestor she could call her own.

Eugenie Hamill
b. 1799 d. 1849
An amiable Mother and a loving wife,
Who of the small-pox departed this life.

In front of the gravestone was a tangle of overgrown weeds and grass—now dry and brittle with winter. "Shame on you, Erastus, for neglecting your mother's grave," she murmured as she pulled the dead plants away. Once the grave was tidy, she knelt in front of the stone.

"Good afternoon, Great-Grandmother. My name is Neenah and your grandson George is my father. My mother is Foo-Tai Sun from Suchow. That is a city in China." After telling Eugenie about her life, she ended, "My Chinese ancestors will tell you I was a misfit in China. And as you can see, I'm a failure here, too. Sarah will send me away when she finds out what happened today. I really want to stay. I'm desperate. Please help me."

The sun was low in the sky, and it was getting colder. The damp breeze off the river made her head throb. She hoped Eugenie would hurry up and give her a sign.

"Neenah Hamill!" A voice echoed across the cemetery.

Neenah's eyes widened. She hadn't actually expected an answer.

Then she realized it was a man calling to her from the road. She scrambled to her feet and saw Joe Arthur, the driver from the station. He waved from his wagon. "Miss, your grandmother is frantic with worry. The whole town is looking for you."

Neenah glanced up and down the empty road. *How hard could they be looking*, she wondered, *since she'd seen no one for hours.*

"Let's get you home," Joe called.

She scrambled to her feet and started toward him. Then she remembered her flowers and ran back. Placing the purple blossoms on Eugenie's grave, she whispered, "I suppose a ride home is helpful." Then she added, "But I hoped for more."

As she climbed into the wagon, her head swam. Joe grabbed her arm to save her from falling.

"Are you all right?" he asked, as kind today as he had been that first night.

She nodded, hugging herself to keep warm. She had

missed her lunch and walked for miles—no wonder she felt light-headed. "Do you still have that blanket?" she asked through chattering teeth.

"Of course," he said, wrapping the blanket around her shoulders. "We'll have you home as quick as lightning."

"Lightning?" Neenah groaned, peering at the sky. What else could go wrong today?

"It's an expression," Joe said. "Sit back. I'll get you there soon."

"Thank you," she mumbled.

They rode up the hill in silence. Sarah spied them from the window and came running outside, clutching her shawl to her chest.

"Is she hurt?" she demanded.

"Mrs. Hamill, she's fine. Just a little cold. And hungry, I think," Joe said. "Why don't you get her inside? I'll call off the search in town."

"Joe, we're very grateful," Sarah said. "I'm sorry for the inconvenience."

Neenah climbed down, a little unsteady on her feet.

"Where have you been, you inconsiderate child?" Sarah demanded, grabbing Neenah's sleeve and dragging her into the house.

For such a little woman, Sarah is very strong.

"Take off that wet coat," Sarah ordered. "I went to fetch you from school, but you were gone. Mr. Chapman said you were in a fight and you ran away." She took Neenah's coat and hung it up. "I don't know which was worse."

Neenah wished Sarah would lower her voice. "I . . . couldn't stay there," she mumbled.

"Mr. Chapman was very concerned about you," Sarah said loudly.

"I doubt that." If only she could think clearly, but she felt dizzy and ready to throw up.

"Don't you dare mock your teacher," Sarah snapped. "You've humiliated me in front of the whole town. What were you thinking?"

Neenah struggled to remember the order of events. "Mr. Chapman wouldn't listen to me when I told him I could read perfectly well."

"No one likes a braggart," Sarah said.

"Then Letty's brother put a toy mouse in my lunch."

"A prank?" Sarah's eyebrows lifted. "You put everyone to all this trouble because of a harmless prank?"

"He sang a horrible song about Chinamen. And told me to go back to China." Before Sarah could make that unimportant, too, Neenah went on. "I told him to stop. I grabbed his shirt. And he hit me."

"That doesn't give you the right to hit him back," Sarah scolded.

"He hit me first," Neenah said. "I didn't want to fight." Did Sarah expect Neenah to swallow every slur and attack as though they meant nothing?

"Young ladies do not brawl in public." She glared until

303

she was sure she had Neenah's attention. "Ever."

"I didn't want to be insulted anymore," Neenah said slowly, realizing how true it was.

"And then, on top of everything else," Sarah went on as if she hadn't heard anything Neenah had said, "you ran away like a criminal."

Sarah led the way to the kitchen. For once, Neenah welcomed the warmth, imagining all the water in her clothes and hair boiling away into steam. Pointing to the chair, Sarah ordered her to sit down. "We have to talk."

Every part of Neenah hurt and she wanted to lie down so badly, but she did as Sarah told.

"Mr. Chapman said you can go back to school, if . . ."

Neenah crossed her arms and shook her head violently even though it was painful. "I don't want to go back."

"That's not up to you," Sarah said. "You can return if you apologize to the class."

"The whole class?" Neenah repeated. *Why should she apologize to them? None of them had done the right thing when Billy started his tricks.* "I won't do it. They were awful!"

"I don't care," Sarah's voice was icy. "You promised me you would behave. Is it so hard for you to obey me?"

Obedience. Neenah hated that word. She'd tried so hard to be obedient for Mama, for Sarah, even for Mr. Chapman. It got her nowhere. "China is my home. I won't let them insult it," she said, gritting her teeth. "No matter what you say, I won't apologize for defending myself."

Eyes narrowed, Sarah threw down her ultimate threat. "Then you'll just have to go to boarding school."

She said it. It's almost a relief.

"Fine," Neenah said loudly. "Send me away! You don't want me here. No one wants me anywhere." She pushed her chair away from the table and stood up. "It won't matter where you send me. I'll never belong."

She spun around to go to her room. But she kept spinning. The room went sideways, and she tumbled to the ground. She heard Sarah's panicked voice, "Neenah? Neenah!"

Then it all went black.

chapter *Thirty-Five*

"She's waking up."

The scent of cherry tobacco filled her nose. Neenah's eyes flew open to see strange blue eyes staring into hers. She screamed as she scrambled away from the unknown man. Her head collided with the sloped ceiling.

"It's all right, Neenah. This is Doctor Clemson," Sarah said kindly. Neenah had never heard that voice from her before.

"Welcome back, young lady." He smiled under his limp, white mustache.

She was in her own bed. Neenah glanced out the window. The morning sun was shining, but it had been late afternoon and gray when she got back from school.

Her whisper barely reached the edge of the bed. "What happened?"

"You fainted, and I sent for the doctor," Sarah said.

"You have a fever, and I wager your head aches?" Dr. Clemson said.

She nodded, then regretted moving her head. She fell onto the soft pillow, her skull ballooning with pain.

"I think you have the 'flu.' I have two other cases in town." The doctor's hand was cool as he laid it against Neenah's forehead. "How long have you been feeling ill?"

"A few days." Her faint voice sounded like a stranger's.

There was a little gasp from Sarah. "Why didn't you say anything?"

"I didn't want to be a burden," Neenah replied.

"Oh, child," Sarah said, looking guilt-ridden. "I wish you had told me."

Dr. Clemson patted Sarah's hand. "Mrs. Hamill, the flu can be serious, but Neenah seems pretty healthy. Keep her still and warm. Make sure she drinks tea and water."

Sarah nodded after each instruction, adding them to a list in her mind.

"Send for me if her condition changes, but she should be fine in a few days," Dr. Clemson said, as he put on his coat. His soothing manner reminded her of Master Li.

Sarah offered to show him out. "I'll be right back, Neenah," she promised.

After he left, Sarah returned with a teapot and a mug. "I've sent for Erastus. He'll be home tonight."

Neenah groaned. "All I ever do is make trouble for you both."

"Don't be ridiculous." Sarah's tart answer for once was not directed at Neenah as she poured the tea. "You're sick. You were sick when you went to school. Neenah, you should have told me."

"I'm sorry."

"Stop apologizing. I should have noticed. Now lie back and have some tea."

Expecting sweet black tea, Neenah was surprised by the grassy smell of green tea. Her eyes met Sarah's over the rim of the mug.

"I thought a taste from home might help you feel better," Sarah said. "And I've noticed you don't like your tea sweet." For once she looked unsure of herself. "Neenah, I tried to make you like sugar when you were used to something different. I'm sorry."

Neenah stared. What was Sarah really saying? Because Neenah was fairly sure she wasn't talking about sugared tea.

"It's all right," she whispered. "Sometimes different is good."

When Neenah woke up again, it was dark. A warm pressure on her feet told her that Jin Mao had found his way to her bed.

"How do you feel?" Sarah asked. She was knitting in the corner by the light of a single lamp.

Propping herself up on her elbows, Neenah realized the ache in her head had faded now. "I'm better. How long have you been there?"

"Not long," Sarah said, shrugging. Judging from her pale and exhausted face, she was lying. "Are you hungry?"

Supporting Neenah's back, Sarah fed her spoonful

after spoonful of hearty beef soup. When she was done, Neenah snuggled deeper under the blankets.

"Neenah, drink this," Sarah said, offering her a glass of water. "Do you need anything else?"

"Can I have my doll?"

Sarah looked surprised. "You have a doll?"

"In my trunk," Neenah said. She'd hidden the doll away ever since that first day when she had offered to become more American.

"Certainly." Holding the lantern up, Sarah lifted the trunk lid.

Too late, Neenah realized what else Sarah would see in there. The doll was nestled among Neenah's old Chinese clothes. Sarah drew in her breath. "I thought these went into the rag bag."

"I didn't want to lose everything from home," Neenah admitted. "But I put them away. I know you don't like to see anything Chinese."

In the greenish-yellow light of the lantern, Sarah's face looked as though she might be ill as well. "Is that why you hid this?" She gently placed the doll in Neenah's hand.

"I didn't want you to throw her out, too."

Sarah's hand went to her mouth. "I never meant to . . . your doll is safe," she said. "Does she have a name?"

"Sun."

"Isn't that your mother's name?"

"She looks like Mama," Neenah said sadly.

Sarah pulled her chair closer to Neenah and began to knit, a thoughtful expression on her face. Neenah turned on her side so she could watch the smooth motion of Sarah's hands—it was as soothing as . . . Mama making tea. Fatigue set into her bones and Neenah drifted between wakefulness and sleep.

"Thank you for taking care of me," Neenah whispered.

"Your mother isn't here so it's my duty to look after you," Sarah said, staring down at her wool.

"Number One Boy tended to me if I was sick, not Mama."

The clicking of Sarah's needles paused. "I'm sure your mother worried for you just the same."

Neenah was too tired to watch her tongue. "No. I was a burden to her."

Sarah put her knitting aside and leaned closer to Neenah. "A mother's love for her child is the strongest kind there is."

"Not my Mama. She sent me away and didn't even cry when I left." As if the word *cry* had unlocked her own grief, Neenah's eyes filled and brimmed over.

Sarah's swollen knuckles made it hard for her to grip, but she squeezed Neenah's hand tightly. "I don't believe your mother didn't care about you. Why else would she send you all the way to America?"

"Because she wanted to get rid of me."

"She sent you here to have a better life, even knowing she might not ever see you again. It was a huge sacrifice. If she didn't shed a tear, it was because she had to be strong enough to say goodbye."

Could that be true? Had it been too painful for her to say goodbye? It would mean so much if Mama had suffered as much as Neenah.

Neenah took back her hand and rolled over on her side, facing the wall. She needed to think, reconsider. She had been so bitterly angry with Mama, but maybe Neenah had been wrong. Mama didn't send her away because Neenah wasn't lovable—the opposite was true.

Did Mama give me up because *she loved me?*

She closed her eyes and thought of her favorite moments with Mama. Watching Mama put on her make-up. Sweeping the bad luck out of the house before the New Year. Laughing while she and Number One Boy bickered. Trying to picture Mama's face, she realized that the edges of her memory were becoming blurry. She pushed her fist to her mouth to muffle a sob.

Sarah was out of the chair instantly. "Is it your head?"

"I miss my Mama," Neenah hiccoughed. "And I don't even have a picture of her."

"Perhaps we can ask George to send one?" Sarah said.

"He won't do it. He doesn't like me."

Sarah *tsk*'ed. "Neenah, he's your father!"

"He was so angry with Mama on my account. He didn't want to take me to America—she made him do it. He's ashamed of me because I'm half-Chinese."

"Why would you think that?"

"I heard him say he hates everything about China." Neenah had never told anyone, not even Number One Boy, the whole story of when she had met her father on the dock. But her illness had weakened her usual defenses, and the truth poured out. As she talked, she could see Sarah's eyes glistening. "I can't help who I am, Sarah," she wailed.

"Sweet girl, of course you can't," Sarah agreed with a long sigh. Straightening the blanket and tucking it around Neenah's body, she said nothing for a few moments. "I've made the same mistake as your father. I judged you for being different. But you have every right to be proud of your culture. I was wrong to ask you to forsake it."

"I understand," Neenah said, her eyelids heavy. "You don't want a Chinese in your family."

"But I never meant to make you feel unwelcome . . . but now I see that is exactly what I have done." As if to herself, Sarah asked, "How can I fix this?" A voice shouting from downstairs interrupted her.

"Sarah! Neenah!"

Erastus's heavy steps pounded up the stairs. The door swung open, and he stormed in. "Neenah, I came back as soon as I got Sarah's note." Still wearing his winter coat, he knelt by her bed. "How are you?"

Wincing from his loud bellow, Neenah whispered, "Better."

"Shhh, Erastus. Stop your fussing," Sarah scolded. "Our granddaughter is doing just fine. It's a touch of the 'flu.'"

"*Our* granddaughter?" he asked, his eyebrows lifted hopefully.

"Well, of course," Sarah said as if it had never been in doubt. "You sit with her while I get your dinner on the table. Don't wear her out—she needs her sleep!" She came to Neenah and kissed her on the forehead. Speaking for Neenah's ears only, she said, "Tomorrow, if you feel up to it, we're going to open up George's room. I think we will both find it very illuminating."

After she had gone downstairs, Erastus pulled up a chair. He stroked her hand as she drifted off to sleep. It was the first time she had ever gone to sleep in this room without worrying about the morning.

chapter *Thirty-Six*

"Are you ready?" Sarah asked.

With Sarah's quilt draped over her shoulders, Neenah nodded.

"Remember this is just between us. Erastus doesn't need to know," Sarah said as she inserted the key in the lock.

"It will be our secret," Neenah promised. She had only shared secrets with two people before, Number One Boy and Erastus.

Now there are three.

She stepped inside her father's room. It was the mirror image of her own—the same windows, the same high bed tucked in under the sloped roof. Her entry kicked up motes of dust that danced in the air before settling back on the surfaces. By the door, sticks of incense lay on a small tray made of onyx. Neenah lit one with a match. Closing her eyes, she inhaled the smoke. In an instant, she was back in her mother's parlor.

It smells like home.

"I recognize that perfume," Sarah said, wrinkling her nose. "When George is home, the house reeks of it."

"It's sandalwood."

Mama's favorite.

Her slipper caught on the edge of a carpet. She glanced down, and her breath caught in her throat. She knew this rug. The design of green, blossoming trees and butterflies on a golden ground was heartbreakingly familiar. Without a word, she slipped off her embroidered slippers and let the soles of her feet remember the smooth silk.

A bemused smile on her face, Sarah watched. "I do like this rug," she said, lifting up the corner and examining the weave. "It's exquisite. It's made of knotted silk."

"Mama liked it, too," Neenah said.

Sarah looked startled. "She has the same rug?"

"Exactly the same," Neenah answered as she glanced around the room, hungry for more reminders of home. There was a green jade dragon on the bookcase. She ran her finger along its ridged back. "This is a very fine piece. My father must have spent a fortune to buy it."

"When he brought it home, I assumed it was some heathen whatnot."

"Dragons are very important in China, Sarah," Neenah said seriously. "They symbolize power and strength."

"Like eagles in America?"

"I think a dragon would always beat an eagle."

"Hopefully, we'll never have to find out," Sarah said with a smile.

Neenah barely paused to admire the deep-red, lacquered armoire, although it was clearly very old and valuable, because she had spied something far more meaningful. The blanket, not quite wide enough to cover the featherbed, was made of raw yellow silk.

"Don't tell me, your Mama has the blanket, too?" Sarah asked, rubbing the fabric between her thumb and forefinger.

"She made it." Neenah recognized Mama's distinctive stitching on the seam. Putting aside the quilt, she pulled the blanket around her body. Was it her imagination or did it smell of her mother's jasmine perfume?

"George has kept all of this for years." Sarah's gaze traveled around the room. "This is not the room of a man who hates China."

"No, it's not," Neenah said, sinking into a carved armchair at her father's desk. "I was wrong about that."

"We've both been mistaken," Sarah said quietly, "about many things." She blew dust off the clock on the nightstand and started to wind it. "I don't know why I bother to wind it. It will just run down again."

Of course, the clock was a duplicate of the one in her mother's parlor. Mama had said George gave it to her. Neenah half-smiled, remembering Number One Boy's pronouncement, "Unlucky." How did George happen to have a second unlucky clock? And two rugs? Did he buy both at the same time? Or did he purchase these things when he knew he was leaving? Did they remind him of good times or torture him with regret?

"Did you see this?" Sarah asked, pointing to a scroll tacked to the wall.

Refusing to abandon Mama's blanket, Neenah drew close and examined it carefully. In the center was a detailed drawing of a Chinese steamboat, a shoveling contraption attached to the back. It looked as though it was powered by a waterwheel.

"It's a contract for the dredging of the canal between Shanghai and Suchow," Neenah said.

"You can read that funny Chinese writing?" Sarah asked, impressed.

Neenah nodded. "I can write it, too—but Mama says my calligraphy is terrible."

"I only know one alphabet," Sarah said. "I'm sure your handwriting is fine. What does the contract say?"

"It's between the Mercantile Association of Shanghai and the Osgood Company of Troy, New York."

"That's George's company," Sarah said. Mischievously, she added, "It looks as though the Chinese needed an American dredge."

"But they put it on a Chinese boat," Neenah pointed out. The dredge was awkward and ugly, but it looked efficient. "It is Chinese *and* American."

317

"Like you," Sarah said.

"Like me," Neenah repeated. Her eyes swept the room finding instance after instance of Chinese and American things working together. Like the tight-fitting Western suit hanging in the Chinese armoire. Or the jade dragon guarding the American novels. But it didn't always work perfectly; Mama's blanket wasn't quite the right size for the American mattress. Neenah didn't always fit in well, either.

For the first time, Neenah realized not everything had to be either Chinese or American. Neenah's two halves offered more together than they did separately. It was a welcome revelation. "Sarah, do you think I can be both American and Chinese at the same time?"

"I think you can," Sarah said. "Someone who can bring both cultures together would be rather . . . formidable."

Formidable! Like Sarah. Like Mama. Like the Pirate Queen.

"Then that's what I shall be," Neenah decided.

She opened the top drawer of George's desk to find a leather folded frame, worn from handling. It fell open and Mama's face, mysterious as always, stared back at her. It was a formal photograph: Mama wore a heavy, silk-embroidered jacket, and her tiny lotus blossoms peeked out from beneath her wide pants. She was only lightly made-up which made her seem younger. More vulnerable.

This was the face Neenah wanted to remember. She let out a sigh of joy laced with longing.

"Is that your mother?" Sarah asked.

Neenah jumped; she had forgotten her grandmother was there. She nodded, not trusting her voice.

"You look like her."

Sarah couldn't have said anything kinder.

Sarah went on, "I think George must have loved her very much."

Neenah had to agree. Here, George had created a shrine to his past with Mama, just as surely as Number One Boy had a shrine to honor Buddha.

"He never said a word to us about her," Sarah sighed.

"She never spoke of him, either," Neenah said. "They both like to keep secrets, I think."

"I wonder why he left her?"

"Mama said he wanted to go home," Neenah said slowly. "I think she was too proud to ask him to stay."

"Why didn't she come here?" Sarah said. "We would have made her welcome."

Neenah's involuntary bark of laughter made Sarah blush.

"I hope I would have tried," Sarah said.

"Mama loved China too much to leave," Neenah said. She thought of telling Sarah about Mama's lotus blossoms, but she decided against it. Sarah wouldn't understand.

Now that Neenah had made her peace with her mother's decision to send her away, she didn't want Sarah to think badly of Mama for any reason.

"What's that?" Sarah asked. Tucked in behind Mama's picture was a second one. Neenah teased it out so she could see what it was.

"It's the Longhua Pagoda," Neenah said happily.

"Like your embroidery?"

Neenah nodded, staring at the frame. At the base of the pagoda, two small figures posed for the photographer: a man in Western clothes and a Chinese woman holding his arm for support. Although the faces were too small to see clearly, she imagined that they were smiling, very much in love.

It was all too much to take in at once. Neenah wilted in the chair, abruptly exhausted.

"Back to bed, young lady."

Neenah let Sarah lead her to her own room. "Can you leave my father's door unlocked?"

"Yes. And if George has a problem with that, he can tell me himself."

"Do you think he will come back?" Neenah asked. But for once, the answer didn't worry her. He could return. Or not return. Neenah's place in this house was safe.

"Eventually. But I doubt he will stay." Sarah hurried to add, "Not because of you. He just always wants to be somewhere else."

For her whole life, George had always been somewhere else. "I never knew him," Neenah said. "But I feel better knowing that he loved my mother. And for her sake, I think he also loved China."

"Seeing all of George's treasures through your eyes, I can see why you love China so much," Sarah said thoughtfully as she tucked Neenah into bed. "You nearly broke my heart when you said I was throwing away your Chinese memories. I never meant to do that." Sarah's voice caught. "I was only thinking of myself and what the Eva Rushbridgers in town would say. I never considered how you felt."

"It's fine, Sarah," Neenah said. "Now that I've seen that room, I won't ever forget where I came from."

"Do you want to go back to China?" Sarah asked, tensing as though she feared the answer.

Neenah drew the blanket up to her chin and considered. Did she want to go back? China was her whole past . . . but was it her future? "I don't know," she said at last. "I think I could like America."

Now that I have Sarah and Erastus and Jin Mao.

"Good. That's settled then."

"My father won't try to send me away, will he?"

"Over your grandfather's dead body," Sarah said. She laid her hand against Neenah's cheek. "And then he'll have to deal with me."

chapter *Thirty-Seven*

By Saturday, Neenah was almost completely recovered. Nevertheless, Sarah insisted she lie on the couch in the parlor in front of a crackling fire. She dozed, Sarah knitted, and Erastus read the paper. Neenah woke up to hear them talking about her. Keeping her eyes shut, Neenah hoped they would forget she was there and speak frankly.

Erastus said, "She has to go back to school eventually, Sarah."

"Not until she's apologized to her teacher," Sarah replied.

"He should be fired for losing our Neenah," Erastus said loudly.

"Shhh, you'll wake her," Sarah scolded. "Neenah did fight with a student and run away. He can't just overlook that behavior."

"That's the teacher's story," Erastus said. "What did she say?"

Sarah's needles clicked faster and faster.

"Sarah?"

"I didn't let her tell me," Sarah burst out. "I was scared and angry. Then she fainted a minute later."

Erastus must have been puffing harder on his pipe because the room began to smell of his cherry tobacco.

In a timid voice that was totally unlike her, Sarah asked, "What do you think I should do?"

"We should find out what really happened," Erastus said.

Outside, there was the telltale sound of a carriage on the gravel drive. Sarah went to the window. "It's Lucy van der Smith," she said. "What on earth is she doing here?" She bustled out of the room to beat her guest to the front door.

Neenah muffled a groan.

"I thought you might be awake," Erastus said, peering at her down the length of his pipe.

"I have to go upstairs," Neenah said, throwing off the blanket. "I can't face Mrs. van der Smith."

"Don't you dare move," he ordered. "Lucy van der Smith wouldn't say boo to a goose. Why are you afraid of her?"

"Her son is the boy I hit," Neenah confessed.

"That brat?" Erastus guffawed. "I hope you hit him hard."

"Hard enough." She gnawed on a torn thumbnail. "I'm in trouble, aren't I?"

"Were you defending yourself?" Erastus asked. She nodded. "That's good enough for me," he said. "But Sarah might have a different idea."

As if he had summoned her, Sarah poked her head in. "Oh good, Neenah, you're awake," she said. "There's someone here to see you."

Neenah swung her legs off the couch. Erastus, without a word, moved his chair closer to her, a giant protector. She noticed again how similar Erastus and Number One Boy were. They both would defend her against anyone . . . except Sarah and Mama.

Mrs. van der Smith pushed Billy ahead of her as they came into the parlor. He looked miserable, tears streaking his cheeks. His nose was swollen and bruised. She felt a little guilty about that.

"Mr. Hamill, Sarah, Neenah," Mrs. van der Smith said. "I'm sorry to stop by unannounced."

"That's quite all right," Sarah said politely.

"This morning Letty told me everything that happened on Monday. I'm so mortified. You know how much I value your friendship."

And Sarah's business.

"Billy would like to say something to Neenah," Mrs. van der Smith finished.

"I'm sorry, Neenah," he said in a nasally voice.

"Sorry for what?" his mother prompted.

"For putting a mouse in your lunch," he said, staring

at his scuffed boots. "And being mean. And hitting you."

As Erastus heard Billy's list of offences, his face got redder and redder. "Rotten little rascal," he muttered.

Sarah put out a hand. "Erastus, please. This is between the children."

Neenah looked at Erastus. She mouthed the words "What should I say?"

Still glowering, he shrugged as if to say it was up to her. *Just like Number One Boy*, she thought. They always had plenty of advice until the moment you really needed them to tell you what to do. Sarah gave Neenah a hard stare; her instructions were clear as glass.

"I accept your apology," Neenah said quickly.

"And?" Sarah asked, her voice lifting.

"I'm sorry for hitting you back," Neenah mumbled.

"Good." Sarah swept her hands against each other. "All's well that ends well."

"Thank you for being so understanding," Mrs. van der Smith said. "It's been so difficult at home with my husband out of work. He talks wildly sometimes and Billy misunderstands."

"It is all right, Lucy," Sarah said.

"We'd like to make it up to you, Neenah. You must be quite bored staying home for so long. If you like, Letty could come over tomorrow after church and keep you company."

Neenah did not like the idea at all. But then Sarah

narrowed her eyes. "That would be very nice, Mrs. van der Smith," she said meekly.

After they had left, Neenah said, "I don't want Letty to visit."

"The sooner you make your peace with her, the better," Sarah said.

"What did Mrs. van der Smith mean about her husband?" Neenah asked.

Sarah gave Erastus a quick nod.

"Lucy's husband is out of work," Erastus said. "He went to New Jersey for a good job at a steam laundry. But the factory owner replaced all the Americans with Chinese workers because they were cheaper. He had to come home and look for work here. He's been angry ever since."

"That's very sad," Neenah said. "Is that why Letty and Billy don't like China?"

"Van der Smith spouts a lot of nonsense all over town," Erastus said. "But it has nothing to do with you. He's just hurting."

"Financially, the family is struggling," Sarah said. "Lucy's store only brings in so much money."

"That's why you bought all my clothes from her," Neenah said, appreciating how generous Sarah had been. And how discreet.

"She is an excellent seamstress," Sarah said, not admitting anything.

• • •

"Dinner smells good," Erastus said coming into the kitchen. Sarah was putting the finishing touches to a lamb stew while Neenah removed biscuits from a baking pan. "When do we eat?"

"In a few minutes," Sarah said.

Erastus took his seat at the dinner table, and his foot knocked against a satchel. "What's this?" he asked.

From the stove, Sarah said over her shoulder, "Neenah's schoolbooks. Lucy brought them."

Still holding a hot biscuit, Neenah's hand froze. "I forgot. Mr. Chapman gave me some work to do at home." She realized the biscuit was burning her skin, and she dropped it on the table.

"How much work could there be?" Erastus asked. "Let's see what you have here." He lifted the bag onto the chair.

"No! It's fine. I can manage the . . ." She tried to grab the satchel away, but Erastus was surprisingly quick.

"What are you hiding, Neenah?" he asked as he pulled out the McGuffey Second Reader and opened it to Lesson One. "The cat. The mat. The cat sat on the mat." He slammed the book on the table. "This is for babies, not you! You can read my newspaper—I've seen you do it."

"Calm down, Erastus," Sarah said.

"I supported universal education," he said. "I don't mind paying the taxes. But I do insist that she learn something!"

Her face red, Neenah said, "I told Mr. Chapman that I could read, but he didn't believe me."

"You should have insisted," Erastus said.

"He said he'd punish me with a rod if I said anything more."

Erastus's fury filled the kitchen. "He said what?"

Sarah said hurriedly, "He has to keep order in the class."

"I'll set him straight," Erastus said.

"No, let me do it," Sarah demanded. "You've got the farm to tend to. I'll make sure he understands that Neenah is quite capable—she just needs a little help."

Neenah had always dreamed of having a family to defend her—but was that what she really wanted? Did the Pirate Queen send someone else to fight her battles?

"Grandfather, Sarah," she began.

Sarah looked up from ladling the stew into their bowls.

"Please don't talk to Mr. Chapman. I would rather prove to him that I can do the harder work." She pushed her bowl closer so Sarah could serve her. "As soon as I learn to write in English, I will catch up to Letty and Abigail."

Their silence went on so long that Neenah grew worried. She looked up to see Erastus grinning broadly.

Sarah turned back to the stove but not before Neenah saw the delight on her face.

"That's commendable," Erastus said. "I'm proud of you, Neenah."

"As soon as I've done the dishes, I'll start practicing," she vowed.

"I'll clean up tonight," Sarah offered. "You have work to do." She got up to get Erastus a second serving of lamb stew. As she passed Neenah, she squeezed her shoulder and whispered, "I'm proud of you, too."

No one, not even Number One Boy and certainly not Mama, ever said they were proud of me before.

chapter Thirty-Eight

Sarah looked up from her knitting when Neenah stepped into the parlor and twirled in a circle. Her skirt billowed around her.

"Very nice. And for once you aren't squirming like you have ants in your pantalettes," Sarah said, looking gratified.

Mama used to complain that she had crickets in her tunic. Maybe the one thing that was the same in both China and America was Neenah.

"I fixed the scratchy part." Neenah bragged, turning out the lace collar of her dress so Sarah could see. "I sewed in a silk lining, so it doesn't itch."

"That was clever," Sarah said. "And you don't notice it at all. In fact, the dress fits beautifully."

Neenah looked down. The skirt fell exactly below her knees. While it felt odd to have her legs exposed, it was nice that she didn't have to hide her feet.

Sarah glanced at the clock. "Letty will admire it, I'm sure. She should be here any moment."

Neenah returned to the argument she had already

lost the day before. "I don't see why I have to spend the afternoon with her. We don't like each other."

Sarah put her knitting aside. "This is a small town. You can't avoid each other."

"What will we do all afternoon?"

"Why don't you show her your little shrine?" Sarah glanced at the small table in the corner. With Sarah's permission, Neenah had made a small altar with items raided from her father's room: the onyx tray, incense, and the photograph of the pagoda with her parents in the foreground. Mama's dragon mahjong tile had a place of honor. At home, there would also be a statue of Buddha, but Neenah had not even suggested that. Sarah's tolerance had limits.

"Letty will make fun of it," she muttered.

"Maybe. Maybe not." Sarah put aside her knitting and patted the cushion next to her. "Come here, Neenah. I want to talk to you."

Neenah took a seat wondering if she was in trouble.

"I know there's no love lost between you and Letty," Sarah began. "But now that you know about her family situation, I hope you might be a little more patient. It's not easy for Letty."

"Letty was rude! She didn't tell the teacher the truth . . ."

"You took offense very easily." Sarah held up her hand to quiet Neenah's objection. "There's an expression . . ."

"Another proverb?" Neenah groaned.

"Love your enemies because they tell you your flaws."

Number One Boy said things like this all the time. *These maxims were useless in both America and China.*

The crunch of gravel alerted Sarah to their guest's arrival. "Just remember," she said. "If we insisted on perfection, none of us would have any friends. Give Letty another chance."

Only if she apologizes first.

. . .

Neenah joined Sarah on the porch. Letty, looking as obstinate as Neenah felt, climbed down from a fancy, black buggy. To her surprise, Neenah saw it was Mrs. Rushbridger rather than Letty's mother holding the reins.

"Hello, Eva, Letty," Sarah said.

"The van der Smith's wagon lost a wheel," Mrs. Rushbridger said. "I thought it would be charitable of me to give Letty a ride."

"I'm sure Letty's mother is very appreciative," Sarah said, her tone not matching the compliment.

Letty hopped down, her face sullen.

Mrs. Rushbridger watched Letty, clearly expecting her to say something.

Finally Sarah intervened. "Letty, you owe a thank-you to Mrs. Rushbridger."

"Thank you," Letty said, spots of red appearing high on her cheeks.

In spite of herself, Neenah felt a tiny bit sorry for Letty. Neenah knew a busybody when she saw one; it was clear Mrs. Rushbridger gave Letty a ride to collect fodder for gossip.

Mrs. Rushbridger glared at Letty then turned and smiled sweetly at Neenah's grandmother. "Sarah, you were missed at church today." The slight malice in her voice battled with her fake smile. "It doesn't look good if the new president of the Ladies' Benevolent Society misses the Sunday service."

"Neenah is much better, but I didn't want to leave her alone just yet," Sarah said placidly, not taking the bait. "The whole family will be there next week."

"All of you?" Mrs. Rushbridger asked, eyes widening as she noticed Neenah's new dress and properly pinned up hair.

"Even me?" Neenah whispered.

"All of us," Sarah said firmly.

"Aren't you worried about what the Ladies' Benevolent Society will think?" Mrs. Rushbridger said with raised eyebrows.

"I don't care what they think," Sarah said. "Neenah is family."

In front of the others, Neenah couldn't tell Sarah how

much that meant to her. Instead, she reached for Sarah's hand. Sarah squeezed back, but not too hard due to her rheumatism.

"How broadminded of you, Sarah," Mrs. Rushbridger said. "Not everyone would welcome a Chinese to her bosom."

"Recently, I've discovered I had a lot of mistaken ideas about China. Luckily, Neenah was here to teach me the truth. If by chance you are ever interested in learning something, Neenah would be happy to teach you, too." Letty gasped and Neenah bit her lip to keep from grinning. "Thank you for dropping by, Eva, I hope you have a nice afternoon. Goodbye."

Sarah motioned to Neenah and Letty to go inside.

As she and Neenah walked down the hallway, Letty whispered, "Golly! No one talks to Mrs. Rushbridger like that!"

"Sarah does," Neenah said with satisfaction.

Once in the kitchen, Sarah said, "I thought you two might like to make some hermit cookies." She handed Neenah a card with a recipe written in her cursive handwriting. "All the ingredients are out for you. I'll come back to check on you in a bit."

The two girls stared at each other, dismayed.

"Sarah, we can't do this alone . . ." Neenah began.

"I'm a terrible baker," Letty said at the same time.

"Nonsense. Hermit cookies are very easy to make," Sarah said. "But you will have to work together."

After she was gone, the kitchen was silent.

"I don't want to bake with you," Letty said, hands on her hips. "You broke Billy's nose!"

"I don't want to bake with you either," Neenah shot back. "And Billy deserved it and you know it." Neenah felt her fists clench. Sarah would never forgive her if she punched Letty, too. To give her hands something better to do, she grabbed the flour tin and tried to open the lid.

"He did not deserve it!"

"Did too!" The lid was stubborn . . . as stubborn as Letty.

Letty stared at her. "You're not sorry at all!"

"Why should I be? He was awful to me, and I bet you and Abigail were in on it." Neenah finally worked the lid off, and it went flying across the table. Letty could have caught it, but she let it slide by and clatter to the ground. "Now look what you did!"

"You always want to blame me for your mistakes!" Letty said angrily. "If my mother could hear you, she'd never have made me come today."

"I don't understand why she did."

Letty folded her arms. "It's only because Mrs. Hamill is such a good customer."

"Then I will tell Sarah we should shop elsewhere!"

Even as she spoke the words, Neenah remembered what Sarah had told her about the van der Smith's money troubles. She knew she had gone too far.

"Please don't do that." Letty retrieved the flour lid and slid it across the table to Neenah as though she was trying to make amends. "Mama is the best seamstress in Baldwinsville."

Neenah's hand went to the pocket hidden in the folds of her skirt. Mrs. van der Smith had kept her promise and put pockets in every dress. She opened her mouth to say so when Letty just had to get in another dig.

"And you need her if you ever want to look like the rest of us. Do you know the story of the Ugly Duckling?"

Of course, Letty had to squeeze in an insult, too.

Neenah gave herself five breaths to calm down before she answered Letty.

"So?" Letty asked when Neenah didn't immediately speak. "Promise me you won't say anything?"

"Why shouldn't I?" Neenah demanded, abandoning her good intentions. "You've been nothing but rude to me."

Eyes on the floor, Letty muttered, "Pa hasn't worked in months. What Mama earns in the dress shop is the only money we have."

Neenah knew what it had cost Letty to say that. She felt terrible. "I never meant . . . I won't say anything to Sarah."

"Good."

Letty paced around the kitchen speaking her thoughts out loud. "Why can't things go back to the way they were? Before the Chinese came and took away Papa's job, everything was fine. I wish the Chinese would just go home."

She means me, too.

This final insult was too much for Neenah to take without answering somehow. She reached into the canister and threw a handful of flour at Letty.

Whirling around, Letty shrieked, "My dress!" Her pert nose covered with powder, she tried to grab the flour. The canister tumbled over, sending a huge cloud about the kitchen. Letty scooped up some of the spilled flour and tossed it at Neenah's face. Soon the kitchen was covered with white powder, like a fresh snowfall on Erastus's fields.

Letty and Neenah faced each other across the table. The flour tin was empty. Neenah looked around Sarah's normally immaculate kitchen and groaned. "Sarah is going to be so angry!"

"She shouldn't have left us alone with the flour," Letty said. She grinned at Neenah's outraged expression. "You look ridiculous," she said.

"Not half as silly as you," Neenah snapped, trying to brush the flour off her new dress. But then she took a deep breath. It was rather funny. They both started to giggle, laughing until their sides ached.

Letty is laughing with me instead of at me.

"Where's a broom?" Letty asked. "I'll sweep up."

"I started it, I will do it," Neenah said.

"Then I should clean the table," Letty offered.

Once the kitchen had been restored, Neenah asked, "I didn't really break Billy's nose, did I?"

"Maybe it wasn't completely broken," Letty admitted. "But definitely bruised."

"I'm glad it's not broken," Neenah said honestly. "But Letty, all I did was fight back. It was Billy and a lot of his friends against me." After a moment, she confessed the truth even though Letty might use it against her. "I was scared."

"I didn't know that," Letty said. "Abigail and I only saw the end of the fight. We'd gone behind the school." Looking shamefaced, she confessed, "We were avoiding you."

As Neenah swept up the last of the flour and dumped it in the bucket for the chicken's dinner, she reconsidered the scene with Billy. "You really didn't see how it started?"

Letty shook her head. "If I had, I hope I would have told Mr. Chapman the truth. But then again, I might have stayed quiet. Billy is my brother." She held out a flour-stained hand. "I'm sorry it happened."

I can't ask for more than that.

"Thank you," Neenah said. "I accept your apology."

She felt such relief wiping the slate clean. Carrying grudges was exhausting; Neenah was better off without them.

"We had better make the cookies or Sarah will have something to say about it," she said.

Letty agreed. "Do you have any more flour?"

"We'll need to open a new sack. It's in the larder on the bottom shelf. You get that, and I'll find the raisins."

Letty went to the larder and a moment later called out, "It's too heavy for me to move."

Neenah joined her and together they tugged the twenty-five-pound sack of flour across the floor.

Who would have thought that we could do anything together?

A box behind the sack fell over as the flour shifted. Letty reached into the cupboard to right it. "Look at this, Neenah," she said, showing her a box of rat poison. "Is this how men in China look?"

Neenah's smile faded as she took in the vicious illustration. The box of Rough on Rats Poison showed an exaggerated drawing of a Chinaman with a queue and a coolie hat. He was holding a rat above his mouth as though he were about to gobble it up. Anger rising, she read aloud, "They Must Go! Clears out Rats, Mice and Bed Bugs." She turned to Letty. "Is this why you think we eat rats? Because of nonsense like this?"

Letty gulped. "It's just an advertisement. It's harmless."

"It's an insult," Neenah cried. "It's making fun of Chinese to sell poison."

"Don't take it so seriously. No one would think . . ." her voice trailed off.

"You believed it!" Neenah accused. "Remember the soda shop?"

"I didn't mean it," Letty muttered, but she wouldn't look Neenah in the face.

Knowing that they could never be friends unless she could make Letty understand the problem, Neenah thought for a moment then asked, "What if I said all Americans ate . . . maggots or drank blood?"

Letty's back stiffened. "That's disgusting."

"Exactly," Neenah said, hands on her hips. She waited for Letty to figure it out. It took longer than Neenah thought it should but finally the other girl saw it.

"I guess I'd be angry if anyone said that about my country," Letty conceded. "I don't blame you for being upset. I didn't think about what I was saying before. I'm sorry." With a rueful expression, she added, "I don't know anything about China, do I?"

Thinking of the shrine in the parlor, Neenah said, "I could teach you."

Looking embarrassed, Letty said, "My father wouldn't like that. He hates the Chinese. He lost his job . . ."

"My grandfather told me," Neenah said quickly.

"I wish I could tell your father that I'm sorry about his job. But also that it's not my fault."

"I know that," Letty said. "But he is so angry all the time. He says things, and Billy believes them. I should know better, though."

Maybe there was a chance for Neenah and Letty to be . . . if not friends, then at least not enemies. Neenah extended her hand. "Let's start again. My name is Neenah Hamill. I'm pleased to meet you."

Letty hesitated, then shook Neenah's hand. "I'm pleased to meet you, too."

An hour later, when Sarah poked her head into the kitchen, Neenah and Letty were giggling as they stuffed too-hot cookies into their mouths.

It wasn't that hard to make a friend after all.

Epilogue
May 1879

Sarah threw open the windows in the parlor. A breeze, laden with early summer, rustled Neenah's stack of notepaper.

"Put that letter away," Sarah said. "They'll be arriving soon."

Today was the annual Ladies' Benevolent Society picnic. Mrs. Sarah Hamill, president, was the hostess. Sarah and Neenah had scrubbed and swept and polished for a week straight.

Erastus was even more on edge; he was going to reveal his big surprise today. No matter how Neenah begged, he wouldn't tell her what it was.

"I have a few minutes still," Neenah said, glancing at her father's clock. It lived on the writing table in the parlor now. She liked to think of this clock and her mother's, ticking at the same time on opposite sides of the world. It made Mama feel a little closer.

"I'm going to check on the food," Sarah said for the tenth time. Mrs. Rushbridger would be waiting to pounce on any misstep. Neenah hoped the other woman wouldn't fault Sarah for the Chinese tang yuan dumplings. She had used Number One Boy's special Szechuan peppers and she was afraid it would be too spicy for the Ladies' Benevolent Society.

She dipped her pen into the ink bottle, sparing a thought for Number One Boy who would love to buy ink ready-made without having to grind it and mix it himself. She began to write in English (she couldn't bear for Mama to see how her calligraphy had deteriorated without practice):

Dear Mama,
  I hope this letter finds you in good health.
My grandfather, Erastus, and grandmother, Sarah,
are very well and send their good wishes.

"It is better to make the break clean," Mama had said. But Neenah had a say in the matter, too. With Sarah's encouragement, Neenah had begun writing to Mama every week. It might take as long as six months for a letter to make the journey in one direction, so she had not yet had a reply. In fact, her first letter might not even have arrived yet. Neenah liked to think that any morning now Mama would tell the Mandarin Foo-Tai, "My daughter has written from America."

My father was here but now he is away again.
He said I can live here forever.

Outside Erastus greeted friends, mostly the husbands of the Benevolent Ladies. She could hear the excitement in his voice as he parried questions about his surprise. Everyone in town was dying to know what on earth Erastus Hamill was up to.

She picked up her pen again.

My grandfather hired Mr. Stanton, an artist from New York City to paint my portrait. But before he does that, he is doing a secret painting on the barn! My grandfather told me it is a gift for me and made me promise not to look. Today all will be revealed.

"Neenah! Come outside." Erastus's enthusiasm was contagious. "It's time!"

Placing her pen on the blotter, she hurried to join her grandfather on the porch. The road was filled with buggies and wagons. High in the tree next to the front door, Neenah spied Jin Mao hiding from the invasion of strangers. Neenah sympathized, but as she scanned the crowd she realized she recognized almost everyone.

In a small town, no one is a stranger.

Letty and her mother had been among the first to arrive. Even Billy had come, although he immediately ran off to chase the chickens in the orchard. Over the winter,

Letty and Neenah had become friends with only a few arguments about the other's wrong ideas. Neenah had taken Sarah's advice about remembering that everyone had faults. It helped that Letty's father had gone to Utica for a job in a shoe factory.

Sarah was standing under the elm tree, chatting with Mrs. Rushbridger. They had an excellent view of the huge oil cloth draped over the front of the barn. Sarah was relishing the older woman's curiosity. Neenah glanced at the artist, Mr. Stanton. He sat in the rocking chair on the porch sipping lemonade, looking pleased with himself.

Erastus swung his bell. The clanging silenced the crowd and they gathered around. "Thank you for coming today," he said. "My lovely wife Sarah, has arranged a delicious lunch, but first I'd like you all to see something special." He beckoned for Sarah to come up and join them on the porch.

"Everyone here knows that our granddaughter, Neenah, has come all the way from Shanghai, China, to live with us. We're very proud of how she's taken to our American ways, but we've learned a lot from her, too. To honor the land of her birth, I asked Mr. Stanton," he pointed his finger in the artist's direction, "to paint something special. He's recreated one of Neenah's favorite places in China right here at our farm."

Neenah stared at him. "Grandfather, what have you done?" she whispered.

Grinning widely, he said, "Stay right here." He moved to the barn where a piece of rope was attached to the oil cloth. "Let's count down, folks," Erastus shouted. "Ten, nine, eight . . ."

The voices joined together until they reached "one." Erastus tugged, and the tarp dropped.

The gasps from the gathered crowd were nothing to Neenah's shock. Mr. Stanton had painted an enormous mural that looked like a portal to China. The Longhua Pagoda rose fifteen feet in the air against a traditional Chinese landscape of low rolling hills. There were no lustrous dragons, but the hills were the exact same color as the jade one upstairs.

Neenah's chest tightened as if she had too much joy to be contained in one body.

"What is it, Erastus?" a woman from the crowd shouted.

"It's a pagoda!" he answered.

Voices erupted with a barrage of questions. Neenah could make no sense of it—she was too busy taking in every detail of the painting.

"Do you like it?" Sarah's voice brought Neenah back from China to Baldwinsville.

Dashing away tears, Neenah bobbed her head up and down. There weren't words for how much she liked it.

Pleased with Neenah's response, Sarah said, "I thought it was a foolish idea, but in the end that artist did a good job. Even Eva Rushbridger can't complain."

Sure enough, Mrs. Rushbridger was staring at the mural with a bemused expression.

Neenah started to speak, then cleared her throat and tried again. "But it's so big!"

"We want everyone to see it," Sarah said simply. "Erastus is thinking of changing the farm's name to Pagoda Hill."

"What do you think, Neenah?" Erastus demanded, taking the two steps to the porch in one leap.

"It's beautiful," she said. She stepped into his arms, and he enveloped her in an enormous hug. He pulled Sarah close, too. Wedged between the very tall Erastus and the tiny Sarah, Neenah felt entirely at home. This was a family. Maybe not the one she had thought she wanted—those dragons were sneaky in their wish-granting—but a family, nonetheless. Her family.

Late that afternoon, after everyone had gone, Neenah returned to her letter.

My grandfather painted the Longhua Pagoda on the side of his barn. Everyone who passes by will know that in this house, China is not forgotten. Just as I have not forgotten you.

Love,
Ning

Author's Note

When I was six, my mother brought me to visit a great-aunt in Baldwinsville, New York. My mother wanted to photograph some family heirlooms. There was a long scroll with an architectural drawing of a dredge and hundreds of Chinese characters. A silk fan fascinated me because the faces of the people woven into the silk were painted on slivers of ivory. And there was an oil painting of a solemn little girl, not unlike me, with green eyes and dark hair. After that visit, we went to a farm on top of a hill. There was a brick farmhouse and a large red barn. It was a typical farm in every way except for the enormous pagoda painted on the side.

The little girl was my great-great-grandmother, Neenah. She was born in 1866 in Shanghai, China. Her mother, Sun, was Chinese and her father, George, was an American. His family lived in that farmhouse. George brought Neenah to America in the late 1870s. The family hired a painter to paint a pagoda on the front of the barn for the enormous sum of $400 ($10,000 in today's dollars). The mural is still there, and the farm is called Pagoda Hill.

The Pagoda Hill barn in New York in the late 1800s

Neenah was born exactly a century before I was. Her story fascinated me, especially the unanswered questions. Why did Neenah come to America? For that matter, why had her father gone to China? Why did her mother stay behind? When you think about it, painting a pagoda on a barn is a very odd thing to do. Was it to relieve Neenah's homesickness or was there more to the story?

I had several clues, including photographs of Neenah's mother and father. For my story, the key was a photograph of Neenah's mother, Sun. She is clearly a "lady." You can see her impossibly tiny feet in the picture. Until the end of the nineteenth century, most upper-class women had their feet bound as children. These women could barely walk.

Ning as a young girl in Shanghai

Foot-binding was a tradition in China handed down from mothers to daughters for a thousand years. Typically, the process began when a girl was between the ages of five to eight. Her toes were broken (except for the big toe) and then bound flat to the sole of her foot. The foot was bent almost double so that the toes were as close as they could be to the heel. Then her mother tightly bound the deformed foot with silk cloths. The girl was forced to walk long distances, balancing most of her weight on her big toe. The goal was to break the arch of the foot. Over two years, the wrappings were made tighter, and the shoes the girl wore became smaller. A successful

Sun Foo-Tai, Ning's mother, and George Hamill, Ning's father

foot-binding resulted in a "golden lotus blossom," or a foot that was only three inches long. The practice ended abruptly at the end of the nineteenth century due primarily to the efforts of Western anti-foot-binding activists.

Although Sun's feet were bound, Neenah's were not. In family photographs, you can see her feet are normal size. (Most of the women in my family have long—some would say big—feet.) Sun was a woman of status; wouldn't she have wanted her daughter to have "lotus blossoms" like hers? But would an American father permit his daughter to be crippled deliberately? I think her parents decided she would be better off in America and so Neenah came to Baldwinsville, New York.

The prejudice Neenah encounters in this book was real. The few textbooks that talked about China were wildly inaccurate and suggested that the Chinese were less than human. The misconceptions about the Chinese— they were fleeing starvation in their own country, they ate dogs and rats, they gambled and were unclean—were widespread. Cartoons and advertisements from the era portrayed Chinese men as ominous or ludicrous figures.

During the depression that followed the Civil War, there was widespread resentment of the Chinese living in America because Chinese workers accepted lower wages and American workers feared for their jobs. There was a famous instance in 1870 in Belleville, New Jersey, where a steam laundry owner fired his American workers and brought in sixty-eight Chinese workers to fill their jobs. Although Letty's father is fictional, I imagined that his bigotry toward the Chinese comes from losing his position in a similar way. The song that Billy and his friends sing was a common one and sums up the cultural biases against the Chinese.

American prejudice resulted in legislation restricting Chinese immigration. Neenah encounters the Page Act of 1875 which was designed to keep Chinese women out of America so they could not marry workers already in the country. By 1882, the US government had passed the Chinese Exclusion Act of 1882, which made it illegal for Chinese workers to immigrate to America. This was the first time in American history that immigration to America was restricted based on nationality. The Act was not fully repealed until 1965.

Ning/Neenah had to make a choice: would she be American or Chinese? Or could she somehow live an American life and still honor where she came from?

As it turns out, in real life, Neenah coped quite well. Sarah became a second mother to her. Neenah married her schoolteacher, John Chapman. Teachers in the late nineteenth century were often only a few years older than their students. However, since he left Neenah for her seamstress (leaving Neenah with eight children!),

Nineteen-year-old Neenah in America

I made Mr. Chapman an unsympathetic character. Neenah divorced him and raised her children with Sarah's help. Neenah inherited her grandfather's property.

She never returned to China, nor did she see her mother again. George, however, did return to Shanghai periodically. He brought Sun photographs of Neenah wearing her mother's the jade necklace. (For the purposes of my story, I made Neenah a little older. We think she actually came to America when she was five or six.)

George, continued to wander. But he stayed in touch

The author's mother at the Longhua Pagoda in Shanghai. She is wearing her great-grandmother's jade necklace, the one that Ning wore and treasured in the novel.

with Neenah. He died by suicide in 1896 at the age of sixty-three leaving a journal with instructions that it should be sent to his daughter. Neenah lived until 1936. Neenah and George are buried together under a handsome granite gravestone along the shores of the Seneca River. I borrowed this cemetery for Neenah's chat with her great-grandmother.

When I began to write this novel, my mother gave me Neenah's Chinese doll and a pair of tiny hand-sewn shoes that had never been worn. I was in awe that these most cherished belongings had crossed the oceans over a century ago. We also have a very British-looking clock that was made in Shanghai.

My mother was the first of Neenah's children's children to return to Shanghai. She wore Neenah's jade necklace in front of the Longhua Pagoda.

Pagoda Hill Farm is no longer owned by my family, but the current owners are delighted with Neenah's story and consider themselves caretakers of her memory. The pagoda is still painted on the barn to the surprise and delight of anyone passing by. *View from Pagoda Hill* is my way of honoring Neenah's journey and her story.

Sources of Inspiration

To help me tell Neenah's story I was inspired by many of my family's heirlooms—the contract for the dredge, the clock, and numerous photographs. Neenah's doll, fan, necklace, and shoes were especially inspiring. Details about Neenah's trip to America are partly based on the travel journals of her father, George Hamill. Unfortunately Neenah left no record about her voyage. These days it is a fifteen-hour direct flight from New York City to Shanghai, but in the 1870s the journey could take three to six months depending on the type of ship you took. Neenah's journey on a mailboat was one of the fastest ways to travel.

To Learn More

I've collected a wide variety of resources about my family, nineteenth century Shanghai and Baldwinsville. Please visit michaelamaccoll.com/view-from-pagoda-hill.

Acknowledgments

Neenah's tale was always a family story, but I needed a lot of help to write *View from Pagoda Hill*. I'm grateful to all of you.

Carolyn Yoder was infinitely patient with draft after draft, always guiding me to a better story. Susan Krogulski asked the tough questions that helped me get to the end. Barbara Grzeslo designed the book and cover and as always did a phenomenal job.

Patricia Reilly Giff encouraged me to write this book over a decade ago. She never forgot, often reminding me, "Michaela, your Chinese book has to be written."

Ramin Ganeshram offered key insights about Neenah's experience as a newcomer to America, and the choices she might make to fit in. Special thanks to Veronica Chen Guerreiro for reading the manuscript and providing valuable feedback from the point of view of a first-generation immigrant from Shanghai. The editors from Thinkingdom Children's Books in Beijing kindly offered very helpful comments.

Artie Steenstra and his family, the current occupants

of Pagoda Hill, welcomed me into their home and shared their artifacts. Sue McManus at the Shacksboro Schoolhouse Museum, a tireless keeper of Baldwinsville's history, was generous with her time and the records in her care. In Shanghai, Henry Hong was the perfect tour guide and showed me the few places in Shanghai that still exist from the 1870s. One of my favorite memories of Shanghai was having noodles with the monks at the Longhua Pagoda temple cafeteria.

My critique group, Sari Bodi, Christine Pakkala, and Karen Swanson were there for me at every step. Krista Richards was my sounding board during innumerable coffee dates and once even in a sea kayak.

My mom, Barbara Burns, read multiple drafts and together we tried to puzzle out the relationship between Neenah and George. We both wish we could know more about Sun. As always, thank you to my family for being so supportive. Rob, Rowan, and Margaux, I love you guys!

Picture Credits